The Spoon Knife Anthology
Thoughts on Compliance, Defiance, and Resistance

Edited by N.I. Nicholson & Michael Scott Monje, Jr.

Owned by disabled workers, NeuroQueer Books extends the
Autonomous Press mission: Revolutionizing academic access

Autonomous Press is an independent publisher focusing on works about disability, neurodivergence, and the various ways they can intersect with other aspects of identity and lived experience.

ISBN-10: 0-9861835-8-X
ISBN-13: 978-0-9861835-8-4

Cover art and NeuroQueer Books logo design by Selene dePackh. The one in this book. The one that wrote the great story. I know, there are a lot of great stories in here but you know the one, the one we gave her credit for. Anyway, stay tuned for more NeuroQueer Books from Selene. And until those are ready, check out more art at: http://asp-in-the-garden.deviantart.com/

Table of Contents

Part II: Fiction

Part III: Memoir

What is a Spoon Knife? An Introduction

The first question I got from my partners and blogging friends when I started talking about spoon knives was "What is that?" Every one of them had heard about Christine Miserandino's "The Spoon Theory," of course, and they could tell I was referencing it, but none of them seemed to be familiar with traditional woodworking tools, because they didn't see that reference or its connection to activist work. Not at first, at least. Once I posted some pictures of various spoon knives and the bowls they were used to carve, the idea caught fire.

To start understanding the idea of the spoon knife, you need to start back at "The Spoon Theory," that wonderful, dynamic metaphor for living with chronic pain and disability. If you've never read the original essay, it's worth the time, and it is available online at www.butyoudontlooksick.com. In it, Ms. Miserandino details how she used a collection of spoons to symbolize her pool of resources when a friend asked her what it was like to live with lupus. As she detailed the tasks of a regular day, she took spoons away, to show how her energy had to be spent. At the end, when there was only one spoon left and the only item on the list– dinner– was likely to take two spoons, it helped to drive home the choices and the careful safeguarding of resources she has to make as she plans her daily activities.

The essay is a powerful statement about the importance of long-term planning, of not doing everything, and of prioritizing self-care. At the same time, though, it also begs a question: How does one get more spoons? To extend the idea in her original essay, each day is treated like a table, and each table is set with a different number of place settings. Sometimes, there are more spoons than you need to do everything on the list. Sometimes, though, there are not enough. That complicates planning. What if there was another way, though?

Interdependence, that principle that governs so much of the way that disability and disabled cultures are constructed, seems to suggest that the whole room does better when we are willing to send extra spoons to other tables. That, at least, is the organizing principle in most of the activist organizations and groups I've been involved with, whether they are formal or informal in nature. What about when the whole room is packed, though? How do we get more spoons when everyone needs them?

The answer is the spoon knife, that old woodworker's companion that looks something like the tool it is used to make, only sharp and nasty and quick. A spoon knife is used to carve the bowl, which makes it curved, like a melon baller. It shaves away the unnecessary parts of the wood in layers, too, so it has to be sharp and strong, to keep slicing and slicing until it has peeled enough to make a depression in an otherwise smooth stick. It looks thin, like something made from an old beer can, but in a master's hands, it rewards patience and precision.

If we're keeping with our extended metaphor, though, then we still have to ask the question: *What is a spoon knife?* We know what our symbol does, but what in our community is capable of doing that thing– cutting away layers of what shouldn't be there, to leave us with the ability to do more, reach further, and nourish ourselves more successfully. What looks thin and weak, but nonetheless digs deep channels into reality?

My belief is that the spoon knife is a story. For some, it's an expression of solidarity that refills our emotional reserves even as it bolsters the morale of the one who offered support. For others, it might be an example that provides the cognitive scaffolding needed to get out of an abusive situation, or even just to recognize one in the first place. It's also possible for it to be a confrontation, a reality that will not yield to our need until we learn to wield it and to control its damage with unwavering precision.

It's fitting that the spoon knife looks both weak and menacing at once, because story is a thing that can be blown away on the wind, or it can slice away the people around you by revealing what lies underneath your initial presentation. And, at the end of the day, a spoon knife is absolutely nonthreatening unless one chooses to make it otherwise.

If I'm right, then this collection of knives will provoke new spoons when the right kinds of readers connect with them, providing the things those readers need to navigate their own daily tasks and challenges. And who knows? Maybe a few of them will look into this volume and see more than spoons. Maybe those readers will see the possibilities that arise when you study the uses of the knife. And you know what? We will be waiting for them.

Michael Scott Monje, Jr.
Kalamazoo, MI

❖　❖　❖

Dedication: How to Time Travel in a Closet

to Aunt Jean

Let me show you the magic of time travel.
I've materialized next to twelve year-old me,
just before the instant you first cracked your hand
across her face. You can't see me, but I can see
you, her, and how you ruined her in slow motion

over six years: blading your words into her, and
stamping your red handprints and your Bible belt welt
lines into the parchment of her skin. Daily she had to
regenerate missing parts: a hand, a slice of ass cheek,
a hunk of clit severed and sacrificed to YHWH,
a clump of fizzy black hair, a lump of heart muscle. Yet
daily you pruned her: I still see trails of blood ellipses
on the polished pine fallow floors

of that old worn dirt-brown brick house,
which is where I stand *right now*,
next to her, in front of you. I am a Time Lord,
signaling backwards along my own timeline
to collect those parts of me you amputated
and I store those in my closet, a timeship powered
by the grey walnut inside my bone shell

head. I've piloted back to this moment to see you
as you were, a skeleton carrying your own ruined self –
a hungry ghost, deflated shriveled skin, mouth unhinged
to scoop up stray bits of the love you never got –
over your shoulder. You clobbered the girl that I was

with your miserable sack of nothing, beating into me
the whippings *you* got as a girl. But know that
I am rebuilding myself:

I have the technology, I am learning how
to regenerate, and I am reincarnating as a queer
man. Are you surprised? I am becoming what you
hated most. To prove that I'm right, I can just
jump to other spots in my timeline and listen to
your broken-record tongue's needle skip:
on repeat, I hear *faggot– faggot– faggot–*

and little else, except for *retard, freak,* and
nappy-headed. But *right now,* I stay in this particular
moment, invisible, next to twelve year-old me,
my gaze fixed on your raised right white hand,
its wrinkled marble almost bloodless
except for the scarlet sun exploding
just beneath the limpid skin of your palm.

N.I. Nicholson
Ashland University

Part I: Poetry

Carillonist
Alex Conall

My mother believes
I am the perfect
heterocis
daughter
with a few disappointing flaws
like being feminist
like not dating men
this is what I tell her:

the silence loud as church bells

My father believes
I am the perfect
neurotypical
daughter
with a few disappointing flaws
like few social skills
like executive dysfunction
this is what I tell him:

the silence loud as church bells

I cut my hair
from mid-back to mid-neck
almost pixie
now I see myself in the mirror
I do not know what my mother sees
but she has never once said
she likes my new hair
this is what I tell her:

the silence loud as church bells

here is how to clean a bathroom:
remove towels to laundry
spray vinegar on surfaces
– wait, remove items from surfaces
now Windex the mirrors
now spray vinegar on surfaces
wipe down surfaces
– wait, toilet cleaner needs to sit
pour toilet cleaner in toilet bowl
now wipe down surfaces
sweep floor
– wait, move items back to surfaces
now sweep floor
wait wait wait
now scrub toilet
put out clean towels
hurrah done
– wait, forgot the bathtub
my father says I've done it wrong
this is what I tell him:

the silence loud as church bells

I study women's studies
I study queer studies
after what my mother says
about women's studies
not being a real field of study,
when I talk about my studies
this is what I tell her:

the silence loud as church bells

work work work
People People
stress stress stress
eight hours then home
and the dishwasher needs emptying
after dinner I didn't eat
it can wait till morning
my father says it shouldn't
this is what I tell him:

the silence loud as church bells

research apartments on my own
search out potential roommates
must be okay
with my four to midnight work shift
with my queer trans divergent self
(I come up empty, but
that kind of works for me)
moving day in seven weeks
round up every spoon in the county
I will *make this work*
and when my father says
I should wait on finding furniture
and when my mother says
I don't need to hurry planning meals
this is what I tell them:

the silence loud as church bells
loud as lightning
loud as voices
loud as tears

BODY::FORGETTING

Andrea Abi-Karam

waiting for fracture

body full of whatever. body full of red genderless nothing– a
blank hole--it costs so much

to maintain this body. it just wants to consume and consume
and burn it all away too fast

until i gnaw at the fingertips– i get cold easily– hard to
maintain my skin sealed to the

bones below to the meat beneath to– itself. the environment
tries to pull it apart– make

little entrances for itself– ports– to communicate
information ports to channel energy

into the surroundings as if it's not enough to just be here they
want the full download the

full externalization of what we've tried so hard to keep sewn
strictly in. skin just a shell. a

case for your new iphone 6. congratulations! release your
innermost secrets through your

fingerprints. eyes just a mirror, body just a case for desirable
information.

every body is consumable.

every body is consumable.

after we grow up, we're just waiting to be consumed.

confuse the consumer. confuse the entry. box check,
unchecked– skin wants to plug

in– desire exchange, desire energy, desire heat, desire
connection beyond this soft

border. my skin is my border against whatever bullshit the
world readily presents.

sometimes it's frozen. sometimes its rigid. sometimes it's soft.
elastic. caves in when you

reach for me. sometimes it's strange to me but clear to them.
cold & warm. cold & cold.

body as empty
body as untraceable
body as nothing left to sell
body as needing to sell
body as lost
body as not wanting to be found
body as cut off from the rest
body as cut off from you
body as looking at another body
body as watching another body
body as wanting another body
body as desire
body as watching you (be careful, no wrong moves)
body as wet yellow lines on the street
body as wet for another body

body as the final frontier, the uncharted map, the last
renewable resource

body as the last most satisfying thing to waste, and be wasted

body as full of poison full of misperception full of trauma

body as needing extraction pull each wire out from the skin of
the arms slowly, one by one, until the connection is broken
and electricity no longer shoots down the hips in the street

body as ever extracting, ever rejecting, ever pushing out the
poison as it comes and comes and comes

body as waiting.
body as sick of waiting
body as the buzzing swarm, the tidal wave, the earthquake, the
drought that finally accumulates into the fire

body as sick of all of this
body as getting sick all over this
body as so dehydrated
body as dying within all of this
body as dead next to other bodies
body as never really being dead.
body being dead next to other bodies as a gesture
body as archived in a warehouse full of servers somewhere in
vermont

body as what's next. i pull wires out of my skin daily, tucked
away just below the surface of the screen. I tap on them to
make them activate, thicken, awaken. I tap on them at the
inside of the elbow until they become thick. until they become
material. so they become something to hold on to, something

that is known. tap on them again until you're sure. i take a new razor blade out of the package from the hardware store and make an incision on my forearm close to the inside of my elbow. i massage it open. i pull the wire out slowly careful not to pull anything else out at this time. the wire is wet from being on the inside on my body. it won't short out– these wires were built for the body. i drop the wire into a clear plastic bucket at my feet where it rejoins the wires it used to connect with inside my body. communication exoskeleton. ports on the inside of my wrist that just can't connect. body as waiting to connect. body as never connecting. body as needing to connect. body as alone. body as desiring control of the body.

cold & cold. i reach behind my head to adjust my temperature settings. i look for the little ridged plastic wheel tucked behind my hair right where the skull meets the spine. hot & cold. I push it two clicks to the left to warm up. the skin has imperfect insulation.

i pick at the thinner wires that reach out of the tops of my arms. pull them out quickly, a little resistance and then the skin lets go. break down the communication pulse between my body and other bodies.

body as needing to name myself
body as needing to name you
body as needing to name this
body as needing to forget but being unable to
body as making me tired
body as landscape
body as electric landscape
body as signals hovering
body as having coordination problems
body as having trouble remembering

body as remembering anyway
body as territory
body as my territory
body as machine
body as machine waiting for the extra buzz
body as discipline
body as scheduled to fall asleep

there are interruptions to the body's regular schedule.
nightmares. dreams of you dying in an earthquake under the
collapsed frame, studs tall and thick. dreams of you drowning
in a lake midsummer. pulling the body out from under. pulling
the body out from the water. interruptions. glitches.
misfirings in the body's disciplined network. the body that
suffers is the body of the other.

body as needing to forget.

i hold my memory in my hands. at least what i could pull out. i
pulled them out each one by one. i pulled them out from my
ears. white strings that curl up readily in my hand. as if
resting. as if always resting always waiting always holding--
always waiting for activation. some of them are no longer
white, clouded more of the heavy grey the sky gets when it's
not ready to wake up. more brittle, the curls they make in the
palm of my hand are wider, crescents unwilling to curl up
tight. they're not ready to wake up, buried deep. they must be
stroked before activation pushed on turned on lit up. they are
not forgotten. the body knows them in a different way. not in
flashback not as frames in motion but as muscles who
witnessed it in their own way.

i feel something unravel within me throughout all of this.

body as wanting to fall apart

body as wanting to fall apart at the angles
body as being forced apart at every angle
body as wanting to fall apart
body as so small but still so uncomfortable with itself
body as floating below
body as pretending some of itself doesn't exist
body as not wanting to exist
body as wanting to escape the container of the skin
body as wanting to escape the cover of plastic sheets
body as wanting to eat a lollipop
body as breaking the barrier
body as breaking down
body as consuming itself cell by cell, wire by wire
body as not made of cells
body made of thoughts, feelings, desires that make the body
shake

Something Wicked This Way Comes

Athena the Architect

*[**Editorial Note:** This poem was originally produced to bridge
    the Transgender Day of Remembrance and Autistics
    Speaking Day events for 2015.]*

My fourth year participating I have to come on strong,
so let's start with the shit at least half of you will read wrong:
I've been working too diligently at speaking clearly
to hear you tell me which day is set aside for me speaking,
so fuck the first to the nineteenth.
I decided to speak when it's time to count bodies.
It's always been my role, the place I'm put is underneath,

either supporting or working to earn a basic recognition of my
    humanity.
I'm not doing chores no more,
and I'm done front faking an expected presence
when I would rather run screaming from being alone with you,
but that's not expected decorum in a men's locker room.

I learn to be a blur, finding space for myself in deception.
Clinical observers have always called our pace of learning
    manipulative,
and it's a term they use for resistance, too, and when pain is
    expressed,
but apparently it's not manipulative to tell a child
that the reason you hit her in the face after school
was because you lost your medication
and your diagnosis says "depressed."
Luckily I have a brother who stands between me and the
    others,
a swift quickness, work horse harnessed and capable
of pulling my workload when the others aren't observing,
and over time he becomes faster, until they can't observe him.
He's a blur of motion that they find unnerving,
and he uses it to keep me from being alone with anyone
who looks past my body, sees me, and decides I'm for them to
    play with.
My quicksilver bullet, my headmate,
my prolific novelist-cum-suicide Herman Hesse acolyte,
he's eventually going to catch his end,
but until then, he's the one who protects us when artillery
    shells hit.

I'm finally finding my body in the year my siblings mostly
    expect to be bodied,
transitioning at the life expectancy for those of us who come
    out in their teens,

and I see the faces around me when I go out presenting
    publicly,
wearing makeup without hormonal support, my face like
"Fuck you! Quit staring, I got shit to do and I'm walking!"
And that's only possible because of what he did for me,
but one of us has to go this year, and he already put himself
between the shooter and another fighter in the family,
so I have to remember him, along with the sisters who had
    more courage than I did,
who came out when we were little, then got statisticked and
    became
part of the reason I can't stay hidden. I'm sorry, kids.
I wish I'd been strong enough to fight when it would have
    made a difference,
but the moment of merit hadn't happened,
and I was too busy protecting myself from the next blow to
    know
that there were people ready to help stop the next hit from
    landing.

I'm writing thirty novels to help him go, because people need
    to know
the process by which we became possible, so they can benefit
if the moment of merit is something they also need to
    accomplish.
I was professionalized by people who taught me to look deeply
into the way I supported other writers in my community,
but the support they seemed to need was nothing that fed
    them,
so there were always congratulatory dinners if they could be
    afforded,
long tales to regale the host, singing for supper until an
    invitation for a workshop could be extended.
The result was that their support for emerging artists lacked a
    certain focus to the tutelage,

because the business they were engaged with was old enough
     to be, by default, simple.
While they were wondering how it was that they worked at
     nothing but novels
and watched years pass between them,
I skipped the bistros where they lamented and spent nights
     going toe to toe onstage,
putting performance poetry out through clenched teeth,
trying to find a way in modern vocabulary
to lament the relationship between mathematics and
     medicine,
sharing sensory impressions of medallion necklaces
like a motherfucking golden chariot of the sun,
shooting arrows of flow like fire into everyone,
and defending my title from someone with big lungs and ninth
     grade educational formalities,
but a vocabulary with more grace than ten holy men
and a sense of rhythm that glossed over syntactical departures
with a scaffolding that bridged the audience's differences in
     idiom.
And if I wanted to get half of what was in that hat for
     groceries,
I had to be on top of him with a ferocity that masked the fact
     that he would practice with me.
Every poet in the pack was a brother, but only one of us got to
     eat.
You're surprised at how I work? This is how I had to be.
It made me. Fuck you if you think a novel in eight years is an
     accomplishment,
I had to do a fresh three minutes of perfection once a week to
     keep my car filled up with gasoline.

So getting the spit out in time is what he did for me,
moving quickly, Quicksilver slipping past teeth,
flow lightly like lightning moves until he'd punch you,

but in the end that was not for me.

You see, the truth is
his presentation isn't the rhythm
of our movements,
so when he does his thing
it disrupts our control,
eventually collapsing
the somatic unity,
meaning he will work
until he's melting me.

You see, he's fast,
but she's weird, and
though it looks like his anatomy,
he's really just her beard.
Now that he's departing,
I am finding transition completes me,
and that means I'm no longer standing
hidden, whispering over your shoulder
and teleporting away before you see me.
Instead I'm standing strong,
whipping your ass telekinetically
and spraying cover fire from fingertips
like a social-justice-positive Palpatine.
Don't fuck with a Sith Slytherin witch bitch
who's had a recent loss in the family,
because I will cut you with something
that isn't even physical,
and you will realize alignment change
happened right before your eyes
and now the villain has a mission
and she's out avenging.

I got lit up like this when I was without him

and a genderfae Katniss Everdeen
took cover from enemy fire where I was hiding,
and then that warrior said to me the things
I needed to hear to understand what I was meant to sing.
They said

"I'm using a fucking bow,
The city is flying,
None of this makes sense.

Parents try to kill me when I say 'please,'
And contracts don't matter,
Even when I have all the signatures,
Because I can't speak for my experience
if I'm talking.

This is actually what they say.
So don't try to make sense,
and if you are too wounded to come with,
that's fine,
there's no judgment,
but I have to go back out there and draw fire,
and I have to trust the others
to tell me where the snipers are
when I put arrows back into their armaments,
so I can't stay here and coddle you through this.

If you lock the door, your brother will be sent,
or else someone from a rescue team,
but if you follow me, I'm not here to save you,
and you will be expected to be avenging."

That was all it took to make me see,
I couldn't leave K to do this knowing the Mockingjay
was just intentionally providing bait

with no cover fire, and no way
to recover ammunition, so,
knowing the enemy could now see me because
my brother wasn't a distraction,
I sprang into action.
I didn't go through that door,
I blew it into shrapnel shards to create environmental hazards
and then we went to war.
Now, when they see me I subvert their gaze
with my witchy ways,
turning their intentions in their heads
and making my fingertips provide the pyre
to burn their targeting sensors before they fire.

So now, it's your moment,
as we prepare to say the names of the dead,
this makes no sense,
and I don't expect you to magically have the strength,
but if you follow me, don't expect rescuing,
I am out for avenging,
And what I need are recruits, not complications,
so I understand if you stay hidden.

For the rest of you,
it's time we went to the *Gaslight Village*
to learn what we need to win this,
another site on my trail of origins.
Fuck a wack, narcissistic cyborg with religious visions,
this isn't the age of Ultron,
it's the age of the Heirophantess,
and this isn't the fulfillment of an incredible wish,
it's the coming of the Scarlet Witch.

Here's this year's dead list:

Papi Edwards, Lamia Beard,
Ty Underwood, Tasha DeJesus,
Yazmin Vash Payne,
Penny Proud & Bri Golec.
Don't get up from your seat yet.

Kristina Reinwald, Sumaya Dalmar,
Keyshia Blige, Mya Hall,
I'm not even getting very far,
Vanessa Santillan, and
London Chanel,
Mercedes Williamson,
Jasmine Collins,
And I'm not sure I even know all of them,
Ashton O'Hara, India Clarke,
K.C. Haggard, Shade Shuler,
Amber Monroe and Elisha Walker.

Kandis Capri ended on August 11 in Phoenix,
And when the list is ended,
Remember that the year isn't over yet.
Tamara Dominguez, Fernanda Olmos,
Sometimes called Coty,
Kiesha Jenkins, Zella Ziona,
And there are just a few more:
Marcela Estefania Chocobar,
Amancay Diana Sacayán,
And Yoshi Tsuchida brings us to
What I hope is the end.

I don't blame you if you stay in here for your safety,
but if you come out, know what it means to follow me.
Now, I have to go,
I hear avengers assembling.

Lament To the Medical-Industrial Division Of the Capitalist Patriarchal Complex

Barbara Ruth

I don't do well in hospitals
don't interface appropriately with the medical establishment.
I'm too damn queer
have too many weird diseases
I bristle loudly
yell about my rights
when I'd be so much more prudent to refrain from telling
everyone
everything about me.

I wish I at least knew if I do it on purpose.
Is it willfulness? Ruthlessness?
Or do I really lose the ability to keep my mouth shut?
I mean
they cut me up
drug me up
shove instruments up and down my openings
then they get exasperated
when I don't play nice
don't bounce back
in the MediCal allotted time
for recovery.

I stay too long in hospitals
have tubes in me
at inconvenient places for the personnel.

My veins are into non-cooperation.
My brain responds idiosyncratically
to fluorescent lights
electro-magnetic fields
all that sketchy shit only kooks believe in.
I'm a gold mine of undocumented anecdotal side effects.
I have these codas to my surgeries that go on and on and on.
The audience gets restless
the doctors pull out their DSMs
alongside their PDRs.

Eventually, they threaten me with shrinks.
It's a game we play:
I say they're uninformed about my disabilities
they say I derive secondary benefits from my seizures.
I think I exercise restraint when I refrain from asking them
about the tertiary benefits they get
from their practices.
They don't show any gratitude for my discretion.
            They call me nuts
            I call them cruel
Eventually they sic the shrinks on me.

Sometimes
I hate it most of all
when the docs
are dykes
or gay women
or homosexual females
or whatever the fuck it is they will or won't admit.
It tears me up
because I'll knock myself out
searching for the perfect, perfect words
so this time she'll get it.
I'll invent new continents

trying to stake out the common ground.
Breathless, I'll broadjump across that chasm
of just who it is
who calls the shots.
Eventually I'll trust her
start to believe we're equals
sister outlaws in a world we never made.
I handle it much better when it's some straight man
who sics the shrinks on me.

I like some docs.
The ones I like do what I ask them to at least most of the time.
Have the good taste to answer my questions
in my vocabulary
like anyone would.
Act like it's no big thing
just because they dress or talk or smile
like regular people.
Neither deny nor abuse their power.
The docs I like
swing pendulums to diagnose
treat patients/harbor fugitives after shootouts with the cops,
live in their cars, in their cells. from time to time.
They tend to lose
their privileges.

Sometimes I think my ideal doc would be
a leftist crip in jail at least as queer as I am.
I'd get her out of prison
and she'd find the cure for environmental illness.
She'd be free   or freer
I'd be well   or better
and then we could be compañeras
plotting to free other crips
in the sunshine

at the ocean
over tea.

When I was six years old
I thought I'd grow up to be tortured by the state.
It wasn't an erotic fantasy
or a recurrent nightmare
just a fact of life
like taking pills so I wouldn't have those fits.
It took me so long to realize The State
would wear white coats
smell of alcohol and formalin
and tell me they were doing it
for my own good.

Some of this is Surely True

Barbara Ruth

I did not choose what happened to me.
I knew it was dangerous, therefore could not resist.

How did I come to vision quest in the hospital?
In the days before,
a Klamath lodgepole man came to me in waking dream,
said he was my ancestor, though I have no Klamath blood I
    know of.

I needed his strength.
He had my back.
But when I unpacked my guardians at the hospital

I found the Dalai Lama instead. He spoke with a Yiddish
    accent. That worried me.
I got busted for talking about His Holiness too much.
and the thought police medicated him away.

What was I truly looking for?
French?
The French language?
Ancestral memory of Alsatian grasses
the flowers of Lorraine?
Dit moi.
Donne moi.
Tell me what to give away.
Who can help me find my way?
What language holds the words I need?
Must I learn new alphabets, teach my tongue new diphthongs?
Who should I follow through the blind times?
Where are the guidelines, who will cut the braille into the
    paper,
into the skin?
Can I learn those letters, learn to touch, not see?
I have been to where there is no sight. And where there is too
    much.
If my eyes and ears will not find focus then I will rest
in breath
in taste
in touch.
Each has its secret tones.

Why do they hold me here?
I do not accuse myself. I accept no guilt. I will make the
    diagnosis and it shall be called grace.
Begin with that.
Imperfection cannot make it fall away
even when I fall.

My sad lusts.....
my addictions and deceits....

Still, some of this poem is surely true.
Imperfect Buddha tries so hard
to breathe in
the koan, still unsolved.

The List
Barbara Ruth

I meet women through the online personals.
It's a good way for me
because cyberspace is more accessible,
because I am a woman of words.
I flirt double entendrely,
but it's not cybersex I want.
Before long I crave the press of flesh to flesh
so I'll need to give you
The List.

If you would come to me
you will need to deconstruct
your ideas of how humans meet and mate.

We cannot go out for coffee.
If we find a restaurant accessible enough to rendezvous
you cannot have a glas of wine.
I'll probably meet you in a park,
be prepared to change locations several times

because of the cascade of things which make the world
unwelcoming to me.

Don't adorn yourself
with perfume, makeup, essential oils. Aromatherapy
is out.
You'll have to change
your shampoo, laundry products, deodorant and sun block –
      are you still with me?

Did I mention I'm a fat woman?
Not the fattest, but fat enough to have "grossly obese"
scrawled on the pages of my medical chart.
Idle diet chat will shut away my heart.
Don't expect, "I wasn't talking about you,"
to open it back up. I've heard it before.
It's alright to use the word "fat"
say as well:
voluptuous
zaftig.
Mean it.

You can't wear wool or polyester if you want my fingers
to brush against your clothes without catastrophe.
Maybe I should tell you now, sometimes I seize when I come.
Did I mention I'm epiletic?
Did I tell you, don't call 911?

I'm a radical anarcha-feminist
trying to be peace
and I will listen to KPFA for hours
and cry because of bombings and landmines and torture.
Sometimes when I'm visually assaulted by all the American
      flags
draped on the urban landscape

I forget about being peace. Can you help me start again?

I'll want to go to events where we will be searched
for security reasons
(of course we'll have to change our seats several times
because of ordinary people
with their ordinary scented products
who sit too close.) We may have to leave before it starts.
I'll phone and email, maybe get you involved,
trying to make events accessible,
then likely be too sick to go.

I'm Potowatomee and German
Jewish and French
recently I learned I'm a bit Welsh as well.
I have no country.

Like many women here and now
I take anti-depressants which make it hard to come.
Don't say, "It doesn't matter." Of course it does.
But it's not the end of the story.

If I really love you
in the night I will hang on to you in and out of sleep,
cry in your arms
want you to rub me hard
and barely enter me at all.
Wholeheartedly I will try to make love to you the way you
        want.
But I'll get tired, my hands might shake
I'm likely to collapse.
I don't promise to be the best lover you ever had
(although my orgasmic seizures
might make me the memorable, in that regard.)

I love to play
and I will hold your secrets.
I will also write them down.

It will not be easy to make your way into my bed.
(Yours, no doubt, will be inaccessible.)
I'm a lot of trouble.
I'm worth it.

Behaviorism Everywhere

Elizabeth J. Grace

I am real
Even living in your Internet.
How I feel
You know less about
Than I do,
Though I cannot breach
This keyboard
Trying to tell you.

Muscles taut and trembling;
Guts churning in
Sweat drenched innards,
Mixing with blood
From secret lacerations
Of a million mental pains
I do not know how to cry out–
But it's nothing to you
Because I am "nice."

The medical masters say
Behavior is everything:
I am only what they observe.
A to B to C–
There's nothing to see here
Move along–
Agency and self are illusory
If they are disabled.

You know this is wrong
Yet apply the same
Standards to me:
I do not cut so must not bleed.
I am not cruel so must not feel.
The least I could do
Is tell you all my business.

Oppressor and oppressed
Confessor and depressed
Stop stressing. See:
Pressed from all sides
I now declare I care
With raring equanimity.
All y'all can take a knee,
Kiss my stoic kindhearted ass
Equally. You choose for you
And I for me.

Now step up and use
Your compassionate imagination
Or leave me alone
To break in glorious silence
Before I try again.

Don't Tell Me to Stay Calm (a rantina)

Harriet Grace

Don't tell me, again, how much
I don't need to worry. Don't tell
me that I'm fine. Don't tell me
how I am, when what you mean
is you don't want to have to change.
Don't tell me. I don't want to know.

By which I mean, you don't want to know
what you don't know already. How much
you've already decided, and won't change
no matter what I may or may not tell
you. You've already decided what I mean.
You've decided for me

what's in my best interest. You'd have me
the way you like me, the way you know
I can be: polite, quiet. You'd mean,
cheerful. You'd mean, happy. But much
of the time, what you're calling happy, I'll tell
you, is for me, compliance. A change

in your tone: compliance? Change
your mind about what that might mean to me.
I've changed my mind about what to tell
you, I think. I've changed what I know
to suit you, again and again, so much
I'm exhausted from it. I mean

tired. Dead tired. What you mean
isn't interesting, not anymore. Change

won't come on your time, will it? How much
I've forgotten of what it's like to be me.
Don't tell me what I know,
and what I don't know. Don't tell

me that everything's fine. Don't tell
me about my best interest. Say what you mean:
that your life is the only way you know
it to be, and you can't imagine changing
your mind. You can't imagine mine. You and me,
we're not the same, though so much

of what we need could be summed up
like this: I don't know how to change me.
There's so much I meant to be.

Last Night I Saw a Photograph

Harriet Grace

Last night I saw a photograph
of a man I'd loved.
He'd not been kind; nor had I.
Though I didn't know that then.

Though I didn't know it then,
I'd love women, and he'd love men.
Back then, I'd made him swear again
that I made him laugh,

and last night his photograph
reminded me of what I'd been

when I was young, and so was he.
He could now be my son,

though I didn't think so then,
but now, his face blurred, turned
away, it seems like the years
have rubbed the distance from the lens

Last night I saw a photograph
of my lover who'd just died.
He'd not been kind; no, nor had I.
Yet now I saw his ravaged face

and through a kind of brutal grace,
there I found the universe
in a photo taken in reverse,
though I didn't know that then.

To Give It a Name

Harriet Grace

To give it a name
is to make it small, you said.
You said, I don't want this to be
small. I want to let it grow
into whatever it might become.

To tell you the truth,
I wasn't even listening.
I was leaning
into your neck, breathing

the scent of you, mown

grass and salt and nothing else
could have held me then.
But now, alone, hearing again
that birdsong that I've known
since I was a child

I wish I'd asked you:
what is made smaller
by a name? This birdsong,
the tilting trill, embroidered cry
staggering from azaleas –

would it be less for being
named together with others
who share its cry? After all,
it knows its song. So
do those who need to hear it.

My cousin's three-year old son
held his small arms open wide
as I said goodbye.
I love you so, he cried.
What's your name?

Neurodivergency

Jessica Goody

"At last, I began to consider my mind's disorder a sacred
    thing." - Arthur Rimbaud

I survived the Holocaust of birth,
the poison palace of the womb.
One quadrant of my brain is blank,
oxygen lost like air from a broken balloon.
In my mind's eye, that hollow is dark,
a clotted cave of scar tissue. Elsewhere,
brain pathways are lit like switchboards,
thoughts blinking like turn signals.
You can see the nerve-socket glow,
trace its trail from synapse to cell.

The ego delights in taxonomy, sorting the population
into neat categories: "normal", "perfect", "strange".
Imaginary words, transient and impossible
as the ever-shifting horizon.
All neurodivergency is the same.
The tic and twitch of Parkinson's Disease
isn't all that different from the spastic's spasm:
The complicated electrical mechanisms of the mind
are controlled by the same mental motherboard.

The brain rattles in a dance of the ancient trickster god.
Numbers and letters flicker on the page like butterflies
defying capture, evading lepidopterous nets and corkboards.
Perhaps the silence of the autistic, the selective mute
is a defense mechanism against society's noise,

the volatile verbosity of Tourette's
a simple refusal to let his subconscious go unheard.

Being Handicapped

Jessica Goody

Being handicapped is a lifestyle unto itself.
Those who were born able-bodied
and transfigured into the afflicted
due to old age or accident can't comprehend
the subtle but certain difference.

Even war veterans, victims of
catastrophic mishaps and natural disasters,
however battle-scarred, don't know exactly.
Their point of view is one of grief, as if something has died.

And it has. They can no longer ambulate; their legs
Are heavy paperweights, dangling uselessly from hips
Bitten with shrapnel.
They mourn their former lives, their physicality.

It is all the more galling because
their days of Herculean feats are now gone.
Cops, firemen, soldiers, whose personas were founded
On saving lives, facing danger, fighting for the common good
Are no longer able to slay society's dragons.

But what of the ones
Who had no such glory days,
who were "born that way":

Disabled.
They envy the ease with which other children move,
their speed and precision
as they run, kick, dance and dive.
they regret not possessing such abilities
Even though they never knew what it was like.

I remember, as a child
Waking at dawn, tiptoeing to the patio,
Stepping onto the yellow-painted wooden deck
silent, eager for a taste of freedom.
My clandestine excursions, solitary and tame,
Were merely an excuse to stay barefoot a little longer.

Had the grown-ups known I was awake,
they would have proceeded to dress me
in long white knee socks, cuffed
over the hard tree trunks of my braces.
Once strapped into my legwear, they remained,
solid and unforgiving, until I was undressed at night.

Being handicapped is oddly like being an athlete:
Spending hours stretching, flexing, pulling, straining
One's body in order to reach
the ultimate physical capability.
For us, the "ultimate" is being able
to hold a fork, button a shirt, or write a straight line.
I could not tie my own shoes until I was twelve years old.

The tyranny of the wheelchair,
which seemed a luxury to the kids
Who on field trips had to trudge
from bus to museum to exhibit to gift shop.
What they didn't know is the way
the wheels clattered over the cobblestones,

Which nobody thinks about nowadays
except in the historic places
where people go to sight-see.

The way the chair rattled, jarring me so
that I nearly slid from my seat;
the way my body felt every line, crack and pothole,
every blemish in the asphalt, every loose pebble,
and the way store aisles are never wide enough.

The narrowness of staircases, the smoothness
Of walls lacking railings and bannisters.
The way the barest incline
is an Everest to be perilously crossed
When your body cannot support itself,
possesses no balance in its equilibrium.

For Karen
Jessica Goody

I feel the strain in my own arm muscles
As, strapped to crutches, you concentrate
all your strength to shift mere centimeters.
the poles dig into the ground with a rhythmic click.
The leather bands cut into your arms,
unyielding as a tourniquet.

I was born asleep
at six months old, like you.
They said you would not survive.
They said the same to me.

Had I been born a mere three years before, the advances
which kept me alive would not have existed.
I cannot imagine how you did.

I have no memory of the white box
in which I existed, to ensure the steadiness
of pulsing organs
And could have just as easily
been the box they put me in to die,
My shoebox-coffin buried in the backyard.

How did you do it in the days
before hyperactive technology,
When record players with fragile needles held music,
when gas stoves heated the meals?
Did you light the pilot light with a match, lickety-split,
the snap of the pip-head against the thumbnail,
or did you struggle, hands shaking,
to merely hold the speck of wood,
to strike the match without breaking it, as I do?

Were your legs always cold in the omnipresent
gingham dresses and tartan schoolgirl skirts,
not encased in blue jeans (unladylike
and impossible to pull on flailing legs
and spasming feet) despite the winter wind?

I bet when the polio vaccine was discovered
you cheered, not simply for the succor, the relief
the eradication of a succubus disease,
but because you knew all too well what lay behind
the colorized March of Dimes posters,
their hand-tinted portraits of the afflicted,
rosy and angelic.

You knew the unwilling, unrepentant clench of muscles,
the tenseness of tendons, the agony of being forced
to sleep in unnatural positions, splinted and exhausted
from the strain of rigidity and the lack of rest.
The years when physical therapy was your only extracurricular.

You are more familiar with hospitals,
their rhythms and protocol
Than anyone without a medical degree should be.
How many meals have you eaten off of metal trays
In rooms of bilge green, bruised and infected mauve,
and industrial beige?

Have you tallied those long days and nights?
How many of your years have you spent isolated, infirm,
      invalid
Amidst glass thermometers and sterilizing ovens,
rubber tubes and white nurses' caps?
The thick, vicious needles, bitter medicines, the trespass
Of strange hands giving you sponge baths,
your body left clammy and violated?

You waited every year for your life to begin,
like Miss Haversham in her moth-eaten trousseau
believing that every new surgery,
every expanse of time spent bed-ridden and immobile
would bring a miracle:

That you would stand straight,
you would Walk, you would wear ordinary shoes.
You would be able to keep time with the rest of the world,
instead of sweating, straining, to pull on a sleeve,
turn a key in a lock, dial a telephone.

Fabulous Fringes
Leah Kelley

(*In response to being described as a radical fringe element...
Bring it!!*)

I love the edges of things
places of intersectionality
where ideas meet
thinking is broadened
perspectives are shared

there is beauty in the edges
the fabulous fringes
that decorate our interactions
and build understanding

Liquid Man
Leah Kelley

15
I see you perched on the edge
A balanced droplet
Reflecting back the whole world
Defying gravity
Rocking softly
Regrouping
With gently swayed rhythm
Considering
Owning your body's movements

Choosing curled still solitude

23
I see you sliding down a wall
The edge that keeps you
Gives solace
Defining your space
You say awkward
Some might accuse: flop
(they know not)
I see ownership of liquid beauty
You puddle on the floor
Relaxed fails as a descriptor
Your words are spinning
Weaving thoughts
Spinning
And I can hardly keep up
But the vision of your
Wall water self
Exploring concrete edges
That anchor
As your thoughts
go to places far and wide
The naturalness
The beauty in the authentic
The message in that move
Is nourishment
Joy

52
I see you reflected
And reflecting
And dazzling
Water in water
Connections

Ripples felt as you move
Flowing
Seamless
Sound and movement amplified
Emotions intensified
The Butterfly Effect
Transformative
Connected in the wake
Or the wave
The pebble in the pond
Affecting one other
We pool
Liquid
Reflected
Movement

15, 23, 52
I see the silent power of your liquid ways
Refusal to be contained
Stuffed down
Boxed in
Shaking off shame's plea for a discrete mopping
Water protests, in all its liquid forms:
Drops, tears, puddles, pools, and oceans wide
To combat the stream is folly
It is to miss the moment of perfect stillness
Where the whole world is reflected
That convex bead
Tenuous balance held forever
In the present tense of poetry
Defiant
Destined to be triumphant
This is the power of persistence...
Rail against the rock
And honour yourself in all your watery forms

Two Months Of Outpatient Treatment And All I Got Was An Updated Comfort In Sondheim

Lucas Scheelk

[Certain details omitted due to privacy]

A new guy [he was new to me] came in to Group Therapy one day, and my paranoia was set off right away. An unexpected man. My breathing was tactical, my chest tightened, my admissions limited, and eventually I became non-verbal. When I told the therapist the next day what had happened, all I was told was that men would, "come in and out of the group".

I haven't disclosed [since the initial intake] that I'm autistic. I'm not there to defend myself.

Hyperfocused on a painting placed on the wall across the room from me during group therapy. The picture within the painting was cut up into squares and rearranged into jumbled patches of color *["and light"]*. The other people in my group exuded their tales in almost epic proportions. I tried to find the colors on the painting that matched the lyrics from "Color and Light" in *Sunday in the Park with George*. This happened on a Tuesday.

Just before Group Therapy session started, I heard someone mutter the r-slur in conversation. I coped by tracing a tree pattern on the carpet with my eyes. I turned again to Sondheim. Same musical as before, but this time, from the song "Move On": "*Notice every tree*".

One Monday wouldn't have been possible without taking an Adderall before leaving the house, then proceeding to drink 3 cups of coffee throughout the morning. I needed to be functional to get through yet another Group Therapy session.

The next day – same drug intake formula.

We started the day rearranging words on the table. The second hour was Arts & Crafts. My hands smelled like glue and were covered with glitter as I placed mosaic tiles on my tray. I allowed myself to doodle on my folder during Group Therapy, the last session of the day, so I had something to do with my hands.

The focus without the panic... I was actually able to talk through the whole 8 minutes.

I've been asked, at least once, if I'm at outpatient because of a legal requirement. People just can't figure out why I'm there in the first place.

A different person, at the end of their last day, told me that I was brave for seeking treatment, especially "at a young age".

When my Mom's anger started being directed at me again, I called a friend to temporarily remove me from the situation. My friend offered me a place to stay long term, should I need. My instincts made the decision before I did.

Thursday. Mid July. By the time I arrived at outpatient that morning, I had already been awake for 24 hours, worked an eight-hour overnight shift, and hadn't eaten since before work.

I had three cups of coffee within the first hour.

I had one Adderall left. I was saving it until the next day, when I'd go visit 2 of my Grandmas graves at Fort Snelling for the first time.

During the last hour of outpatient, I was told that after the session, I'd be having a "monthly treatment plan" with my therapists.

I had no notice.

The 3 therapists and I sat inside a tiny office, with the door closed. I could feel them all staring at me, as if their pupils were nudging me, trying to get my full attention. I thought I was getting kicked out of outpatient. My thoughts were scrambling to piece together what I did wrong.

I had no time.

I had no opportunity to prepare my answers. It took a long time for me to respond to a suggestion that I should find a long-term therapist.

When I was allowed to leave, my lungs moved as fast as my legs.

My panic attack intensified at the light rail station as I was waiting for the train. I had to take my last Adderall. I needed to feel like I wasn't going to die.

Thursdays. Middle of the month.

"These meetings always happen on a Thursday. We scope out who's around."

Do not trust those who give zero notice.

Exactly 7 days after my last Adderall intake. Thursday.

Same lack of sleep. Same overnight shift on Wednesday night. Thankfully, no surprise meeting.

I asked the person in charge of Arts & Crafts hour if I could sleep.

After suggesting sleeping in the waiting room (I cannot comfortably sleep near people I do not know – paranoia), and going home (I wouldn't make the bus trip without falling asleep), the person in charge then said:

"If you slept in here it wouldn't count as you being here. We couldn't charge your insurance company if you're only here for 2 of the 3 sessions in a day. But then that's probably not a worry for you, since you're not paying for it."

I tried my best to hyperfocus on my phone during Arts & Crafts.

I fell asleep no less than three times during Group Therapy the next hour.

During Group Therapy one morning, I dissociated. I think... Did I?

I was going through an episode where a middle aged white guy (never seen him before) had just raised a gun during a film showing. I thought that if I hid myself and the closed captioning device I was using below the chairs, I wouldn't be noticed. Is it possible to have an episode from something that's personally never happened to you?

I pulled myself out by repeating in my head, "*Notice every tree/understand the light*".

When I received the paperwork back from the UNEXPECTED MEETING – under the Strengths portion of the assessment, the first thing listed was, "Employed".

The same assessment diagnosed me with Major Depression.

Was close to a meltdown during a Group Therapy meeting. I can't deal with hearing non-autistic people talk about us when/especially when I don't feel safe enough to disclose my identity.

I gathered up my arts projects at the end of the day. My instincts made the decision before I did.

Missed two outpatient days. No phone calls. Not even to ask, "Are you alive?"

At my friend's apartment, a painting was born in a burst of concentration.

A black canvas, with green glow in the dark acrylic stenciling.

NOTICE EVERY TREE

UNDERSTAND THE LIGHT

The letters glow before I sleep. When I sleep.

Over two weeks since I left. Outpatient contacted my Mom.

Who in turn was hostile at me over it when I visited her.

Do not trust those who first rely on secondary testimonies about your mental health, over your experiences.

The only reason I visited Outpatient (in the lobby, before hours) was so then I could try to discreetly get discharged from the program (not in person with a therapist, but not over the phone, and definitely not after going through a group session).

I was handed a phone number. So much for discreet.

My Group Therapy leader, after a month since I left, called me. Left a message.

Just before my phone shut off for 3 days due to low funds.

Each day, I believe I have enough executive functioning to go back to Outpatient to begin the discharge process.

Each day, the paranoia that I'll be forced back creeps in.

I'll find another way.

"*I chose and my world was shaken/So what?/The choice may
have been mistaken/The choosing was not/You have to move on.*"

!Vivá la Frida!
Luis Lopez-Maldonado

Fresh roses adorn your head
Twist in and out of your perfect *trenza*
(ironically known as the *Frida* braid)
Round like a *tortilla*
Ribbons here and there
Red White and Green
Rojo Blanco y Verde,
The way your earrings fall south
Your silk *rebozo*
The Gold ring your *Diego* gave you
Ese Panson!
You light a cigarette
And converse with the stars
In the Blue House
La Casa Azul
Sitting on an old chair
Diego nowhere to be found,
His shirts reeking of whores
His lies tattooed on your chest
His *mentiras* tattooed on your *pechos*
You bleed like an open wound
And lay frozen, dead with silence.

Frida: You close your eyes
And make weird noises
(moans and groans of sex and desire)
Your black eyes pin me down
And I can see flecks of laughter
Inside of them, deep down
As you bite bitter fruit
And stare at the yellow moon
Pregnant with light
Hanging in the air like *mangos*.

Thirty winters and
Thirty springs
Will never be enough
To erase your face
Your masculine eyebrows
Your full lips
Your *faldas largas*
Your aching paintings
Your blind love,
But it might be enough
To say a prayer or two,
(to *La Virgen de Guadalupe*)
Look up into the blue
And try making sense of it all,
Nodding at everything the *gringos* say
Their eyes of wax and
Wine and oil.

But time passes by
Everything passes by,
And in the distance
Beyond fried roses and limp trees,
Constellations burn into nothing,

Into everything–
The Blue House
No longer blue
The blood stains
No longer stains,
But art.

A Found Poem On Saturday Morning, South Bend, Indiana

Luis Lopez-Maldonado

Inspired by Ta-Nehisi Coates

Last Sunday
A satellite closed the miles between us
White America's Progress
Was built on looting and violence
Stood in defiance of their own God
Life, Liberty, Labor and Land
A 12-year-old black boy tearfully hugging a white officer
Fail
Perfect houses with nice lawns
Cookouts
Tree houses
Sad for my country
Sad for you

The killers of Michael Brown would go free
I have never believed it would be okay
Eric Garner chocked to death for selling cigarettes
Renisha McBride shot for seeking help

John Crawford shot for browsing a department store
Men in uniform drive by and murder Tamir Rice, a 12-year-
    old child
It does not matter
It does not matter
It does not matter
Your body can be destroyed
Escape
Survive
Streets
Black History Month:
Intimate violence
The babies having babies
HIV
Michael Jackson
Ice Cube
Malcolm
Jim Crow
Chocolate City
Our history inferior

Black skin
Black kings
Black blood
White America

Here is what I would like for you to know:
Heritage
Sprit
Soul
Body
Brain
Wings
You will misjudge
You will yell

You will drink too much
I am sorry that I cannot save you–
But not that sorry

Moving in before school starts, South Bend, IN

Luis Lopez-Maldonado

Outside the night breathes
What's left of summer,
Blooming roses
Flying June bugs
The distant fields of corn
But there is nothing left inside of me,
Pray the gay away, they said
Pray the gay away
Pray the gay away, brother:
How has life come to this?

I gobble down a bag of Flaming Hot Cheetos
Take a sip of black wine
Scratch my dry hair
And across the street a cookie crumbles,
A little white girl staring up
Pointing at the dead constellations:
Delight has to be somewhere.

Fear coils around me like a rattlesnake,
At Wal-Mart customers ask me if I work there.
Students ask me if I am an international student.
And I laugh at them.

Tell them I don't work there.
And I'm not an international student.
I am a professional bitch!
I am from California motherfuckers!
Because gay men don't have periods,
But exclamation marks!

Too many degrees and too many *gringos*
Have ruined the Mexican in me,
Now all I have is *Tapatio* in the fridge
Frijoles pintos in a mason jar
Processed organic *tortillas* from Costco:
Keep your flags flying high *Chicano*.

But tonight I am alone in the endless of the night
Outside nothing breathes. You're quite. I blink.
The wooden bench swings your body like a baby;
The moonlight hugs your curves
And I whisper an *ave maria*
Praying to God or the sun
For patience.

Failure

Marc Rosen

I fucked up again
There's so little I seem
To do right these days

I've been arrogant again
By sending an apologetic message
Asking what your preferences would be

I'm being selfish again
It's wrong to show emotion
No matter how patiently I wait

I angered you again
Your words confirm this
Whether I know how and why or not

I betrayed you again
Somehow, whatever I do
I only wound you more

I'm being an asshole again
By writing these lines
I'm an ungrateful bastard

[Picasso Baby]
Fable the Poet

*"We've become a country where
race is no longer so black or white."*
                    - Lise Funderburg from National Geographic

By 2050,
75 million Americans will be able to identify with more than a
    single race.
Meaning most
will actually look a lot like me.

A Picasso -
once considered abstract thought, turned realistic present.

I am sure at one point, you have most likely heard people say:
"Those lips, with that hair?"
Or
"Those eyes, with that skin?"

"That is crazy, but it is not art!"

I personally heard it for the first time in elementary art class.

But
what if Pablo saw the future by gazing into the eyes of his
    paintings
showing him the mismatched features of
humanity and
equality in years to come?

A canvas strategically turned magic mirror, to hang on

museum walls to reassure
"Each and every one of you is the most gorgeous of all.
Ignore any rule, belief, or standard the closed-minded create.

Collaborate and you might make something

beautiful."

When my mother and my donor attempted their
recreation of "The Weeping Woman",
the most common responses to the brush technique they used
    are:

"Where are you from?"
Or
"What are you?"

I now like to say that
Apparently, I am the future.

I am human,
before race was ever used as a chisel or a crutch.
Pre-whips, ripping open the midnight flesh,
showing starry, flickering eyes over
scars and hope that could be seen dying long ago.

Skin showed a journey.
It showed our ability to grow and adapt, be it dampening the
    beating sun rays - *instead* of pride.

Or eyelids molded to an environment with terrain too rough
    to take in with a wide
gaze.

We have forgotten

that our days are numbered.
You can see the thing we focus on most is reflection, instead of
    the direction
we are moving.

Why do we so easily replace hope with hate?

Digging into our history books for life lessons of mistrust, as
    if our great grandparents' parents struggle
should trouble us today.
Yet, it always will.

It is apparent that some of us aren't ready to nurture the
    future.
We are so busy stringing up the past that children will never
    learn to be
monarch butterflies, and break out of the darkness in a world
    that helps us
grow.

Instead
we just train to be monarchs of government because that is
    more
relevant than evolving.

Dear caterpillars,
prepare to fly!

The U.S. Census predicts that by 2080, Caucasians –
those of white European descent –
will no longer be the racial majority in the United States.

And although you will never be able to debate facts –
one being that the majority
rules –

you can choose your voice.

I was once told,
"You will always be seen as a black male."

But I want to be seen as that butterfly.
Two tones collaborating past judgment and flying above a
      stigma.

Because, black is beautiful but
so are the other tones.
I want the orange in my wingspan to be *seen*, not as an
      undertone,
not as an overtone, but a stern tone of voice saying

I am, in flesh and blood, foreshadowing our future.

Instead of covering up my
"What are you?"
I want to be a *WE*.
A W.E.B,
webbed - from Dubois to Marley.
from Barack to Malcolm.
Letting my Xs only be seen as a part of what made me.
Made me a lover of Booker T. Wash, Jimmy Hendricks, and
      Tiger.

Letting what mends the past be the present of life that can tip
      the census.
The best
tip that changed my senses?

"You will always be seen as a black male; you can only pretend
      to be colorblind."

And it is true,
because dark and light hues will always be more prominent
    with *color* being a standard.

There will never be a bandage for racism.
But sporting the crutches after you've started to heal is almost
    as bad as
chiseling away the progress.
Walk, run, stay full stride in the right direction

but be weary;
we are still healing.

Because
Obama's skin is still seen as "the first of its kind."
Instead of
"the first of many to come."
So eggshells planted under the White House carpets
crack every time our nation blames "the one,"

the first,
the original spotlight, museum-framed, and featured Picasso.
Who admitted to being a "mutt,"
as if NOT being a "purebred" is an imperfection.

Dear fellow monarch of another kind,

In 2050 I will be 61 years old.
A well-learned butterfly.
Waiting to be seen as one of many,
proud of my years of flying as an individual.

What is sad is that I will be able to say
"You have it easier now."
But what is beautiful is that I will be able to say,

"You have it easier now."
Nobody thinks you are too dark,
or too light,
or not right.

What's sadder is, if I say it,
I will be bearing the same chisel that will exist forever.

Weather the storm,
be great young caterpillars,
and prepare yourself to fly

free.

[Did You Know?]

Fable the Poet

Did you know
they made pharmaceuticals illegal today?

It turns out:
they are addictive,
if you take too many you can die,
they sway your mood,
they can impair your motor skills, driving, and even
alter your mind.

I wonder -
I wonder how they found this out?
How long could they have known about this?
Did you know?

Oh,
you did?

Well you couldn't have known
I was given early onset memory loss,
walking a straight line, heel-to-toe, over desired memories,
    proudly.
Laughing in the face of death, screaming
"WHAT IS THE WORST THING YOU CAN DO?
TAKE HIM?!"

But *they* took him. They being the ones in my family who act
    more denim than genetic.
And to this day I regret leaving his side.

Mr. Doctor, what part of my grandfather's being helped you
    find and diagnose Alzheimer's?

I know an MRI can help you see the overall appearance of the
    brain,
But did you witness thumbtacks envying his sharpness?

Was it that he knew my mistakes before I made them?
And that he could play wide receiver in family reunion
    football, and call the wide receiver position, while
    remembering his high school routes?

I doubt it could be the steel vault brain that contained
generations of names
of people he loved.

I didn't shrug
when you started giving him the medication-
I cried.

And twice as hard when I was told my name may slip his
    mind.

But I was happy finding his pain, his fear in my life, it was so
    clear.
I had to forget,
like he did.
Because he'd never,
so he chose to-
he had to,

so I did.

I find it deeply upsetting that a side effect of antidepressants
Is feelings of suicide.

I find it even more depressing
that 1 out of every 10 of you hearing this
takes them.
And may proceed to have this on your mind.

Envision yourself on a roof, pointing,
with four fingers judging you back.
A vicious cycle of "I love you" notes, as your digits turn to
    plucked petals in your palms.

You, not you, not you, not you, not you, you, not you, not
    you, and 12 more "not's",

But a million more "you's",
stressing
thinking a pill can fix it all.

Just as Granddad never wanted to put a price tag on his mind,
but did.

Accepting the thought that a doctor
was qualified enough to evaluate him,
trade his memories for corporate-priced capsules.
As though his degree can supersede any doubt.

Not mine.
I find it deeply upsetting that a side effect of an Alzheimer's
    medication is
memory loss.

So if diagnosed wrong,
your son's name and birth date might be gone,
but thank God for recovery.

Recovery,
Recovery.

We forget about that word.
But how could you ever remember when they spoon-fed you
    the recipes to
forget.
Give you security to slip, free fall into one's self-
doubt –
not,
They will save you!

Because you PAID to!
Right?

Well I didn't
and I won't

but I will still smile!
Wishing I didn't make myself forget, and push away so many
    faces

that I'm scared
I will not have enough time
to pull close again.

But hey!
They made pharmaceuticals illegal today.
Who would have known they were bad?

I never would have guessed –
I forgot.
On purpose.
You may have as well.

❖ ❖ ❖

[Don't Mind Me]

Fable the Poet

"This one
was meant to be quiet,"
said doctors about the child,
stillborn. Moving.
Said factors about the lifestyle
I *still* live.
Yet –
soothing me more than the antidepressants.

Because isn't it depressing how life works sometimes?
But isn't it refreshing how life works some times?!

I'm sorry,
I guess that was the "bipolar".
When I can go from my childhood memories like

Saturday morning cartoons –
understanding why I love
ninjas,
pizza,
and turtles.
To not understanding why life's hurdles seem to match Berlin
    Walls,
as I've crumbled to pharmaceutical commercials.
Because the jingles over the symptoms
Matched the dinner bell within.

And I've been *starving* to feel normal.
My own arm always looks a bit more appetizing when I feel
    trapped.
So, smother that?
No!
Where is the salt?

Because I know someone is willing to throw it,
and I might have open wounds that won't heal soon.
So,
if you are going to throw it
could you please pass
on the paper shakers?

It is normal to eat three meals a day,
and this would make a great one.
But,
do we suffer from bulimia
if were coughing up our differences instead of breakfast?
What's normal?
Because sometimes when I reminisce,
I get sad.
Is that depression?

Should life lessons be-

Forgetting that my step dad tried to fight me every day
Because a pill will fix that!
Erase the memory of my grandest father figure, before he
      figures out I
just can't bear to see him change with time.
I was told Alzheimer's would make him forget me,
anyway.

This one time,
I thought about killing myself.
A pill should fix that, right?

That's not *normal*.
But what's normal?

I hear the symptoms are
having both parents
happy and functional.
What you are seeing
is actually what you get
and nothing grows graveyards in closets
behind locked doors and secrets.

Because those skeletons,
if they admit their skeletons,
will be safely swept under the rug out of sight, and out of
      mind.
As if the blind are happier people.

Happy, that's normal!
And not bottling the-

"You won't, because you can't,"

or
"You are too_____ to do it,"
and the
"I wish they never, so I never felt,
not normal."

You shouldn't bottle, unless it's prescribed.
It's not normal.

Well, neither is having my disorder, apparently.
While for some scary reason,
I am labeled a 25th percentile child, and the world isn't
    bipolar.

I ask then,
why does the globe have two?
I've been taught to think my emotion percent is more relevant
    than race
because face it,
with the globe being 20% black, 10% Hispanic, 12% Biracial,
I am forced to equally bandage my issues in the order of:
-Issue
-Get a tissue
-Race

Because face it,
I'm a fucking minority anyway.
A 25% of a 12% leaving me feeling about 3%

normal.

But this,
this is for the paper shakers.
The ones whose hands match leaves in fall,
but don't –

because they aren't normal –
praise it!
Using crowds' ears like medication,
because it's cheaper!
Face it,
the only insurance we ever needed was people showing us
that someone
is willing
to listen.

Genuinely listen.
And even if it's you, this one.
Keep your phone away.
But not the applause,
And look in awe at the people here
brave enough to feel
normal,
trying to feel
normal.

My little brother is nicknamed after the prior who was
      stillborn.
But he -
he *is* moving
through life as a reminder to me
that being still
is *not* why we were born.

Life can SUCK!
But duck a punch and suck it up!
But don't sucker punch the ones lucky enough to find their
      passion
in their sanity.
Doctor to pen,
script to paper.

Chasing an eating disorder by feeling sort of
normal.

Have you ever contemplated suicide?
Do you ever get depressed?
Why at times does it feel like there is nothing left
when there is everything?

The same reason people pay no attention to art, but paint.
Or pay to record
but tune others out.
We all want good listeners
but can't do it our selves so

find out the world's north and south poles are milestones!
And appreciate what you have,
no matter what it is.

Because sometimes you will be the only one who can, or will.

And there isn't a pill to fix that.
That is a fact.

Sleeping with the NT

Sabrina Zarco

Well here I am again
with a new lover, new scene.
I try to convince myself
I have learned what not to do
and it will be an award winning relationship
this time.

I will gladly accept my award for best autistic supershero.
Cloaked in my best indigenous NT rebozo (shawl)
adorned with silver jewelry cuffs of my ancestors
and this time,
this time
my wild autistic heart will not
commit relationship suicide.
Well at least not in the first few scenes.

Those that came before her had great promise
but the challenges of being queer
are sometimes heavy enough
on a relationship.

Im Chicana, Queer, and Autistic
the triple crown of activism and social justice causes.
It's a revolutionary art
just to be me.

I remind myself that
the quirky artist part she adores about me
is really just me
out of my Autism closet.

I wonder how long
before
like in the scene from the movie
about the body snatchers
I am revealed and the stares and pointing will begin.

I can smell the spices coming from the kitchen
a mixture of sweet cultural memories
and unwavering olfactory overload.
She loves to cook.
I don't know how
or when I should tell her.
I try to remember it's a gesture of her love for me
and she is unaware of the assault on my senses.
I smile, mask my distress,
as being tired from a long day
and once again
I attempt to navigate in stealth mode.

I long to tell her how I struggle
when she reaches for me in an intimate moment.
That gentle touch filled with love
how can she even begin to know
that it sends me into physical withdrawal.
Like a thousand spiders
slowly making their way up
and down my body.
I struggle to hide this reaction
and look for a distraction.
There must be a way.

She wants to walk arm and arm
and hang with the crowd tonight

because she doesn't know
Im short on spoons today
not enough energy to keep up.

I wonder how many times
I can push myself to the edge
and then reel it all neatly back in
because she means so much to me
and she knows Im autistic
and "its ok".

She just didn't know
I was going to look like
La Llorna
the weeping woman in the night
uncontrollably crying and rocking
just to release
the days extroverting
on my pillow.

Dios mio
How many times
is internal combustion
with a side of meltdown
acceptable this go around?

I try to play the parts I learned
watching classic movies
but I know its just a matter of time
before the scenes end.
And I'm alone again
looking for another audition.

Mariposa

Sabrina Zarco

Gone are the days I hold my head down and pass.
I am a cis woman in a mans world.
A Chicana in a White world.
Queer femme pansexual in a heterosexual world.
And a Neuroqueer in a Neurotypical world.

One or more of my identities is blamed for
the downfall of the economy,
natural and unnatural disasters,
the loss of moral decency,
and a burden on society.

Seriously?
I didn't realize how powerful I am.

Sadly there was a time
I believed the hype.
Years of internalized oppression
took its toll on my physical
mental and emotional well being.

Like a butterfly
emerging from her cocoon
I am now unapologetically me.

A beautiful intersection
with multiple layers of
life perspectives, experiences
and new adventures waiting to happen.

No more playing oppression Olympics
I stand in solidarity
and embrace all of my intersections.
I am unapologetically me.

Open Loop Triptych

Stephanie Heit

(the understudy waits for cough or stumble **in the wings** an
exchange of pronouns mops up the unsaid she takes keys out
of hidden pockets and cradles grief so I can go to school and
pretend stillness of hands she is the dancer lights off naked in
a studio laughing because I is a slippery vessel that only holds
spine and limbs a coat rack of costume **what will I** wear today
on the other side a trapdoor with hinges that give
unexpectedly I wait for the one I love only mystery shades her
already familiar face after years of hiding **the task of** rerouting
despair to the ocean a sunbather she reaches upward while I
find endpoints to touch what is not my face exhausted
expression of relief **when the tide and all this** water her doing
and I keep silent in arid climates because sight saddens this
detached version fastens itself around neck a slim snap to
sacrifice a part for this steady persistence her beauty marked a
flaw of division she could carry the spring I buried myself and
take away the sin of what has left the eyes a carriage a drawn
exit the joke she remembered when **I forgot how to say** yes
fastened a framework to swing from without danger of noose
and **where I fail she continues** relentless as morning)

(**she** yes she again in silence a misaligned comfort to match
snow in October and the leaves **turn away** her frame slighter

less sturdy from uphill travel slip of step when locomotion
from one corner to the other was a way to speak she writes an
entrance **she does not enter** barren **I enter and she does not
know** to write an exit unlit a tunnel when supposed light and
gentle acceleration instead clash and bump and nothing
reflects the sullen her mother would say ghost and **how could**
as she walked without sound unseen because too much entered
the eye a retina detached and **she pulled inward to live** below
her means the trail to follow entrance served exit when no
other way presented I found her on the kitchen floor we rose
in territories no **one should go** past the unbreakable kept safe
like a doll eyes open and close when tilted **when gravity** is
most kind)

(and she knew how to place hands on another and tilt her
head in comfort but still this jangle of disbelief the date
approaches and supposedly **absent yet I am** and continue to
wear seatbelts when speed is unavoidable seven times a day
ingestion to remember the ribbon laced around finger wife to
capitulation the shiny wrappers line her bag this unloading
channel blocker part of an experiment she leaned to see the
steadiness of tides and **it was easy** one foot then a clear bridge
with forced contraception her genes what would she leave as a
marker to say here and here and especially there the going
eventually **to take leave** and arrival desirable rather she wore
the baseboards down foundation obstacle for **flight**)

because these lines are

Stephanie Heit

a bridge of herring bone tidal patterns lost ships somewhere
bottomed. accompaniment jack hammer saws of construction.
this build up to break down. (I must write these lines before
going further.) completion of five / ten words before step. this
is going slow. so the foot wobbles unsteady transfer of weight.

how to stand on exposed stone?

creekbed awake and stumble slosh around outstretched fingers
hold. the test of edges. sustain the weight of a body in transit.

how much does escape weigh?

outline of a person once here and then. what makes it across
and how the lines get filled shaded nicks scratches. skinned
knee still blood and sting almost forgotten. eye sight keen
attuned to make out tunnel openings / contrast of a gate
bolted close. remember the double locked doors and pending
certification. importance of answering their questions
correctly. on a scale of 1 to 10 with 10 being you are...

where are you?

I am lost in Malá Strana on the way to touch bullet holes in
                    Terezín where the tunnel is a
                    long walk of echoes and.
                    no hands.
I am on a ferry eating pomegranate seeds in the Aegean.
I am on the psych ward and the pen stops.

(I need to write) five / ten words to take another step but they
have taken my possessions. have stamped my hand with an IV
and stolen the contents of my stomach. torn throat and tired
but they open the door every fifteen to make sure I am still

                                                    breathing.

palms on unbreakable window to distinguish outside. (from
inside.) tucked away for weeks in a corner of this mountain
town with nothing to cut. through this sheen of they want me
to smile. they want to shock the light back in my eyes.

IfindtheVltavaIfindthebluelineatPiraeusIfindtheroadtotheligh
thouseatPointBetsieIfindthe bookshelvesofthegirlIusedtobe.

and this tumult and balance. I have fallen these words
unworthy. bridge. sag and disappointment I leave the bag at
the hospital and walk. through locks. (this is the dream
version.) something left behind. traces around the eyes / scar
marked wrist. preparation for tightrope walk for this river I
breathe across.

[two weeks in a sanitarium]

Thalia Rose

two weeks in a sanitarium
/
he is in charge of admission, this polish man with no
eyebrows, he picks at your skull to check for lice - *hey, you
know there's something seriously wrong with you right? you need
treatment* - you are angry, the tearful kind of upset, so you

bandage yourself up with dainty laughter *yes, of course* are you being battered with a baseball bat? is that a part of the healing process? you do not want to be in that windowless room for as long as staff keep you there
/

you accept the exchange, my story for yours, as you like stories and you have as many freckles as allergies, once you took lametical and it gave you steven johnson syndrome in which all your skin fell off, you glory in pain though so there was a strange pride when your fingernails slid down your fingers like butter and nurses had to hold your eyes open so the skin on your eyelids did not decay further while you told me about this i thought of the small angry polish man
/

flies buzz outside of the barred windows while you are laying bare-chested on the bed, eyelids shut as i read you the story of an old woman who went to bed and never woke up you say this story is scary
/

broken skin grows back you tell me even though friends avoid you and on the rare days you are well enough to attend school the silence saturates the air with pungent piss-stain sickness when you called the ambulance they thought it was a prank because your sobs sound like laughter until then you had never imagined talking static noise while the other line was unsympathetic
/

waking up with a body that rejects itself is inflamed gums and losing a lot of your hair. it feels like when you climbed a steep san franciscan hill to watch the fourth of july sky - the clouds ate the fireworks and the constellations were covered in smog
/

still the food on my dinner plate is as enormous and repulsive as the hair loss we encountered pale meat looks like deep-fried eyeballs and i felt impure enough to mash my teeth together and grind my food into a clump of possibly eaten meal

/

i sat in the land of hives and scrubs until i felt myself melt through the common-room chairs, first time i held your hand i explained how the stoplights from the hospital windows were one of the few things that made me happy, i dreamt of the oil painting traffic, smeared by the tallest trees in the world, i could hear where the cars came from but not where they were going

Part II: Fiction

Testimony of the Teen Ogre

Andrew M. Reichart

I insisted on putting this in writing so that, among other things, there can be no ambiguity as to my intent. Here's how I stalled Dr. Hariss till the camera crew arrived. My formal request follows the main narrative.

For starters, please forgive the fact that you can't take my word for this, given my actual and alleged divergences. But think it through: that's nothing special, that's always the case, whoever your narrator. If we're not taking someone else's word on faith, we're taking our own perceptions and cognitions as fact. But our senses only give us access to a small sliver of all phenomena; and we know that our self-narratives are post facto confabulations. Yes, I am saying that certainty is impossible. If you want to call me an epistemological nihilist, I'm ok with that, but don't mistake me for a moral nihilist. On the most abstract level I may agree that nothing means anything, not even ethically, but you won't convince me that my actions have no grounding in rightness. Their material effect serves as their own justification. On this basis I also thereby assert you should find my testimony credible. You may call this circular reasoning. I'm okay with that.

When I found Jeannie hanging in her room, at first I was surprised. Did Dr. Hariss really consider her a threat? Could he believe that her delusion (i.e., that he's possessed by a demon from Hell) crept dangerously close to the truth? Did he off her just for being such an incessant loudmouth about it, as if that might someday inspire someone competent investigate and discover the truth?

Funny of me to jump entirely past the option that Jeannie might actually have committed suicide. But of course she did not. I knew this not because she wasn't "the type" – there is no "type" – and not because her faith supposedly prohibited it; her faith also guaranteed her an eternal euphoric afterlife, and the ideologue will pick and choose which bits of dogma, if any, they wish to apply or disregard. No, I knew this had been done to her simply because I knew her conviction. She was dedicated to exposing Dr. Hariss as a demon, even if she died trying.

Seemed to me she posed no threat to him, though; if anything, she provided cover, because her version of the story was obvious nonsense. If she had ever produced a shred of evidence, then some concern on his part might be justified that she could inspire someone to follow up on her line of inquiry. But nothing she pointed to had any significance. Had she discovered, for example, his old manuscripts in a distinctly different handwriting? Or learned of how he used to drink two pots of coffee a day, then stopped cold turkey when he came here? No; her accusations lay along cryptic esoteric grounds which failed not because her cabalistic and astrological analyses were flawed – she seemed quite good at that stuff, such as it is. But all her work was predicated on the mistaken assumption that this was a demon of christian mythology. Nothing of the sort. Hariss was in fact a telepathically mind-swapped Yithian time-traveler from either the distant past, before the evolution of humanity, or from the far future, after our extinction. Not a demon at all, but an alien. A being just like the two fiends from Yith who bodysnatched my parents when I was a boy, and who righteously died by my hand while still occupying those hosts.

So why would Hariss risk attention with this stunt? Actually, as the only one left who was onto his game, I was the only one likely to spot that this suicide was faked. Did he intend to convey some kind of message to me? The next time I saw him, in the dining hall, the look he gave me made it clear: a threat. He knew I knew what he was, and he wanted me to know he knew. Might he even intend to pin her faked suicide on me? The thought gave me a momentary pang of concern, but nope, too convoluted. First prove it was faked, possibly exposing evidence against himself; then somehow prove it was my doing, me with no motive. Implausible all around. No, he was just trying to show me that he meant business, he'd stop at nothing, human life had no meaning to him, and I could be next.

So be it. Proving him the killer would be even more implausible for me, given my status as an inmate of this asylum with an extensive record of delusional raving (falsely so called, given that the Yithians are entirely real; but credibility is independent of fact).

So I would have to destroy him a different way.

I began bluntly.

The next day, in group with Dr. Megalon, I simply volunteered the opinion that Dr. Hariss had killed Jeannie.

Megalon and the whole group knew my history. How I had killed the Yithians who'd mind-swapped into my parents' bodies. How I first came here after spending weeks catatonic in cold solitary in the filthy county jail, a rare break in my lifelong peace of mind, traumatized with regret for having stranded my parents. Wherever in timespace they'd been swapped to, into whichever alien bodies, whether the beetle-people of millions of years hence, or the weird tentacled cone-creatures from before the dinosaurs; or perhaps somewhere else, even more distant on the timeline of the people of Yith and in stranger bodies still. And everyone sitting in circle knew how, a month after I had axed to death their human bodies, killing their Yithian infestation along with them, my parents had sent me the telepathic message assuring me they lived contentedly enough, wherever they were, and that their pride in my unflinching determination more than outmatched any inconvenience on their part. This communication from beyond the aeons restored my natural equanimity, enabling me to calmly endure the empty ritual of my trial, followed by the arguable inconvenience of my permanent incarceration here.

It does help that I am never bored: I spend any empty time meditating, aka staring into space, which only serves to further deepen my equanimity.

Perhaps a word about why I have no qualms killing Yithians. I could go down a path of argument that they are not "people," but that's bullshit, epistemologically and ethically. I could say it's self-defense; that line is typically ethically legit, and someone stealing your body seems fair enough reason for 'any means necessary' whether they take it from outside or from within. Thinking larger scale, if we fuck them up whenever they send scouts like this, perhaps they'll skip us entirely whenever their "current" bodies face extinction and they have to flee, en masse, into a planetful of new hosts. But regard for humanity frankly does not motivate much action on my part. As a species we are fucking awful.

For me, my most real reason to kill these folk is that they're fucking fascists, and all fascists must die. Their existence is predicated on serial genocide. If they made the slightest effort, they could find a way to occupy bodies not otherwise in use, rather than displacing the minds of an entire species into another biosphere light years away just in time for a supernova to burn them into interstellar dust. These people are super-geniuses, with a fascist society capable of organizing a project on the scale of finding and telepathically colonizing a planet. They could figure something else out, if they tried. Uplift? Clones? I don't know, they're the super-geniuses. So fuck the immortal folk of "Yith," whatever that long-gone place may have been. Kill fascists on sight, that's an uncontroversial ethical principle. (Even so, is every Yithian a loyal goosestepper? (Metaphorically, of course, in the case of the Permian cone-people.) What if they're a refugee? Bah; you're still bodysnatching. If we figure out a way to just force-switch you back, we will; till then, fuck you.)

So I told Megalon and the group of my fellow inmates:

"Dr. Hariss killed Jeannie."

This received crickets, a non-response it pretty well deserved, these folks rightly skeptical of my claims more or less across the board.

Crickets; so I continued, now announcing to them for the first time: "He's a Yithian, like the ones who took over my parents. I don't know if it's a coincidence, or if he came here after me. Spy, cop, assassin, heck it could be personal revenge: after all, I did murder two of them, coulda been *his* parents, ha ha." More crickets. "Anyway, Hariss probably killed Jeannie to scare me."

Given my history of axe-murdering people whom I claim to be infested with Yithians, this lands me gently in our own solitary, which is marginally more comfortable than County.

Dr. Hariss came to visit me quick. He acted patronizing and unperturbed, as usual, but clearly wanted to know exactly how I saw through his disguise. "So," he said, half to me, half to his henchman in white behind him, "how did you see through my disguise?" He laughed, a tad loudly. His henchman said, "heh," with a half-grin.

I began by explaining, "One of my more philosophically-inclined fellow inmates defined the word 'epistemology' as something along the lines of, 'How we know what we know.' I believe he said it encompasses not only the study of our perceptions, deductions, inductions, etc., but also the various degrees of certainty we can reasonably have about both the reliability and unreliability of any of these. As well as whether we should care, although that's perhaps more the domain of ethics. Or aesthetics?" Hariss scowled and his brow furrowed with gratifying annoyance so I continued my verbose, opaque digression. His henchman's eyes glazed over, which made me smile.

I continued, "Since all sensation is merely an approximation of a small fraction of the external world, and since even that is then further distorted by the processes of perception in the nervous system – and perception is so strongly fueled by emotion, expectation, bias, cognition, etc., then clearly no one can ever truly be certain of anything, even things as concrete and unambiguous as whether rocks are hard and water is wet." This conclusion is such a severe exaggeration of my actual view as to approximate satire, but I sought to unsettle him.

"Add to this my diagnosis of schizophrenia, and it is only reasonable for me to apply this skeptical view to my own impressions with rigor, even though any 'inaccuracy' in my ideas or perceptions is not necessarily intrinsically different from anyone else's. Nonetheless, if we are being rigorous, we are being rigorous."

He tried to interrupt, but I barreled on through him before he could complete a syllable. "Although, if we are being rigorous, it must be acknowledged that my diagnosis is based solely upon one delusion, and any other symptoms I may seem to have could be attributed to other forms of neurodivergence."

"Plus the small matter of killing your parents," he got in.

"The bodies of my parents," I said, staring into his eyes, "infested by the likes of you." I scrutinized both his human material body and his Yithian astral body for any sign of reaction, and both of them cringed ever so slightly. Nothing substantial, but amusing nonetheless. I wondered whether by keeping him off balance I might get him to tip his hand or make some misstep. Not that I needed more proof; I could see his inhuman alien soul plain as day, same as I could with my parents.

"In any event," I proceeded, "whether my diagnosis is complete bunk or not, whether it's attributed to me by the mundane meat-grinder of so-called justice or was given to me as part of a collaborationist plot with the parasites of Yith– " another flinch, plus his Yith-tail flicked irritably like a cat's– "rigor demands regardless that I treat even my own perceptions with skepticism. Therefore, although I have since childhood had some degree of what is sometimes called the 'second sight' – most simply defined as the ability to perceive certain aspects of the astral plane, the aether, the Otherworld, the Realm of Faerie, call it what you will – I must attribute at least as much skepticism to such experiences as I do to what most people would presumably describe as 'everyday phenomena.' Where does this leave us, you may ask."

"Not exactly how I would phrase it," snapped Dr. Hariss, "I was thinking more along the lines of 'will he ever get to the point,' but do go on."

"Well," I said, "this means that just because I could see the hideous Yithian parasites occupying my parents' unwilling host bodies" – a barely-perceptible clenching of the teeth there; funny that an interstellar time-traveling telepathic vampire should be thin-skinned – "I couldn't assume I saw things rightly. Even though I was only fourteen, I was smart enough, or skeptically enough inclined, to know I might be seeing things that aren't there. Other visions in the past had sometimes proven accurate – such as certain encounters with ghosts, gateways, and the so-called 'Boogeyman' – but most sat inconclusive. Also I knew myself, and the vagaries of the adolescent mind, well enough to know that possibly, as doctors later claimed both in court and here, my visions of twisted, grotesque, spiny, sneering monstrosities" – another jaw muscle working slightly, heh – "clinging to my parents could easily just be some sort of hallucination spurred by my own discomfort at growing older, increasingly seeing the flaws of their mere humanity, weird sexual tension, the usual stuff. Then again, I had no such issues before my visions began.... The extreme equanimity that typifies my peculiar neurodivergence had been in place all along and hasn't wavered much, from my near-tearless infancy, to my indifference to peer taunting, through the competently-executed double-demon-killing followed by trial and imprisonment here. So, adolescent hormones seem an unlikely stressor. Buuut... rigor. Might I have repressed some such anger or resentment so deeply that even I could not see it, for it to only burst forth as hallucination and delusion? Presumably possible. Therefore, we must resort to material evidence."

Here I fell silent, staring at the beady black eyes of the immaterial Yith-body contiguous with Dr. Hariss, watching my final statement sink in. It waited, braced, for me to continue. I didn't.

"Well?" spat Dr. Hariss.

I stared dispassionately into the beady demon eyes. It had surprised and gratified me how easily I was able to agitate the creatures infesting my parents, and I smiled faintly at how 'Hariss' showed the same vulnerability.

"Is there a point to all this?" he snarled. "Your exigesis or rant or whatever this is? I'd love to know what 'material evidence' you have about me. Do you have it in here with you?" He chuckled, gesturing to the empty room.

I smiled faintly wider and shook my head slowly.

He stared angrily at me. "I won't be played by you, Max," he growled.

"Surely not," I said.

"Explain!" he shouted.

"My parents," I began.

"Screw your parents!" he said. "Tell me about me!"

At this even his loyal orderly looked at him askance. As Hariss pulled himself together, I continued: "My parents." I watched him bite his tongue. I smiled, paused a moment longer, took a breath. "Had fallings-out with all close friends and family. As we know from my trial, nothing unexplainable by mundane reasons: coulda been stress, drugs, nervous breakdowns. Quit their jobs, withdrew their savings, but nothing odd enough to earn them the attention of even the state tax board, much less the paranormal wing of the FBI, if such a thing exists. So no one bothered to look, because no one took my testimony seriously – understandably enough, mind you; and they wouldn't have found anything anyway, I'd wager. If anyone had examined their papers, would, say, an abrupt change in handwriting been revealed? It would not, because my parents' parasites dutifully destroyed any and all such papers first thing upon arrival. Something which you may have done yourself with Hariss's personal effects."

We stared into each others eyes. I drew out the pause for a long moment.

"Not, however, with, say, handwritten manuscripts preserved in digital archives, or photographs of blackboard writing, or anecdotes in old colleagues' blogs about how Hariss used to drink two pots of coffee a day. All of which and more can be obtained online via clever usage of an internet search engine, as I have done, and as has been done under my direction by my man in the press. Who is currently using these materials in his next move. Which shall remain undisclosed for now."

Dr. Hariss looked half-baffled, half-enraged, with a crust of incredulous. "Your 'man in the press.' How do you have a 'man in the press'?"

I shrugged, refusing then, as now, to disclose my methods of contacting the outside world. "He has my full testimony, and I have alerted him that you have escalated to actual murder – why Jeannie and not me directly, I confess I can't fathom – and that I may be next. I gave him this notification immediately before heading to group to make my announcement, and you can likely expect the aforementioned 'next move' shortly."

"'Next move,'" scoffed Hariss. He leaned in and whispered to me, too quiet for his orderly to corroborate, "Jeannie was but a step in a gourmet performance. Your turn is soon, but I'm going to marinate you a bit longer."

It should be around this moment in the video that the

cameraman and his crew, having made their way through the facility, arrive at my room. The orderly panicking with his hands up. My masked man in the press asking, "Dr. Hariss, how do you explain your sudden change in handwriting two years ago?"

Then Hariss grabs my throat, snarls "You little shit," and I dislocate his thumb. Shortly after this is when you come into the tale, moments after my man and his crew have made their escape.

So. As for my formal request, I and my attorney demand that my evidence, as presented to the aforementioned cameraman and his crew and posted by them online, be given thorough consideration, regardless of preconceptions of reputability or legal status; and that this evidence not only be applied to my assault charge against Hariss, but that you reopen my matripatricide case and reconsider my old testimony in full, in light of this new information.

Of course I don't entertain any such likelihood; you think I'm crazy, and anything that fits my story must simply be a lie, an illusion, or a mystery. Fine. My trademark 'uncanny' equanimity serves me well in this regard. As you can well see, I have an adequate degree of mastery over this place to provide for my own comfort.

In closing, though, I presume your entire purpose of this inquiry has been to get information from me that will help you find my cameraman and his crew. Of course you'll get nothing; the only reason I stayed behind at all, rather than escaping with them, was to stall you just as I stalled Hariss. Given how agitated you have been, and how often you have pestered me during the admittedly extremely lengthy time I have spent composing this document, I feel reassured that I've succeeded. I confess to being very, very amused that my efforts to stall Hariss have now served double duty here in their recounting. Perhaps this unhelpful attitude will jeopardize any chance I might have with my aforementioned request, but as I said, I'm okay with that.

Monday, Past Blue

Barbara Ruth

September 13, Monday, Past Blue

Light through the partially drawn curtains, bustling sounds in the halls. New day. I was wrong, it's not a bar, but I don't recognize it as a hospital room I've been in before either.

An intern comes in, one of Dr. Chen's, but I don't remember his name. Maybe - maybe, he can tell me what has happened to my mind.

"Good morning Mrs. Isabella. I hear you had a rough night."

"Please. Can you explain what happened to me? I don't think it was a dream. But what I thought happened– " I stop, as images of my lover and my best friend here in this room, filled with hatred and disgust toward me flood through my body. Except that was in the bar. And we were never there. "What I thought was true couldn't have possibly happened."

He looks at me strangely. Did I say that wrong? Is he reacting to something about the way I look? "I have to look at the tapes," he says hesitantly.

What tapes? This seems like confirmation that I am under constant surveillance here at this hospital. Well, maybe in this case it can help me. I want him to look at the tapes. *I* want to see the tapes.

Another intern comes in. Maybe they're residents, I don't know how to tell the difference. I think I like this one, although I can't recall her name either. "Please," I hear the begging in my voice, and I don't think of myself as a person who begs doctors for anything, but I'm so desperate to know what has happened to my mind. I thought last night was real, completely real. How can I tell in any minute whether I am dreaming, hallucinating, or part of consensus reality? And if I can't tell, if I don't have that basic orientation, then I am, by my own definition, insane.

They turn to one another, exchange a look I can't interpret, possibly because I can't really see them. I wish I could wear my glasses. Why can't I wear my glasses? I know there's a reason but I forget what it is.

"You're smart," I say to the woman. "I think you've been kind to me. Please. Please please tell me. You know so much I don't - help me."

The man says. "Do you think she should be NPO just in case?" I scramble through my memory banks, trying to find that acronym. I know I could define it once, but now I have no idea what it means. What's wrong with me?

The woman shrugs. "Has she seen anyone besides residents and interns this morning?"

"I don't think so," he answers. "Not yet."

"Then let's make her NPO just in case." She turns to me and says, "Ms. Isabella, don't eat or drink anything this morning."

"Why? I think I've been drinking water this morning. No one ever told me not to eat or drink here before." Something flickers in my memory banks. "Are you planning to operate on me?"

They don't respond. Is the answer to that question somewhere in the tapes? How am I supposed to interpret their silence? How am I supposed to interpret anything around here?

"Oh good," the man says. "Here's Dr. Gray. We'll let you speak to her privately." He nods to the other resident and they leave.

"Hello, Ms. Isabella. What happened here last night?"

"I fell out of bed. Maybe I fell out twice. And then I was –
nowhere. Just nowhere. No connection to anything or anyone.
I couldn't feel the Dalai Lama, I couldn't feel my friends, my
family, I couldn't feel G-d. What is that? What is that in your
brain when you can't feel anything?" For the first time I'm
glad I'm seeing a psychiatrist. Isn't that who knows about
consciousness, about the mind? But she doesn't answer my
question.

Instead, she asks, "What else happened?"

Then I remember how much I don't trust her. I feel torn
between my need to conceal myself from her, for fear of what
she'll do to me, and my need to tell her anything I can, in the
hopes she'll explain this in some way I can understand.

"I hallucinated. I know now it was a protracted
hallucination, but at the time it was horribly real."

"What were these hallucinations?"

"Just bad things about me and my friends. I was very
certain we weren't in the hospital." I must keep myself from
blabbing everything to this untrustworthy bitch.

"Where were you?"

"I don't know. Maybe a bar. It was surreal, the whole thing
was surreal. It's distressing to think about it."

"I think you'll feel a whole lot better if we adjust your
medications."

"Stopping Dilantin would help a lot. I know I need to
titrate down, but the people who come with my pills keep
saying I'm not allowed to have less Dilantin, only the
prescribed dose or none. I don't want to go back into status
epilepticus. Can you make a schedule for reducing the dose
and getting off it safely?"

"That's not what I had in mind," she said. "I think we need
to increase your psychiatric medications."

"I was thinking Ativan might be helpful. I've taken it
before and I know I'm not allergic to it."

"You're already on something much stronger than Ativan. And clearly that isn't enough. You need strong medication. Right now you're on Respirdal. I think we need to increase that and add Abilify."

I've never heard of either one of them. I'm not in a position to go look them up on the internet. Maybe I'll get lucky with meds. Maybe they will help. But it would help so much just to know what happened.

"What is that, when I feel like I'm in the void, in nothingness. How does the mind do that?"

"I wanted to do another MRI when I heard about your episode last night, but I understand you wouldn't allow transport to take you to the machine." I start to respond but she cuts me off. "So maybe we can do something here. I'll just ask you some questions and we'll see if that will help me assess what happened. Let's try counting backwards from 100 by sevens. You remember that one."

"How can you be so cruel? I'm desperate here. Yes, I refused to go to the MRI machine. I remember screaming and screaming when they came for me, there in the bar/the hospital room/the void. And you must remember that I can't bear the 'count backwards by sevens' routine. What are you testing, how much it will take before I become catatonic?"

Did I have a psychotic break? What ripped inside my head? They must have seen the tapes by now. Why won't they tell me? Can't they figure something out from that? And who the hell can help me understand it?

How can I find the Dalai Lama again? How can I survive this place without him?

"I'm not going to count backward by seven or any other number. I'm never going to do that again. It gives me vertigo and it gives me a migraine. I can get those effects on my own, thank you very much, without your torture tests."

I stop talking. I shut my eyes, put on my headphones and just stop talking. Because really, what is the use?

This has been an excerpt from the novel *Lying in Beds I Never Made.*

❖   ❖   ❖

T-Bone

Elizabeth J. Grace

"Eli. Wake up. Come on, man, are you dead or something? Psst. Hey Eli, wake up."

I could hear Jim[1] whispering and could feel the determined rhythmic pressure of his large hand on my shoulder. When I finally decided to open my eyes I could also see the outline of his head and shoulders peeking out from his sleeping bag, not by any natural light but by the thin fluorescent haze coming from the shelter staff's office.

"Get real. What time is it anyway?"

"Time to meet Billy and T-Bone."

"Right, in the middle of the night?"

"I've gotta go for a walk." Jim spoke in that quiet, urgent tone he'd been using quite a bit ever since before Christmas, when he and Julie had to split up to get shelter for their kid. They'd all come from Montana in the '74 Vega for some construction work, but the job fell through. Living in a car midwinter worked even worse with a two-year-old, so she had to tell them at West Women's[2] that he'd left her. And he had to leave her. The man never said much after that, and showed

---

1. Names changed because I didn't know how to find them to ask. T-Bone really went by T-Bone.

2. Real names of shelters open in Portland, Oregon in 1987. Most are extinct.

even less emotion, so when he did speak you got the impression there was some reason bigger than you could figure.

"O.K. You tell the office and I'll collect my braincells." I stuffed both the sleeping bags in his Army duffel and was pulling my cap down tight when he returned. He picked the bag up high over his head so he could see better not to trip on anybody and I followed his route carefully. Having everybody so close together on the floor was great for keeping warm but you had to concentrate to walk. Opening the door was like walking into a meat freezer. I turned up my collar and wished my gloves weren't the fingerless kind, but Jim didn't seem to notice the cold. He walked slowly, looking leaner than ever with the wind against his clothes. It was still dark outside, but from the streetlights reflecting on the river I could see him sort of chewing on his teeth, the way he always did when he thought about missing his family.

"Let's wake up the guys," I said. Whenever the three of us – T-Bone, Billy and I– got together and set our minds to it, we could get Jim to laugh. Billy was about my age, seventeen, but he continually insisted he was twenty-one. He had big, smirking brown eyes and a tiny little nose and carried his guitar with him everywhere. Nobody believed much of what he said and he didn't expect them to, as long as they had a good time listening. Billy and I would improvise crazy nonsense songs on any subject we could think of (usually sex or the President) and T-Bone would dance around and laugh that infectious deep-belly laugh of his.

Seeing T-Bone dance was comical enough– he was 5'8" and weighed about 225, all of it in his arms and shoulders, making him look like a spinning-top or a cartoon sailor. But if this didn't crack you up there was no getting past his laugh. He'd start with a bearlike rumble, then laugh deep and round and open like he was playing Santa Claus, then soon he'd put his hands on his hips, throw his head back and shake so hard there wasn't any sound. By this time we were all laughing too hard to be singing and we just had to give in to it, even Jim. Then when we could breathe again T-Bone would tell us rowdy stories of his Navy days and we'd laugh all over. Yes, these guys could really get your mind off things, and that's just what Jim needed now.

We walked silently across the bridge, me setting a faster pace and Jim sort of following without ever getting behind. We passed the lighthouse mission and United Clothing, Cindy's Adult Books, the abandoned Greek restaurant and J.T.'s yuppie bar. We took a right at the Catholic chapel with the statue of Jesus and passed the Satyricon nightclub with all its graffiti.

Then, sooner than I'd expected, we ran into Billy, leaning against the bike rack where you wait for Sisters of the Road to open.

"Hey dude," I greeted him, "been sleeping in?" He didn't answer; maybe he was groggy. I continued: "Where's T-Bone?"

There was a pause. Billy seemed to be fascinated by the designs in his Guatemalan-weave bracelet. I was about to repeat myself, thinking he was in his Twilight Zone mood, when Billy finally spoke.

"Kicked," he said simply.

"That's not funny, Billy." Jim was so quiet you could hardly hear him. Billy kept fiddling with his bracelet.

"Projects filled up, and Joe's; old sailor froze to death."

That was all. I looked at Jim then. He was crying.

Apology Power Struggle

Kassiane A. Sibley

Say you're sorry!
No.
Say you're sorry!
NO.
Apologize.
But I'm not sorry.
That isn't very nice.
I'm still not sorry.
You can say you're sorry she feels that way. Just say sorry.
But I'm not.
She feels bad.
She should feel bad.
I wasn't sorry when I took my toy back from my brother.
When my first words upset my mother. When trying to comfort a
classmate got taken as rude.
Say you're sorry.
No. I would do it again.
Hitting me won't make me sorry. Time out won't make me
sorry. Taking my books won't make me sorry. Yelling at me
won't, & calling me names in front of my whole grade will not
make me sorry.
Apologize.
But I am not regretful.
Then we will beat you. We will starve you all weekend. We
will try to shame you. We will sexually assault you. We will do
everything we can think of to break you.
Say you're sorry.
I'd do it again in a heartbeat. **NO.**
You're too stubborn for your own good. Submit. Bend.
Stop being defiant. Comply. Follow the script. Say you're

sorry.

I don't tell lies. No.

Then we will hurt you in many ways, utterly without remorse. For your benefit you will have hypoglycemic seizures in an antique shop. Destroying your homework is for your betterment. The dent in your skull is to teach you to be sorry.

Are you sorry?

Of course not. It's for your benefit. This hurts me more than it hurts you. Apologize.

NO. I will die before I apologize for something I don't regret.

They tried to call my bluff.

I'm still. Not. Sorry.

The Longing

Nina Fosati

"Sybil, wake up. Come on, it's time to wake up now." A hand firmly, insistently shakes her shoulder and she groans, trying to wave the hand away with a feeble swipe. Lifting her eyes, she finds she is sitting in a wheelchair. She is one of a half-dozen lined up along the hallway, waiting for the elevator. Wearily she closes her eyes again, trying to return to the world she'd lost. To a time before age, illness and infirmity locked her in this house of boredom. Better to close your eyes, close your eyes and remember.

She recalls learning to walk through walls; her molecules vibrating apart, searching out the spaces between atoms where she could slip through. The first time she traveled through one wall, emerging in the room next door. She remembers how it horrified her. This ability to travel without motors, to fly without wings. Later she would rummage the ether, exploring the invisible realms hidden beside us, but passing through this one wall, was the beginning. Afterward, back in her body, she understood she could whisper into people's minds as they slept. Planting the kernel of an idea. A seed that would grow into a fully formed opinion, a shifting, an alteration in the world. It's been decades. But she never speaks of it, this ability. All these years she has kept her secret.

In the daylight they call her Sibyl, waving their metal-pierced tongues, la la la, their henna-stained fingers crossed in ancient hexing signs but late at night they come to her, begging, sometimes offering to trade their souls for her intervention. Asking that she rise to where the connections shimmer, asking that she pluck the juddering vibrations between desire and goal. Connecting that which is unconnected. Asking her to please sail to the hidden universe and intervene. "Safiya please," they say, "help me."

"I will do anything," they say.

She has learned objects harbor remnants of emotion, like viruses and bacteria they contaminate her. She stands, holding an unopened letter, the sorrow spattered on it like blood, knowing the news it contains will throb and smart. She brushes the arm of a man intent on harm and then pushes him and his smiling face over. He sprawls like a turtle on his back, yelling, "What the hell's the matter with you? Hey, I only wanted to talk," as she grabs her young sister's arm, running, running as fast as she can.

Yet there are times when knowing does not help. Her daughter, standing in the foyer, excited and trembling, introduces her to a young man. He clasps her hand, saying words of welcome and she stands frozen because her daughter's future pain is searing into her. He with the curly brown hair, smiles and she knows, this one, just by the fact of who he is, will bruise and hurt her daughter. She sees them, her daughter tearful and wounded. Him surprised and sorrowful. She wants to separate them, take her daughter and run, yet she doesn't because she knows it's too late. They've already met. The pain lying ahead is inevitable. There is no protecting her, no warning her, nothing can change this likelihood.

She has learned to see the probabilities, the infinite choices emanating from each soul. The most likely future shining crisp and bright in shimmering beams indicating the most likely path. Mostly she nudges them toward the positive, encouraging the best possible future. But in the early days, sometimes, she gives into anger. She thinks of the beautiful, blue-eyed boy with straight brown hair. She is certain they are meant for each other. The blonde girl, her mortal enemy, stands in the middle of the school bus laughing, reading aloud the love note she has stolen. This one is a mother at sixteen. The boy who hawked a globule of spit at her, its gooey slim dripping down her back as she waits for the bus. That one, he is in jail now, gated away from love and kindness. Manslaughter with intent to kill, they say. Some she can't help. Family and status and inclination making them choose wrong and wrong and wrong again, until their lives are lost, the only possibilities emanating towards hard or harder.

It happened in the end days of high school. Those days of links called friendship, formed for mutual protection. Each wearing their chosen plumage labeled hippie, freak, nerd, turd, word. She carried her oddness with her. The world knowing she was different, knowing only the words weird, odd, crazy. She hadn't yet grown into the name sage, shaman, Safiya. Lonely, knowing none of them were real, knowing their companionship was borrowed. Soon they would leave and the waiting days would be done.

Back then there was a boy. Wasn't there always a boy? This one was fair, his hair so blonde it was almost white, handsome of course, his frame rugged. Shaped by years of farm work. His arms strong and firm. He hugged her as she clung, burrowing

into the scent of him, until finally he detached, pulling her
clawed hands off his shirt with a gentle, "that's enough now."
There was a girl too. She of the tall and thin variety with hair
so dark and long and straight that when they stood together,
arms clasped around each other, they looked inevitable. The
dark and light attracted together as surely as north and south
ends of magnets. Her heart breaking with the certainty she
would always lose to the dark-haired beauties.

She thinks they originated from the same soul stuff in the
ethereal beginnings of time. Jayne is a year younger. Their
class schedules seldom cross but they are quiet with each
other, gentle, careful and respectful. Jayne invites her to her
hushed house, so different from her parents' screaming abode,
where she introduces her to vegetarian casseroles and Tibetan
music. Battered wood tables litter the light-filled rooms of
Jayne's old Victorian. She marvels at the nooks where one can
work uninterrupted, leaving projects in luxurious space to
return to at will. Chaos it seems. So different from the
carefully controlled, cleared, clean, and clutter-free home her
mother keeps.

She tries to obscure her oddness by joining the drama
club. It's the only place she feels she belongs. They are
working on a one act play, written with teenagers in mind.
Knowing Jayne is playing Angel, she agrees to be show runner.
She likes the symbolism of the play, the interaction between
Past, Present and Future (all played by males. The white-
haired boy playing Past.) Each character trying to seduce and
mesmerize Angel; with Death injecting elements of finality
and a creepy counterpointe to the seductions.

Because Angel cannot choose between Past, Present and
Future, she is battered by all three. The last rehearsal turns
disturbing and dark. Jayne's clothing hanging in strips and
tatters, scratches and bruises on her face and body; the
powerful interpretation making her ultimate choice of death
as her lover compelling and understandable. It is powerful

stuff.

Her sense of connection with the play has grown with each performance. Tonight is the last. She is asked to run the ticket table. She fights against the separation but the director is firm. She must stay outside, unable to see or hear the show. Eventually, she sits down on the floor next to the entrance, straining to hear something, anything from inside the theatre.

Her knees bent, she wraps her arms around her legs and allows herself to sink into the floor. The linoleum tiles are cold; the ceramic tiles lining the wall are colder. She closes her eyes and embraces the darkness; seeking the connection with Jayne, seeking a way into the theatre to be with her. The longing compels her. Her breathing slows. She grows colder and colder, finds she is floating through a freezing blackness, when abruptly she finds herself in the theater, able to hear the dialog. The actors are in the middle of the fight. It is raw and intense, more brutal than they have ever played it. The sharp anger erupts from the male actors, they pummel Jayne, emotionally and physically.

It's over. It's quiet. It seems to take forever for Jayne to recover, to sit up and prepare to address her final soliloquy to Death, her acceptance of his proposal. She lies there battered and dazed. The sound of the actor's labored breathing loud in the room. Then a voice, it's her voice but changed, more confident, more commanding: "Jayne, you did it. You finished the soliloquy. You're done. It's time to leave the stage. Jayne I know you did it." The voice is alluring, convincing. Then freezing blackness descends.

She slowly opens her eyes, uncertain where she is, realizing she is sitting on the cold floor, awareness slowly pulling her back into herself. She finds herself repeating the words, "Jayne you did it. I know you did." She looks up and sees Jayne standing in the middle of the hallway, surrounded by the other actors, waking from her trance. Jayne has no memory of how she got into the hallway. She stands shaking and mumbling, "I did it, I know I did it," certain she has finished the final scene. She is stunned to learn she had simply blown out the candle symbolizing Angel's life force, hopped off the stage and left, leaving everyone in the theatre astonished and questioning what it meant.

She never talks to Jayne about it. Soon their time together wanes. The beautiful, blue-eyed boy with straight brown hair finds Jayne and they become a couple. It doesn't hurt very much. She is glad for them. Soon the waiting days will be done. Soon the longing will compel her to cross one last time through the frozen darkness. When they come calling, shaking and punching her chest, she won't be able to hear them. She'll be lost in the ether, searching for the white-haired boy.

Applied Behavior Analysis

Selene dePackh

```
Subject: 17 y.o. female, Non-verbal
```

A crystalline cloud drifted like flowing hair through the afternoon sky. Amelia watched it pass behind the Martian outline of the institutional water tower, thinly veiled by a glinting honeycomb-web of steel filaments in the window glass.

Wizarde Amalle swept the snow-tressed maiden into hir cyber-chariot, clutching the damsel's silken head against hir powerful chest...

The tapping block cracked A-minor yellow flashes into Amelia's synesthetic consciousness. She blinked at the nauseating fluorescent pulse overhead and flailed reflexively. The autism behaviorist set the B-flat red-orange plastic cube aside, grabbed Amelia's hands and held them against the table.

"Quiet hands, please, and look at my eyes when I speak. Don't force me to get your attention that way."

Rising in the air, Amalle saw The Enemy's vulnerable breast. Hir fearsome invention unfolded its ruthless weaponry and took aim...

The behaviorist sighed and leaned across the table to hold Amelia's shoulders.

"Stop rocking, sweetheart. Self-soothing is inappropriate social behavior. Like it or not, this is a social situation, not your private little world."

Amelia twisted away, picking clumsily at the tape over her power-chair controls with an eloquent wail of protest.

The behaviorist gently, forcefully turned Amelia's chin to face her.

"What do you like to do, Amelia? We're stuck with each other for another four hours. We need to find some way to engage."

Amelia flinched from the searing pain of enforced eye contact and shuddery revulsion from unwanted touch. She keyed the synthesized voice of her communication tablet.

"Anything I desire is yours to take away until I give you what you want. I've learned to enjoy hunger and thirst. I love nothing."

She stared out the window again.

The sharpened threads of The Enemy's net shredded the Wizarde and hir love, yet they fought through, bloodied and weakened...

Fat Faggots Must Offer Drugs for Sex

Thomas Kearnes

"What took you so goddamn long, boy?" Margene demanded. "I been calling your name since the commercial." On the big-screen television, a perky blonde with dazzling teeth cooed about the efficacy of scented douche. Whenever Margene needed another wine cooler or wanted to empty the ashtray, she wailed for her son, Dewey, to leave his computer and assist her. He shuffled from the back of the mobile home, past all the piles of cardboard boxes lining the hall, and into the living room where Margene held court. Cigarette dangling from her lips and remote control clenched in her grip, she growled for Dewey to complete the tasks her sloth made untenable.

"I was chatting with someone," Dewey answered.

"You shouldn't talk to people that don't exist."

"Whaddya need, Mama?"

Margene was little more than a skeleton gloved inside pore-ridden flesh. Her ribs, her shoulder blades, and her hips realigned as she looked at her son. Why was it so hard to label her as *frail*? "The methadone ain't kicking in like it should," she said. "We got Xanax left, right?"

"I dunno."

"Well, shit, take a look," she said.

Dewey bowed his head. He couldn't remember the last time he felt brave enough to openly glare at his anorexic, needling mother. Knowing each day brought nothing but more demands, more game shows at thundering volume, more Virginia Slims—the concept of *future* was too painful to contemplate.

The tiny bathroom shared a wall with the living room. While scanning the medicine cabinet, Dewey heard a huckster bark about his batch of used Fords, little kids orgasmic over fruit punch, and finally a plea for those who'd taken a growth hormone to join a class-action lawsuit.

He found the bottle of Xanax behind an empty jar of Oil of Olay. Three or four pills rattled. His reflection in the glass of the cabinet confronted him. His mouth grew long, the corners turning neither up nor down. Fat fuck, he thought. Not fat like your daddy in heaven, but give it time. It's a slippery slope, little pig.

"Goddammit, boy!" Margene cried. "You get lost in there?"

"Just a second, Mama."

Dewey had tricks, maneuvers to make himself more appetizing to the men he approached on the hook-up websites in his room. Most ignored him or wrote nasty replies to his lame attempts at introduction. He pressed his hand beneath his jowls, momentarily mashing his double chin. Relieved that this ruse provided hope, he cupped his hands over his two drooping pecs. No, that asshole kid down the road was right: they were bitch tits. He lifted the sagging flesh of each breast up and to the side. What if his pectorals bulged with firmness as they did in his fantasies?

There were other attempts at self-deception. It was an elaborate series of gestures, rehearsed like a stage soliloquy. In less than a half-hour, Christopher would arrive. Tall, lean, and smooth Christopher with his eight-inch cock. It had taken three weeks of explicit text messages and online chatting to convince Christopher to drive to the mobile home park outside Longview. That, and Dewey promised to provide him with an eight ball of crystal meth for the privilege of sucking that long, thick cock.

The Xanax tablets rattled in their bottle, reminding Dewey he still held it. He planned to persuade Margene to take all the pills. While he wouldn't entertain Christopher in his bedroom, he wished to neutralize his mother to be safe. Christopher knocking on the door and waiting would allow plenty of time for Margene to humiliate her son. When Dewey offered her the pills, she stared at him as if he were a stain.

"You trying to knock me out silly, boy?" she asked, eyes

narrowed to slits.

Dewey shuffled his feet, stared into a far corner. He could hide nothing from her. "Someone's coming over," he muttered.

"You ain't got no friends."

"Yes, I do."

"You never bring 'em here."

"I don't wanna bother you." He gestured toward the television. "Judge Judy is coming on."

Margene lit another Virginia Slim and took the Xanax bottle. "Is he one of those faggots?" she asked, her voice low and froggy, as if the word were difficult to pronounce.

"No!"

"The government ain't paying me to run some queer whorehouse, boy."

"Take the pills, Mama. Don't get excited."

After more pleas to Dewey not to disgrace the Langtree family name, Margene dismissed him. He sprinted back to his bedroom and checked his cell phone for text messages. Nothing. Don't panic, he told himself. Christopher was on his way. Maybe he didn't text when driving. Dewey lay atop his bed knowing rest was not in his future. He'd smoked some crystal meth an hour ago. Without it, he would've cancelled, certain that humiliation loomed. He waited for a knock on the door.

Too wired to sleep, he went into a sort of trance, so fixated on the wheeze from the air conditioning unit outside his window, he failed to register the quick trio of knocks at the front door. Another three knocks followed. Christopher was nearly an hour late. Dewey didn't care. He was thrilled the young man had come at all. Men had flaked on him in the past, even after his promise of crystal meth.

As Dewey dashed to the front door, he caught a glimpse of his mother motionless on the couch. Even Xanax didn't hit that fast. Maybe it was all the wine coolers she'd guzzled since *Good Morning America*. If she hadn't taken the Xanax, maybe he could sneak one himself. He didn't want Christopher to detect his deep-rooted conviction that something would go wrong, and soon.

The vision that revealed itself once Dewey opened the creaky screen door filled the fat young man with hope. Suddenly, his sad and sordid world seemed alive with possibility, with the knowledge this gorgeous man would surrender to him as he pleased and flattered it. Dewey had already decided he would swallow Christopher's load if given the chance. He muttered hello, asked if Christopher had any problems finding the place. Dewey rambled about the hardships of living in the backwoods, how grateful he was for company.

"You got diarrhea of the mouth, big boy," Christopher said, laughing. Dewey stopped at once. The biggest disappointment he'd experienced hooking up with other men was how none of them were witty and charming like in sitcoms and frothy romantic comedies. Instead, they spoke in a primitive language of veiled insults and sexual commands. Christopher, however, possessed a true wit. Better yet, he assumed Dewey must possess one, too.

"I'm sorry, cutie," Dewey said, gripping the doorframe as if he might topple. "I always get so nervous, and my hands sweat, and it feels like I haven't eaten in a fucking week, and– "

"How are you gonna suck my dick if you can't stop jabbering," Christopher said and slipped past Dewey into his home. While he passed, his hand grazed Dewey's love handle. Dewey wasn't sure how to interpret the gesture. This was the worst time to be reminded of his weight... but beautiful Christopher had touched him! The contact hadn't repulsed him. Christopher flashed his host a megawatt grin and casually gazed about. Dewey fought the urge to drag him out the front door. Dewey, however, was too dazzled by his guest to move an inch. Of course, he'd gazed obsessively at Christopher's array of photos on the hook-up website, especially the one of his long, smooth body utterly nude, the image cut off at his neck. Dewey marveled at any man with the discipline– and optimism– to work out.

Even though the age Christopher gave on the website was a mere twenty-two, Dewey believed his guest could pass for a high school senior. An unkempt bush of rust-colored curls drifted atop his head like low clouds at dawn. One of his eyes was a bright hazel while the other was a pale blue. He moved with the staccato rhythms of a tap dancer, all seductive excess motion. His only flaw was that his front tooth was chipped. Dewey's own mouth was full of neglected cavities and rotting teeth stained yellow from his daily pack of Salem cigarettes. He'd lied online when Christopher asked if he smoked. He chastised himself for forgetting to gargle with Listerine before admitting Christopher.

Christopher drifted toward the living room, but kept his head tilted upward, as if waiting for Dewey to begin a proper tour. Margene let out a low grunt. Dewey prayed it wasn't a sign her stupor was lifting.

"You don't wanna see this dump," he said, sliding past Christopher to block his entrance. "I set up the perfect place."

"You put mucho effort into silly things, big boy."

"We have the whole afternoon," Dewey breathed.

"Actually, I only have an hour. My girlfriend needs me to pick up a dime bag. The weed they sell in Tyler is crap." Christopher went on to explain his visit was the product of pure coincidence– and past experience. "You fat boys are expert cocksuckers," he muttered, smiling so wide that Dewey started counting his teeth.

Too much information and too little self-worth led Dewey to panic. Christopher had stopped by for a blowjob and some dope before returning to his girlfriend and pretending her talent for sucking dick came anywhere close to Dewey's. The host rubbed his bulging belly without realizing Christopher watched him. Why draw his attention to that shameful spot? It only mattered how Dewey could please him.

"I picked up the dope this morning," he announced.

"Is it good stuff?" Christopher asked.

"I haven't tried it," Dewey replied, the lie coming easily. He knew these hook-ups were games of deception and concealment. Each man wielded a carefully orchestrated image for the other's enjoyment. There was no shame in this charade. Dewey had joined the website three years ago, not long after his twentieth birthday. His late father had bought the computer years ago hoping to interest Dewey in Tetris and other math-based video games.

"You have a pipe?" Christopher asked. "My roommate always asks all sorts of questions if I borrow his. You're discreet, right?"

"This afternoon is just between you and me," Dewey promised, thrilled to hear those words aloud. Finally, he summoned enough courage to physically guide Christopher toward the screen door still hanging open. He kept gentle pressure at the small of Christopher's back, noticing how tightly his guest's simple black T-shirt wrapped.

"Good. I like boys who keep their traps shut," Christopher muttered, ducking his head to avoid the doorframe. "You let some faggot suck your dick and next week the whole fucking town knows."

"I hate guys like that," Dewey said quickly. "I got a pipe waiting for us."

"Where the fuck are we going?"

"There's a trailer down the street. No one's lived there since Mrs. Zuckerman died last month."

The two young men walked with purpose across the mobile home park. Some of the trailers featured scattershot attempts at decoration or comfort– a wobbly wooden deck, garden gnomes with evil faces, wind chimes that hung uninspired in the still, humid afternoon. Dewey risked a glance through a particular trailer's window as he and Christopher walked past. He wasn't surprised Professor Pete glared back as if waiting for Dewey to see him. That morning, Dewey had struggled with his gag reflex while sucking Professor Pete's spongy, uncircumcised cock, pubic hairs breaking off inside his mouth. Professor Pete didn't accept cash for his dope. Dewey didn't have the cash anyway.

What would a person think seeing him walk with gorgeous Christopher? It was silly to speculate– he knew the answer. He was guilty himself. Obviously, whenever two people knew each other, and one was far more attractive than the other, everyone knew the beautiful one held all the power. Dewey sometimes found himself tempted to invite frankly repulsive men for quick, shameful sex– he was weary of receiving pity. Every bastard who stared at him in frank disgust reminded him of Margene. She had scorned him since his father was killed instead of him on that lonely, icy interstate three years ago. The memory of his father's final sigh sweeping through the overturned pickup cab chilled Dewey. He'd lied when Margene had asked if his father had died instantly.

After another minute of walking, Dewey departed from the pebble-strewn road and lumbered up the steps to a mobile home. He was tempted to glance over his shoulder and make sure Christopher hadn't bolted. His guest, however, clomped up the stairs behind him. Dewey assured himself this man would allow Dewey to please him. *I am not a freak*, he told himself. *I can attract a worthy man. Mama's wrong about me. She's wrong about everything.*

"I'm gonna need to smoke a bowl or two to stay in this shithole," Christopher announced, following Dewey into the empty mobile home. Surprisingly, it was still decorated with taste and thrift. Little touches of warmth littered the trailer: a crocheted maroon blanket folded neatly atop a sofa, bright yellow kitchen curtains allowing the afternoon sunlight, a beige cloth bag holding outdated housekeeping magazines. Nothing, however, could distract the men from the foul, pungent odor permeating each room. How long had Mrs. Zuckerman lay dead before a random relative removed her?

"Follow me," Dewey said with forced mirth. "I've got the bedroom all set up."

"This place reminds me of Grandma's house. Man, I hate that bitch."

"My grandma sometimes forgets my name."

"Actually, I forgot your name, too," Christopher admitted. "Don't take it personal. Names aren't really important, ya know?"

Dewey halted at the bedroom doorway. Christopher was at least talking to him. That was more than some of Dewey's tricks managed. He convinced himself Christopher's candor was a good thing, an indication of his comfort with his homely, heavy host. The downside of having a trick that spoke, however, was how it obligated one to speak in return.

"I'm Dewey," he said. "Actually, it's Dwight, but only my dad called me that. He's dead." He hadn't planned to disclose his loss. The mood was already too delicate.

Christopher grinned and Dewey was reminded of the door greeter he knew from his job at Wal-Mart. He envied people, attractive or not, whose smiles compelled others to trust without reservation. Whenever Dewey smiled, people rarely returned it.

Christopher still smiled, leaning against the doorframe, his spooky eyes alight with mischief. Men so seldom flirted with Dewey, he was ill-prepared to spot it.

"If you can remember my name," Christopher said, "I might let you do more than suck me off."

Dewey giggled, a spontaneous reaction. "Dude, of course I remember your name. I wrote it on my buddy list the first time we chatted."

"Really? I'm glad someone remembers that."

"We chatted over an hour."

"When I'm online, all I see are dicks and assholes."

"Your name is Christopher," Dewey said quietly. He risked a step toward. His guest did not withdraw in disgust. At all these tiny omens of impending success, Dewey marveled. "I don't know your last name," he added, glancing up into the taller man's face. Perhaps Dewey had learned this classic submissive pose from all those black-and-white movies Margene watched after midnight. He occasionally joined her when pecking on his keyboard grew too depressing. He didn't feel safe, however, until she passed out from wine coolers or methadone.

"Unless you're my probation officer, last names are irrelevant."

"Mine is Langtree."

"Dewey Langtree." Christopher brightened. "Maybe it should be Dwight Langtree."

Not knowing how to respond to this oddball kindness, Dewey withdrew into the bedroom, pausing beside the crisply made bed. A quilted comforter with a floral design promised things far more genteel than what Dewey had planned. He slipped the glass pipe from his pocket then fished in the opposite one for the dope. Christopher scurried up to him when he produced the tiny baggie of white crystals.

"Some nice fat rocks in there," Christopher said.

"That's the cool thing about living in the sticks," Dewey said. "The dope is so much better."

"Do you ever sell this shit?"

"I don't know how to be a dealer."

"If you can count cash, there's not much more to learn."

Dewey gazed dumbly at the baggie he held. He and Margene certainly could use the cash. Dewey, however, possessed so little imagination he couldn't fathom life if dealing drugs became his second career. He couldn't imagine anything better than what fate God had coldly tossed in his lap. Margene would want him to walk two miles for more Virginia Slims once Christopher left.

Impatient, Christopher snatched both the baggie and the pipe. "I told you," he said, "I'm on a tight schedule."

"We won't need to smoke it all," Dewey said too quickly. "It's strong stuff. You can take the rest home like I promised." He paused. "Does your girlfriend smoke it, too?"

"I thought you hadn't tried this."

Dewey's heart dropped into his stomach. He felt himself sinking onto the bed, his head bowed like a puppy gruffly disciplined for pissing inside the house. *Now he knows I'm a liar,*

Dewey thought. *Nobody likes liars.* Dewey summoned the courage to glance at Christopher and was relieved to discover his guest ignoring him, too busy loading the pipe with a fat white crystal.

Dewey pretended he hadn't been caught. To his relief, Christopher pocketed the baggie after finishing the bowl and produced a disposable lighter. Dewey watched in rapture as the immense and bright rolls of white smoke escaped his lips. He had always found it deeply erotic to watch men expel crystal meth smoke. He liked to imagine those same mouths ravenous for his own ignored cock. The last man who had sucked him off was so inept that Dewey developed a rash from the irritation.

Christopher took five hits from the pipe before offering it to Dewey, but Dewey didn't mind. After all, Christopher was under no obligation to share. One or two of the men Dewey had serviced hadn't shared at all. Dewey took an enormous hit, sucking on the stem until gasping for breath. He exhaled an endless procession of white smoke, and Christopher chuckled. "Damn impressive, big boy," he said.

"I can do a lot of cool shit with my mouth."

"Let me see that pipe again."

They passed it back in forth, Christopher always taking more hits than Dewey on each rotation. They finished the first bowl and began another. Once that bowl was cashed, Dewey succumbed to the sensation of floating atop a jet stream, fluttering over the continent. For a moment, he forgot Christopher stood before him. The sound of a zipper opening slapped him back to reality. There was the business of the blowjob.

"Get on your knees, big boy," Christopher said with surprising softness. "It's what you want, right?"

"I'm an expert at getting guys off."

"Like I said, you fat boys are the best-kept secret on the internet."

Dewey couldn't understand why no matter how differently

his tricks behaved, the experience of sucking their dicks never changed. Soon after beginning, Dewey lost himself in a torrent of silent commands and stern warnings of how devastating it would feel to fail the man in his mouth. There was no ecstasy until Dewey deluded himself into believing, as always, that sexual subservience all alone can bring one joy.

Christopher actually warned him before he came. Dewey slipped the man's erect cock from his mouth and let the semen splatter his face. Dewey excused himself and quickly washed his face in the bathroom. He didn't want to return and find the bedroom empty, as if the encounter had occurred solely in his imagination. When he did return, he found Christopher lying on his back atop the bed. He wasn't relaxed, though. Dewey noticed the tension in his limbs, his jaw. He dreaded this part of each encounter with a new man.

"How much longer do we have?" Dewey asked.

"I'm too lazy to look at my watch."

"No one's gonna come in. You're welcome to stay."

"Actually, would it be okay if I stayed by myself for a bit? I need to pull my shit together. That was strong dope."

Dewey had never been discarded so gently. Typically, the men couldn't bolt fast enough. Why did Christopher wish to stay by himself? Mrs. Zuckerman had probably died in that bed. Dewey lacked the courage to ask for an explanation. Instead, he shuffled toward the doorway. Christopher called his name. His *true* name, not Dewey.

"Yeah?"

"If you suck cock like that every time, no one's gonna care you're fat."

Dewey couldn't remember the last time someone complimented him with conviction. Unsure if he was smiling, his face contorted into a shape he had forgotten. His only clue was Christopher returning a grin. Dewey silently vowed to avoid the website for at least a couple of weeks. This sweet memory would surely sustain him.

"Now beat it, big boy," Christopher said, chuckling. "You're killing my buzz."

Dewey trotted home, sick with possibility. All the sad, despairing homesteads didn't deter his merriment. He felt he should hum a song, something life-affirming, but he never listened to music. Dewey's life was a silent one, excluding Margene's inescapable television.

His jolly mood curdled when he spotted Professor Pete glaring out his window. Typically, Dewey would've bowed his head and shuffled away... unless he needed dope. Today, however, a surge of guile overtook him. He stood firm, glared at his dealer and shot him the bird. Professor Pete narrowed his gaze. A moment later, the window was empty. The ease of his victory over that odious man stunned Dewey. The vindication mingled with the remnants of his romantic bliss. He couldn't remember the last time entering his home hadn't crushed him like a cigarette butt beneath a steel-toed boot.

He didn't check on Margene before sauntering toward his bedroom. When he heard her voice ricochet through their home, it shocked him. The world had not stopped after all. It never had stopped spinning, desperate Dewey hoping enough gravity remained to anchor him.

"You fat bastard," she brayed. "I know where you were. I know every fucking thing."

Dewey considered slamming his door until something on television distracted her, but he couldn't respect himself if he let that vile woman berate him for the next ten minutes. He wanted to respect himself. Maybe if he did, others would follow suit. He wanted to smile at the shoppers in Wal-Mart and smile wider still when they returned it. "It's none of your goddamn business where I was," he cried. He crossed to the end of the couch opposite Margene. She puffed a Virginia Slim, television remote clutched in her hand. On the screen, a portly weatherman warned about severe weather tomorrow.

"I went back to your room, boy," she said. "I got on that

damn computer you can't live without. What pervert lets the whole world see pictures like that?"

"You can't come in my room," he said. "We had a deal."

"You do things with men that Jesus don't allow."

"You haven't been to church since Daddy died."

"Don't speak to me about that fine man. We both know what should've happened that day. It should've been *your* fat ass we put in the ground."

Professor Pete was a scarecrow easily toppled compared to Margene. Dewey knew she would wear him down until his treasured moments with Christopher were too painful to recall. The horrible woman did nothing but squat on her cushioned throne and demand the world obey. Dewey was the only soul in that world. Margene opened her mouth to speak once more, hot pink lipstick staining her teeth.

"Shut your fucking pie hole, you dumb bitch!"

Margene froze, her gaze turning nervous like a predator who had targeted a superior creature in error. "What did you say, boy?"

"I said shut up, Mama." On the television, the weatherman flirted with the pretty lead anchor. Dewey glimpsed the screen. The weatherman was nearly as big as him, and he was on fucking television. People watched and trusted him.

Margene hurled the remote at Dewey's head, smacking him at his eyebrow. He wailed and grabbed his head. The remote clattered to the floor. He couldn't remember the last time Margene had struck him. She was so small, so puny, she had to rely on words to smother his hope. Dewey knew what he must do. He had heard his late father mutter *Dwight* as they pulled out of the pharmacy, neither of them seeing the big rig headed toward them that awful day.

He grabbed the remote and smacked Margene across the face, the device making a cracking sound as it struck her jaw. The batteries popped out and fell to the floor. She raised her hand in fury and horror. "Boy," she muttered, "I got good reason to get off this couch..."

"You're gonna die in front of that TV," Dewey snapped.

"I need a doctor," Margene mumbled, absently smearing blood across her forehead.

"You need a life," her son replied. He didn't need the excuse of answering the door after an unexpected knock to leave her in pain. It was a trio of knocks, actually. What greeted Dewey was yet another surprise in an afternoon abundant with them.

"You busy?" Christopher asked. He leaned upon the doorframe, the pose eerily similar to a classic James Dean photograph. A man of typical sexual experience would've recognized instantly Christopher's intent, but Dewey was not such a man.

"I thought you had to leave," he said.

"My girlfriend called. Typical bullshit. Don't worry about her."

"What do you want?" Dewey asked weakly. He was terrified whatever happened next would sour their wonderful moment before he left Mrs. Zuckerman's bedroom. He desired Christopher, but he knew desire led to disappointment. Always.

"I'm horny again, dude. I was wondering if..."

From the living room, both young men heard Margene moan. Christopher's gaze sharpened and he turned but didn't step closer. Dewey cherished the revelation this home was now his to control. "Are you alone right now?" Christopher asked.

"Everything's fine," Dewey assured him. "I can handle it."

"You haven't got another stud waiting, do ya?"

Dewey gazed directly into Christopher's odd, shimmering eyes. One hazel and one blue, like birthstones. "If you want me to suck you off again, spit it out." He paused, grinned like a guilty schoolboy. "Sorry, bad choice of words."

Christopher swallowed, his face twitching. Dewey lacked the experience to know most men lose their bearings when forced from hunter to the hunted. "You suck cock like a champ," Christopher finally said.

Margene moaned again. Christopher's eyes narrowed, but he said nothing. Dewey calmly followed him after he drifted outside and down the steps. Dewey left both doors wide open. A neighbor might help if Margene whimpered long enough, he guessed. Christopher required Dewey's mouth. It was possible he would require it fairly often in the future. As they returned to Mrs. Zuckerman's trailer, Dwight Langtree had faith Christopher would call him whatever name he desired.

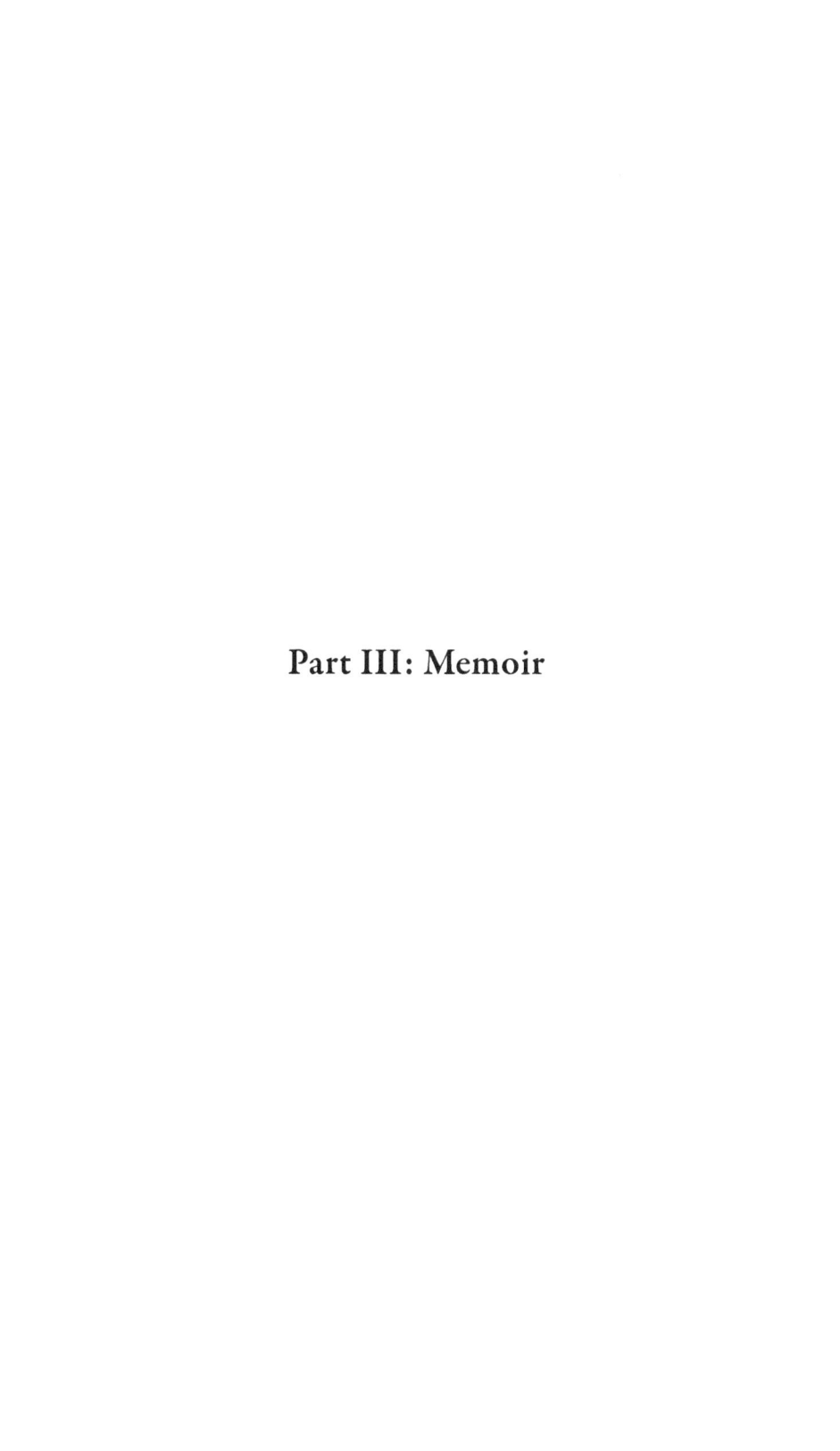

Part III: Memoir

On Pulling Potatoes, Queer Criphood, and My Heartbeat
Alison Kopit

When you weren't looking, I tried on queer crip and realized it was so snug I couldn't take it off. It immediately smelled like me. It was mine, like those brown corduroys and the feeling I get when I'm comfortable in a kitchen. The rhythm of this all started as a dance score, but resonated in "amen," and I can't stop dancing this one, and I know that I don't want to.

Finding queer and disabled in me never made me an outsider– it always brought me in. Maybe it's why I love mulled wine in the crockpot and stocking up on groceries in the winter in case I can't leave. Maybe it's why I like sweaters and cuddling, and the way that I watch movies with the lights on and insist on sleeping on my stomach and will never wear heels again. Maybe it goes back to the memory where I sit, back to the mirror at three years old, as my mom's second grade students act out *Where the Wild Things Are* as I wonder if I would ever be so cool. Or so pretty.

It's not that queer and disabled are similar experiences to me, it's that they are the same. I knew it as home far before I consciously knew it was me. I'm not sure why I know this, but I told my sweetheart over tea and as soon as it left my mouth, I knew it was true. The only way I could ever really articulate queer disability was in stilted academic language. It sounded like I wanted to prove it. But I realized that it's really quite difficult to define what runs through my veins. And anyway, to really write about queer, I might as well write about my first pair of ballet shoes at four years old, what it feels like to roll myself up in the backstage curtain in middle school and the thrill of interpretive dancing in the backstage wings during my high school performance of *Little Shop of Horrors*, while the stars of the show were onstage and completely oblivious to me.

It was never about explaining queerness or disability, but more about pulling potatoes and painted, worn-in jeans, and the way I was so particular about the textures of my shirts and always liked heights and had a high pain tolerance. It was about being strangely good at beer pong and learning to scream. It was the recurring dream that I *can't* scream. Queer and disabled was about what I couldn't do: dance well enough, play pool, fix my bike, crochet more than lines straight across to make the same boring scarf over and over. But those straight lines made the rituals go away for a while. Queer crip. Go figure.

Is queer and crip is why I blaze through stop signs on my bike but wait for the rock-back when I'm in my car? I'm drawn to the subversion, yes. But I'm also drawn to the taste and texture and the sensory world of queer disability. It's so deliciously saturated in the sensory. And I want to eat it up so much that I tickticktick trill mmhm mm mm and snuggle into all of it. I want to get *Really. Fucking. Cozy with it.*

Queer and crip makes me think about the rituals that followed me through my childhood and the compulsion to hide them. The rituals run deep in my veins, and even though they are not always here, they are footnotes that underscore the rhythm of my life. I can't help but count (the numbers on the clock, the sum of the numbers on a price tag, the days that have passed), and alternate what foot crosses the crack on the sidewalk.

I never want to have to choose whether it's queerness or disability that makes me love everything about consent and why I have a soft spot for sex with those black gloves they use in Crashpad. That's never the point of this conversation, and neither is choosing whether it's crip siblinghood or queer family or something else entirely that has kept my heart beating all of these years. Because I know that my heart beats to queer disability, just like it beats to summer camp and fermenting vegetables and crafting and breaking a sweat while I knead bread. It's why I put messages in the spokes of cute bicycles and why my voicemails are painfully long and my first and only tattoo is improvised.

I love queer crip in a way that's fierce, but is still melodic and tender. Queer crip has given me a soundtrack and rhythm to dance to. So, maybe, it's not that queer and crip is important to me, or that the experiences are the same, but that it's my pulse. It's my "what is." And I'm writing it now to see it here, real on the page, because queer and crip is so much more than an individual or a community identity. Of course, I couldn't get it off of me if I tried, but also, it's not just *on* me. It's everywhere. *(We did it!)* Inextricably intertwined.

There's the question of choice. I'm supposed to say "I was born this way," I know, and maybe that would help you understand, but I'd like to give myself a little more credit than that. Yes, there's some luck tossed in. I realize that I'm pretty lucky for this queer, disabled, left-handed bodymind, but there *were* choices. I made a lot of choices. I chose to grow into this one. It was the only growth spurt I ever had, but I suspect a growth spurt is more fun to have at 25 than at 12. I chose to say yes to people, to art, to love, to experiencing the sensory world in this way. I said yes to cripqueering space and queercripping movement. I said yes to dancing in public parks and yes to refusing to feel guilty moving my body against Normal.

So *yes*, sometimes I can't be in crowds and no earplug is good enough to get me through a show, but I like staying home and baking bread instead. Or dancing at home. Or drinking wine in the bathtub. And maybe that's precisely why I love this bodymind. Because when I listen to it, there's peace and healing and repetition and getting my hands in there.

...And truly, what's queerer than that?

Who is Noncompliant Now?

Alyssa Hillary

Who is noncompliant now? I ask because it isn't me, not until later. I don't even learn that defiance – not, "I can't actually do the thing but you're going to take my inability as refusal,[1]" but deciding not to do something I've been told to do even though I *can* do it? I learn that in sixth grade.

Return to that day, go back to the sixth grade.
Read *The Wave* during reading class.
It's really about Naziism and how easily that sort of thing will spread because people are afraid to disobey.
Watch the teacher divide the class into groups and tell us to stand and salute by groups, from the front to the back, each group continuing with the next groups.
Watch the ever-increasing groups stand and salute.
I am in the back of the class. I am in the last group.
I stand. I salute. I start to cry.
I explain my discomfort to the special ed teacher[2].

"If they do it again, you can stay sitting and not do it."

Mind. Blown.

---

1. Thanks to Kassiane Sibley for the idea of people thinking something is "won't" when it's actually "can't." I have dealt with so much of this.
2. Officially, he wasn't my aide. He was the aide for another student who had attached herself to me and who had been allowed to do so by other teachers because she "behaved better" around me, leaving me with some unofficial level of responsibility for her. This teacher is the one who eventually put a stop to that, but before he did, he worked unofficially with me as well as with her. I guess he thought I could use the help. He wasn't wrong.

"I can just... not do it?"

Not as in, "I won't face consequences for not doing it?" As in, "Wait, not doing what the teacher says because I decided not to is a thing that is possible to do?"

I literally had not realized that defiance was a possibility.

Now I know. At least in theory. It will take longer to put it into practice.

Flash forward to ninth grade. I take Chinese in the high school, in a mixed class. Some students are in Chinese II, others in Chinese III. I am officially enrolled in Chinese II, but...

Listen to her teach the Chinese II lesson. It's easy.

Do the Chinese II worksheet. It's easy too. I'm done in 5 minutes, and there are 20 left in class.

I'm bored.

Stand up. Cross the room. Sit down next to the two official Chinese III students.

Listen to her teach the Chinese III lesson. It's not hard, but at least the new words are *actually new*.

Ask for a copy of the worksheet.

Maybe get it, maybe don't.

More and more often, get it at the start of class with the rest of the Chinese III students.

Do the Chinese III worksheet while (only kind of) listening to the Chinese II lesson.

Do the Chinese II worksheet while (actually) listening to the Chinese III lesson.

Laugh when I'm asked which class I am taking. "Both and therefore neither!"

Know full well that I'm not really *supposed* to be doing two classes in one period.

Know that the teacher doesn't care.

Know that the head of languages for the school district doesn't care.

Keep doing the work for both classes.
Learn.

Who is noncompliant?
Does anyone care?

At the same time, I am applying to the study abroad in 西安 (Xi'an) the school is trying to arrange. It would be six weeks living with a host family in 西安 (Xi'an) and attending classes at the local high school, the same classes that our host family's kids take. I am allergic to shellfish – shrimp, specifically, though I'm not supposed to have any shellfish just in case.

Part of the application process is an interview. There are four teachers doing the interviews, to get through the students faster. Each student is interviewed by one teacher, total. Except me.

All four teachers sit on one side of the table, grilling me about my allergy. How bad would a reaction be? (One of the teachers had seen me have a reaction before, and it wasn't much of a much, but the doctor had said that it could kill me. I told them both of these facts.) How much contamination was acceptable before I would react. (How was I supposed to know? I wasn't supposed to have any to test and find out.) What was the proper procedure if I did have a reaction? (If my throat started to close or I had trouble breathing, Epi-pen and emergency room. For just hives, technically the same but probably a Benadryl. Either way, stop eating the food I was reacting to.) Could I teach one of the teachers to handle my Epi-pen? (Yes, but *I am supposed to be the one to carry it.*) Was I sure I needed to be the one to carry it? (Yes. Absolutely. The teacher could have one too, but I had to have one.) Could I explain the questions needed to ensure I didn't have a reaction? (Yes. I did so.) Are all those really necessary? (Yes.) And what if we can't get answers to all those questions? (I wait to eat until I find food where I can.) Are you saying you'd refuse to eat? (If necessary. I don't want to have an allergic reaction.) And on and on. Four teachers, one student, three times as long an interview as anyone else had. I think I am last so that none of my classmates see the grilling.

They don't comply with their own stated method of conducting the interview. They don't comply with how they're supposed to handle a minor student's medical information. They aren't willing to comply with necessities for a student with a medical condition.

Who is noncompliant?
Does anyone care?

I send them a modified version of the release basically stating that if they won't take legal responsibility for my not having a reaction, they don't get to take reality-land responsibility either and I will be handling my own allergy issues.

Who is noncompliant?
Now they care.

I didn't go on their study abroad, even though I had initially been accepted, because they could not handle my medical issues.

Who is noncompliant?
Now they care.

In retaliation for my not being in the program, all of a sudden there *was* an issue with my doing the work for both

Chinese II and Chinese III. The teacher told me I couldn't anymore, and let's just say I didn't take it well. I was in the guidance counselor's office twenty minutes later, because yes this was retaliation, and yes this was about them not wanting to explain why they couldn't manage to bring their top student (and when I was doing the work for both classes, there was no way to deny that I was the top student) on the study abroad trip. If I was only in Chinese II, the existence of a Chinese III would let them claim I was *not* the most advanced. If I was doing the work for both, and top of *both* classes at the same time, they could make no such claim.

Who is noncompliant?
Now *I* care.

"You might not be back in Chinese III tomorrow."

This is her way of saying that this is going to take a while. I'm aware of this, even, but I'm past the point of caring who I piss off, and by this point I even *know* that resistance, defiance, are options. I don't use them much, but for my education? Especially when the person being the barrier is someone who is *supposed* to be supporting my education, not getting in its way?

"That's fine. I don't have Chinese tomorrow. But the day after tomorrow we have a test, and I'd rather take it *with* permission."

Who is noncompliant?
Now *they* care.

For the first time, you can argue that it's me (and they do.) Schools might pretend briefly, but they don't care about the

Antecedent to the Behavior[3] when it's a kid who is the Antecedent, and they'll outright deny it when the head of the foreign languages department for the whole school district makes the Antecedent call.

Still, it works. The next day, the principal brought me the worksheet I missed the day I was kicked out of Chinese III, and I took both the Chinese II and Chinese III tests during the period.

Who is noncompliant now?
Does anyone still care?

Now we go to the summer between eleventh and twelfth grades.
I get a call from the guidance department. (I hate the phone.)
The one remaining math class I could take (and I need one more to graduate) has fallen out of my schedule again, because it's at the same time as Chinese. Should she have dropped Chinese instead?
Of course not.
I'll find a math class elsewhere, and what options are there for my new open elective block?
"Programming first semester and animation second semester are open," she tells me.
"Those same classes you wanted me to take instead of a third semester of creative writing and then digital music?"
"They'd look good for college."
"Anything else open?"
She tells me. Programming and animation are the best of the options – I'm not *uninterested* in them, per se, I just had

3. Thanks to Kassiane again for the Antecedent idea: Sibley, Kassiane. "Here, try on some of my shoes." *Radical Neurodivergence Speaking*. Sept. 8, 2013.
http://timetolisten.blogspot.com/2013/09/here-try-on-some-of-my-shoes.html

them as a lower priority than the electives I already had.

I find another math class, online. I can work on it during school hours if I get a study hall.

I call guidance back to ask for a study hall. (I still hate the phone.)

"Normally we work to avoid giving people study halls," she says.

"I know, but I have an actual reason to want one. Didn't the three guys who had a calc three independent study two years ago get a study hall for it?"

She tells me they did. She agrees, eventually, to get me the study hall.

I get a new schedule in the mail, a week before school starts.

Creative writing and digital music – the electives *I* chose – are gone. The electives she thought would be good for me – programming and animation – remain.

That's not what was supposed to be done.

Who is noncompliant?
And yes, I care.

I go to the school in person this time.

I run into the creative writing teacher before I run into the guidance counselor. I tell her what happened.

It's news to her. She asks what I plan to do.

"I plan to be in your class on the first day of school."

Who is noncompliant?
Does anyone care (yet)?

Next is the guidance counselor.

"Hi Alyssa! We dropped you from creative writing and digital music to get you the study hall!"

"One, I'm here because I got that schedule in the mail

today. Two, no."

"We thought it'd be best for you."

"Well I disagree. Fix it."

"Can we talk about this?"

"We can talk about how you're going to fix it, yes."

"Can we talk about why programming and animation are the classes you should keep?"

"We talked about that in January."

I follow my guidance counselor to her office.

She wants me to think about what will look good on paper, for college.

Too bad for her.

She wants to call my mother.

Fine.

My mother says she'll approve whatever class schedule I will... but not one I won't approve.

She tries to tell my mother the reasons I "should" take programming and animation.

I roll my eyes.

My mother tells the guidance counselor she's not the one who needs to be convinced.

I am.

The guidance counselor asks my mother if she wants to speak to me.

I take the phone. (I hate the phone.)

Mom asks me if she needs to come in to talk to the guidance counselor.

I ask the counselor: "Will you fix my schedule if my mom's next to me telling you to too?"

My guidance counselor sighs.

"Think about this," she tells me.

"I did in January."

"It's August now."

"Yup. A month after I asked for the study hall. Did you wait to drop the wrong classes on purpose?"

There is no answer for that question.

"I just want what's best for you," she says.

"You should probably make my schedule reflect where I'm going to be, then."

She makes a few more excuses, like how someone else might already have taken the spot I emptied.

She fixes my schedule.

On the first day of school, I go to creative writing.

Who is noncompliant now?

It's working.

Now look at my fourth year of college, abroad in China.

I've told the people running my study abroad that I am autistic.

They told all the teachers.

I don't think they were supposed to give the specific diagnosis, just what my needs are.

The administration didn't want me to come.

"People like that shouldn't be in college," they say.

I am stressed.

The way the class is run *really* doesn't work with how I learn.

I do badly on the first exam.

They tell me to drop one of my direct enrollment classes – graph theory or materials science.

I refuse.

She tells me I don't have a choice. (Of course I have a choice.)

She tells me they didn't really want me taking two direct enrollment classes in the first place. (I know.)

She tells me I need to understand that after doing badly on the first test, they need to do something.

I am silent.

I know what would be effective, but they'd never approve it.

Not when they think the answer is to have me in *fewer* classes across town.

I suggest that I take one and audit the other.

I take the finals for both.

I get credit for both.

Who is noncompliant now?

It's working.

Grades come in.

I did better in the direct enrollment classes than I did in Chinese class.

My academic director takes this as evidence that she was right, that I should not have taken two.

I know it is no such thing.

My direct enrollment classes didn't hit my language issues.

My direct enrollment classes depended only on one final, or on one project and paper.

Not the can't taken as won't that is daily homework.

Not the can't taken as won't that is speaking lots in class.

Who is noncompliant now?

It was no one, this time.

At the end of the year, I admit that my taking the finals for both direct enrollment courses had been *totally planned*.

Not from the moment I suggested auditing one and taking one – I had been melting down at the time, and I can't plan anything that devious while actually melting down.

But within a day or so of then, it occurred to me that I could still take the final.

And I laugh.

The academic director tells me not to laugh.

"While there were gains from the two classes, there were also losses."

I want to ask what she thinks those losses were.

I don't have the words to do so.

I know what she thinks, anyways.

She thinks it was my Chinese language learning and grades.

She's right, and she's not.

There were gains, and there were losses.

But the loss was her belief in my innocence.

Who is noncompliant now?

Who is deceptive now?

Who smiles, nods, and ignores you now?

The teacher has learned that I can.

The teacher has learned that I *am*, that I *do*.

Dimensions of Pain

Amanda Sleen

Walking into Twin City Tattoo, I am overwhelmed with the smell of fresh ink, rubbing alcohol, and Vaseline. The scent of sterile equipment and latex gloves permeates its way down my nose, but I welcome it. The smell is familiar and comforting because this parlor has become a second home to me.

There are framed pictures of flash art covering the inside of the shop. So much so, that I can barely make out the painted wall behind them. There are pictures of snakes wrapped around swords, skulls with centipedes crawling out of the eye sockets and daggers lodged inside bleeding hearts. Pictures of solid black tribal designs intricately intertwined with each other and of eyeballs with eight spider-like legs attached to it. There are pictures of roses everywhere. Some have banners with them, some have long stems, some are big and blooming colors of reds and pinks and some are the size of a quarter to emphasize the amount of detail that can be packed into such a small drawing. There are pictures of pin up girls in provocative poses, showing off their long tanned legs, small waists and busty chests, displaying as much cleavage as possible. Some are wearing army or sailor uniforms; others are wearing tight black leather or short red dresses.

Then there are the noises. Even with Led Zeppelin blaring over the speakers, I can still hear the constant buzzing that occasionally dulls when the needle of the tattoo machine injects pigment into someone's skin. The buzzing has also become a welcoming sound, just like the smell of ink. They worked together. The ink combined with the machine. When I hear the familiar noise, I know I am getting closer to my own skin being permanently stamped with a piece of art. I thought of unmistakable buzz and aroma as one thing: a tattoo.

"Hey sweetie," Roger calls to me. "I'm ready for you."

I walk past the front desk, deeper into the tattoo shop. I pass three rooms with other artists tattooing other clients. Some people squeeze their eyes shut as they're being tattooed in places like their ribs or spine. Others wear headphones or read a book because their tattoo doesn't hurt as much on their shoulder or thigh. I wonder if mine will hurt on my forearm.

I walk into Roger's station and am reminded about his large stature. He is about 6'3, heavy set and black. He has tattoos up and down his arms and neck, a graying beard and hands so large he needs to order special latex gloves just so they fit. He is nothing short of intimidating. This is the same thought I had when I first met him back in 2011. But when he starts talking, two things break his threatening demeanor: he doesn't have as deep a voice as one would assume for being such a big guy, and he has a slight lisp.

"How many will this be now?" Roger asks me. He puts on his gloves and starts squirting black ink into small paint capsules. Then he opens up packets of sterile needles and other tattoo equipment. He applies a stencil to my arm that leaves a purple outline of what my tattoo will look like. Then I move to lie on my stomach on his massage-like table and rest my right arm on a separate armrest for him.

"This will be number five," I say.

♦   ♦   ♦

When I was younger, I used to think that every tattoo needed a meaning behind it; that if someone wanted something on his or her body forever, it had to *mean* something. So, when I got my first tattoo, the word "saved" on my left wrist, it meant that I believed Jesus died for my sins and that I would be granted eternal life. It also meant that I was 18 and didn't need my mother's consent or her approval. Nor did I want it.

I remember a dream I had the first night of my newest body modification. I dreamed that I went to wash my hands and with the warm water running over my skin, my tattoo started slowly dripping off my wrist like thick black sludge down the drain. I woke up worried that somehow the ink had disappeared.

After that, I started to become transfixed with it, manipulating my skin, squishing it together and stretching it apart to watch how the tattoo moved with it. I turned my wrist around and around, extending my hand out with my palm facing the sky and making a fist, bringing my knuckles as close to my inner forearm as possible. All while watching how my movement influenced my tattoo. No matter how I moved the skin on my wrist, the ink stayed in place, unchanged. It wasn't even a tattoo anymore. It was simply my skin. It was a part of my body that could never been taken away. It was permanent.

Not long after, I learned that meanings are kind of like feelings in that they change. Sometimes, a tattoo can go from "it means this" to "it *meant* that". However, a change in meaning isn't always the same as regret.

◆　◆　◆

"How's your mom doing?" Roger asks, his body bent over my arm, focused intensely on his inky outline. He asks me this question every time I see him, partly to make conversation and partly because he knows addiction is inconsistent. Over the years that I have known Roger, I have grown very comfortable with him. He has tattooed my ribs, my chest, and right below my armpit. More often than not, Roger and I are physically close during our tattoos sessions. Not only that, but we talk about ourselves too.

I know about Roger's four-year-old daughter Pearl and her mother, his long time girlfriend, Trish. I know that since he creates images with his hands and Trish plays music, they want Pearl to know the importance of art. And I know that they're working hard to get her into a pre-kindergarten that focuses on just that.

Roger knows about my mother. He knows that she has been addicted to drugs since before I was born. He knows that between the ages of 12 and 17, I didn't have my mother because she was in and out of treatments, making empty promises. He knows that after my mother went to treatment at Minnesota Teen Challenge for a year, she became so religious that she forced me to read bible verses about purity every time I left the house. And he knows that after three years of sobriety, she relapsed.

"I guess I don't really know how my mom's doing," I said, returning to his previous question. "I never really do." This hurts to say. I wish I knew how to answer Roger's question. Furthermore, I wish I could say that she was okay, that she was safe, and that she was sober. The emotional pain not knowing my mother's condition is almost unbearable.

He slowly moves the needle on the outside of my forearm but *this* pain is tolerable. It's uncomfortable and annoying but it's not enough to make me cringe or unable to speak. It feels as if someone has drawn the same line on a part on my body over and over with a ballpoint pen. Then, his needle creeps towards my elbow and I squeeze my eyes shut in pain. I inhale sharply and instinctively hold my breath, which you're never supposed to do. My body tenses as I try to sit as still as possible waiting for him to move on from my bony joint. The pain on my elbow is almost as bad as when I got tattooed on my ribs.

◆　◆　◆

The decision to get my ribs inked in 2013 was out of impulse. I had reluctantly attended youth group at my church one Wednesday and my eyes caught on a particular bible verse: Romans 1:31 "Foolish, faithless, heartless, ruthless." Within a few weeks, I endured the pain for two and half hours and etched those words permanently in my skin.

My mother happened to be living with our family at the time and when she saw it, she wasn't happy. Not because it was another tattoo– she had come to accept that they were a lasting hobby I would pursue– but because of the particular words I chose.

"Of all the verses in the bible, why would you choose that one?" She asked in a distraught tone. She sounded as if she was offended. As if the words I chose to get tattooed on my body were disrespecting her faith. A faith we no longer shared. I didn't get the tattoo in spite of my mother, I got is as a memento.

"It's a reminder of how we are without God in our lives," I lied. I didn't want to tell her that most of the reason I got the tattoo was because I just liked the way it sounded coming out of my mouth. But I knew my lie would satisfy my mother with the idea of us all needing God. Truthfully, however, the tattoo reminds me of how I believe human nature is regardless of faith or God.

I learned another thing about intentions and significance that day. Sometimes, the "meaning" comes after the ink.

◆ ◆ ◆

"We're going to take a break now," Roger says and I immediately feel my body relax. I am exhausted from being so tense, so I welcome the break. I stand up from the massage table and hold my arm out so he can lather it with Vaseline. It feels both relieving and painful, like rubbing aloe on a bad sunburn. Then he peels his black gloves off, pulls a cigarette from his pocket, and leaves the room.

I move to the mirror and bend my arm so I can get a good look at what he has done. It was a design I thought of, an arrow that spreads from my elbow to my wrist with katniss plants wrapped and blooming around it. So far, Roger has only done the outline and some heavy black shading. There is no color yet, so it looks boring and empty. While color is not for everyone, it is important to me because it makes me feel different. Different in a way that I can control. It is my choice to include reds, blues, and yellows on my skin and of all the things in my life that I can not control, adding color to my skin gives me a freedom I have never known before. Soon, Roger will be back to put me through more pain for the sake of having a unique tattoo and I am anxiously waiting for him.

He walks back into the room looking refreshed, but reeking of cigarette smoke.

"Ready?"

I nod, lowering myself back onto the table. He puts on his custom latex gloves and reaches for my arm. I squirm with pain as he puts more Vaseline on it. Then he sits and prepares his machine, taking out a new batch of needles. He tests it, letting out a quick buzz.

"Here we go," he says. He brings the needle closer to my skin as I prepare myself to be stabbed hundreds of times per second for another hour and a half, letting colorful pigment penetrate my skin.

"So," Roger says, letting the word hang in the air for a second. He was about to ask me a question I've heard countless times before. "Why do you like tattoos so much?"

It's a statement, it's empowering, and it's exhilarating. My ink is my life uncovered on my skin. They are my inner thoughts exposed as images for everyone else to see. They are constant and enduring, eternal and unending. If nothing else, I can hold onto my tattoos forever.

This is hard to explain to people sometimes, so I've broken up my explanations. To strangers, I tell them that they look cool and what better way to appreciate art than by displaying it on your skin. To friends, I tell them that my paleness makes my colored tattoos stand out more on my skin and it makes me feel confident. And to family, I tell them it's my passion. No further explanation is needed. Despite the answer I give someone, it's always followed up by another ageless question: doesn't it hurt?

No matter who asks me this, my answer is always the same, if not a bit cliché.

"Yes, but pain is temporary." Physical pain, at least. And maybe that's the issue. Maybe the reason I'm addicted to tattoos is because it distracts me from the emotional pain that never ceases. Some people can take a hot bath or go for a long run to put their minds at ease in stressful situations. I can't do this because I have never been given a chance to heal from my mother's decisions. She has never been sober long enough for my family to begin to repair the damage that's been done or restore the trust that has been broken.

When I think about pain now, I remember growing up without my older sister because her father had her taken away after she described a sexually abusive occurrence at the age of three. My mother, younger brothers and I would spend the next few years going to see my sister once a month in a gray building while being supervised by a government employee. Sometimes, my mother would simply not show up, leaving an even bigger gap between us siblings.

I remember when I was 12 and I had just come home to Minneapolis from a visit with my grandma in Moorhead. My mother wasn't home so I asked my father where she was. He angrily told me that she left to be with another man and that she wouldn't be coming home.

I remember when I was 13 and I had to be the mom for my younger brothers. Every morning, I had to wake them up, get them dressed and walk them to school. I had to feed them dinner, help with their homework and put them to bed at night just to wake up the next morning and do it all over again, because our mother was gone and our father was in a coma of depression and narcotics.

I remember when I was 14, and our father had moved my brothers and me into his new girlfriend's house with her kids. I remember sitting next to my cousin one day, looking out of the window and watching my pregnant mother attempt to come inside the house. My cousin and I watched my father push her away to stop her and we saw them scream at each other on the front lawn. We saw my aunt go out and start yelling too, and we saw my mother slap her across the face. We saw the police coming up the street and park in front of the house, and we saw my father practically rip the front door off of my mother's car when she mother got back in it. I remember writing in my diary that night about how much I hated my father. I didn't know it then, but my mother had been using methamphetamines and had come to get my bothers and me and take us away with her.

I remember when I was 15 and my mother had a baby boy with another man while she was high on meth. The first time I saw my new brother was in a meeting room filled with people in suits that I didn't recognize, but I couldn't take my eyes off his vivid orange hair. I remember they took him away from my mother and gave her two years to get sober so she could have him back in her custody. Unfortunately, she couldn't even pull herself together for her newborn son.

I remember when I was 16 and we would visit my mother in treatment after treatment. Each time we would visit, she would promise me that once she left, we would be a family again. Whether the treatment was a year, a few months or even a couple of weeks, she never completed a program. She would check herself out and not come home like she assured me so many times. She would find another place to use and end up right back into another treatment center, making more promises. Strangers, other addicts, would walk up to me and say, "You must be Melissa's daughter, you look so much like her!" I remember I hated to hear that.

I remember when I was 17, graduated from high school and she had been sober for 12 consecutive months, a new record. A couple months later, still clean, she had another baby, with our father this time. And a year after that, we all started to feel like a normal stable family again. We were finally happy.

And then I remember last year when she relapsed.

So when I think about the question of whether my tattoos hurt, I remember that yes, they did, but that's a different kind of pain.

Something Plus One

Bridget Allen

Preface

My first mistake was asking for help.
For trusting.
No.
My first mistake was not wearing a seat belt, and trusting is always a mistake.

♦   ♦   ♦

Labor Day weekend, 1983. I was driving with a friend to a lake about sixty miles from home, Black Flag playing as loud as the tinny factory standard speakers on my Ford Fairlane would allow. After stopping at the last four way stop before the bridge, seeing no one else in the intersection, I began to roll forward. Even though drivers leaving the lake were often drunk, I didn't take the time to double check for cars. A Trans Am ran the stop sign and hit my driver's side door head on. There was a bang of sound and light, and then there was nothing. When I opened my eyes, my pain was intense. I was disoriented, and everything sounded like I was in the bottom of a swimming pool. The impact had popped the cassette tape out of the car. A mixture of AM radio static and gospel music told me to give myself over to Jesus. Convinced I was dead, I felt quite sheepish about getting the whole God-thing wrong. Slowly, it sunk in that I was still alive, my car sat on someone's front lawn, inches from the house. Blood was everywhere, windows, dash, me, but none of it was mine. (My stretchy skin almost never cuts.) I heard screaming, and looked through the blood spattered window to see my friend running down the street crying for someone to help me, blood pouring from a cut on his forehead. Only when he ran back to the car did people notice me. I think it's human nature to tend to the person who screams. I wanted to get out of the car, but the door wouldn't open. Fueled by adrenaline, and perhaps a little amphetamines, my friend ripped the door off the hinges, and pulled me onto the lawn. The grass was comforting, and I drifted. I was told to stay awake, but was too tired. The clouds were pretty. I hurt, but the floating felt good and safe. People were arguing. The paramedics refused to take me; something about my age or insurance. I don't know. A police officer yelled at them. He was so angry. I tried to tell him just to let me rest a bit and it would all be fine, but the words never reached my mouth. Then I was on a stretcher, enduring a horrible, noisy jostled ride to the ER where I was left in a hallway until my mother came with proof of insurance. With no actual examination, they declared me okay, and recommended a follow up visit with my family doctor.

But I wasn't okay. For two days, blood pooled in my head. Back home, I was treated for a hematoma and told I should be better in about a month.

That was six weeks ago. I look better. The bruising is gone, my face doesn't droop, but I don't feel better. I fall asleep all the time. There's a dull, constant throbbing in my head, punctuated by a random sharp pain like someone forced a railroad spike through my eye. There's a queasy vertigo that's persistent, but subtle until it's not. Then I fall down as if someone pulled the floor out from under me.

I'm trying so hard to pick up where I left off, but I can't think. I lose speech, but when I try to write, the words look like blurry gibberish. Text jumps on the page. My hands can't remember how to make the letters.

I'm scared. Scared enough to ask my mother to contact

our family doctor about a neurologist referral. An hour later, I'm checked into the hospital.

◆ ◆ ◆

Day One

Check in was uneventful. I'm surprised to have a roommate. She seems like a nice enough woman about my mother's age. The hospital is usually below capacity, so on previous stays, I've always had a private room. I'm told as soon as a room opens up, they'll move me.

Although it's only mid afternoon, I'm drowsy. As I begin to doze off, a doctor walks in. He's clearly not a neurologist, or he would be doing some cursory examination. He has a broad, open face punctuated by a sloping nose with a sharp bridge, much like a tortoise. I can't decide if he's serene or expressionless. He tells me his name, but to me he is instantly and forever, the Turtle Man. Without asking, he pulls up a seat, opens his legal pad, and begins his pitch.

"I want you to know, you can trust me. Many of the adolescents I counsel are from your school. I already have a sense of how things are for you, of your priorities and values."

I try to be polite. I want to respect the culture and beliefs of my schoolmates, but the thought that my priorities and values line up with those of most of my Catholic school classmates is laughable.

But I'm tired, and laughing will only make my head hurt more. I figure the more I make nice, the sooner he'll go away.

"I saw you on the new admissions chart, and I took it upon myself to stop by and check in on you. You must be going through a lot right now."

"Yes, I'm just trying to get well."

"Is school going well?"

I wonder if this man operates on small talk auto pilot. Is school going well? Is school going well? Let's see, I shattered a windshield with my forehead, and they pulled blood out of my skull with a needle longer than my hand. Now he's looking at a chart with my symptoms listed, and he asks me if school is going well. Polite, I'm going to stay polite.

"Do you mean before the wreck? School was great. Now? It's hard. That's why I'm here."

"Do you get along with your parents? Any issues with them?"

"My father died earlier this year."

"That must have been hard for you."

"Yes, but people die, it's a part of living."

"It seems to me you're trying too hard to be mature about this."

"I'm really tired, and I'm not sure how any of this is relevant."

"Okay, I see you're uncomfortable."

No, really I'm tired. So tired it's not worth arguing with you.

"Do you have a boyfriend?"

I hesitate. This doesn't seem like a safe place to out myself.

"Are you sexually active?"

I should have known. I don't know why, but middle aged men seem inordinately interested in my sex life.

"I don't think it's ethical to have this conversation where I have no privacy."

"I drew the partition. Do you really think anyone else is concerned about our conversation? I take it you're not a virgin?"

I wonder if he could sound any more snide.

"That's complicated."

"How is that a complicated question? You don't have to play naive. Have you ever had sexual intercourse with a boy?"

Not outing myself; good call, but I am really not

comfortable. I feel cornered, panicky. I wish I knew how to lie. Lying would be handy, I'm sure.

"Not willingly."

"So you're telling me you've been raped? By whom? Did you know this young man?"

"Yes."

The Turtle Man stops writing notes. He gently sets his pen down in his lap. His already placid face takes on a new stillness. I will eventually learn to associate this non expression with danger. He makes an exaggerated sigh, the type frazzled parents use when dealing with an unruly toddler, and he begins to speak slowly, pausing between each sentence.

"Sometimes, we make bad choices. We do things we know are morally wrong. Sometimes, those things are so wrong, we can't bring ourselves to take responsibility for them. We try to blame others. Isn't that what happened here? You knew premarital sex with a boy you hardly knew was wrong, so you tell yourself 'he raped me' so you don't have to feel the guilt of your actions."

I can feel tears, but I refuse to let this horrible person see me cry.

"No. I know what happened. You can't make me say something that isn't true. I want you to leave now."

I hear squeaky nurse shoes enter the room. The nurse addresses my roommate. "You called?"

My roommate answers, "I had some questions. Can you wait a minute? I think the doctor over there was just leaving."

As he leaves, the Turtle Man says something, but I can't process the words. My roommate tells the nurse she just wants some fresh water.

When the nurse leaves, my roommate says in a quiet voice, "I'm going to leave this curtain pulled until you're ready to open it. I'm sorry. Some doctors are total jerks."

◆　◆　◆

Day Two

I slept all the rest of yesterday. The Turtle Man used up every ounce of energy I had.

My mother came by this morning with every book in my room that wasn't put away on a bookshelf. I find it hard to read, but it's nice to know the option is there if I feel up to it.

In the afternoon, the Turtle Man returns. He won't make me cry. No one gets to make me cry twice.

"I met your mother this morning. We had a long talk. I'm very concerned about you. We both are."

He wants a certain response from me, and I have no clue what that response is. I make a non-committal hmm noise.

"Why didn't you tell me your mother was pregnant? You must have feelings about that?"

Clearly, the Turtle Man has an expectation of how I should feel, but I honestly don't know what it is. I'm at a loss.

"I'm glad she's healthy. I think she always wanted more children."

"But you must be angry and embarrassed."

I think back to the enormous relief I felt when I found out. For years, when my mother was angry, I'd be told my father had a vasectomy because I was so sickly and burdensome, there was no way to have another child. Not only were all my mother's recent doctor visits not due to some terminal illness that would leave me orphaned, she finally would have the second child I cheated her out of.

"Why would I be? I really don't understand."

"Your mother is having a baby out of wedlock. A baby conceived only a few months after your father's death."

I'm beginning to feel anger at this sexist ass who thinks he gets to dictate everyone else's morals.

"Yes, what does that have to do with me?"

"She betrayed your father's memory. She betrayed your family."

Trying to be civil, I'm still not letting some outsider attack my mother like this. Someone needs to protect her.

"My mother is a woman outside of being my mother. My parents did not have a good marriage, but my parents' relationship as a man and woman is an entirely different thing from their relationship with me. My mother doesn't owe it to me to be faithful to my father, and my father is dead, so his feelings about the matter are totally irrelevant."

The Turtle Man stands up. He begins carefully lifting each book on my nightstand and setting it down. I'm annoyed by the intrusion, but do not want to get drawn offside.

"I find your detachment concerning. You need to deal with this anger if you're going to get better."

I wait until he sits down before I speak again. Despite his short stature, I find his standing over my bed intimidating.

"My only anger is at you condemning my mother. I don't need your Moral Majority conservative Christian views warping everything I say. My father wouldn't have stood for it either."

He seems taken aback. I mistakenly think I've made my point.

"Are you saying you aren't Christian, and that your father wasn't either? That doesn't make sense. Why would you go to a Catholic school if you don't believe in God?"

"Rigorous academics. Multiple dual credit core courses without all the fluff of elective classes. Best way to graduate early with a solid foundation for college."

He changes subject.

"I notice you have a book on Freudian psychology. Did you get that because you're trying to understand your problems?"

"No, I got that because of a debate I was having in my History of Shakespeare class."

"That makes no sense."

I resist the urge to make a cigar is just a cigar joke, out of fear that it will get used against me.

"There's this guy in class. He's nice, but he tries to apply pop psychology to Shakespeare's writings. It's incongruous, especially in a class focused on putting Shakespeare's work into the context of its time. It infuriates me. If a thirty cent used book can help end that, it was worth it to me."

The Turtle Man straightens his back and leans forward in his chair. The sigh returns. His words, once again, slow to a crawl lest I miss anything.

"Listen, I'm going to be honest with you. It's time someone was. These symptoms you're experiencing are not a head injury. They're emotional trauma. Deep inside, you are angry at your mother. You are ashamed of your actions. You have created a pretend rape, so you can absolve yourself. You have created a head injury so you don't have to face your mother's betrayal. You need to begin facing your anger. You need to acknowledge your guilt. Until you can do that, you're not going to feel any better."

The Turtle Man stands up to leave.

"I want you to think about what I've said. I think you'll see the truth."

I am exhausted, and I've still not seen a neurologist. When my mother comes by to visit tonight, I'll ask her to make sure he doesn't come back again.

But my mother doesn't visit.

Some time overnight, staff wake me up. They tell me I'm being moved to a better room. Half asleep, I help with the transfer from bed to gurney and back to a new bed. I drift back asleep happy I'll finally have a private room.

♦   ♦   ♦

Day Three

I wake up early. Before I even open my eyes, I'm beset with a sense of wrongness. There is so much sound. Not that it's louder, but there are too many sounds. I hear what feels like a thousand voices all speaking at once, a television blaring, and chairs scraping the floor with no effort made to stop the horrible screeching sound.

My bed is different, not a standard hospital bed, more like a cheap dorm bed. I sit up and look around. Panic sweeps though my body. While I've never been in one before, it's obvious I'm in a psychiatric unit. I'd lost count of how many teens I knew whose parents put them in a lock-down until they learned to conform.

I haven't stepped out of the room, and already I hate this place. They moved me while I slept, with reassurances that they were moving me to a better room. I thought nothing of it since when I was here for surgery several months back, they moved me three times in the same week.

If I had understood, I would have fought.

I need to stay calm. I'm dizzy so often these days, and mornings are the worst. It will do me no good to announce myself to everyone with a spectacular fall. I'm sure I'd be accused of melodrama or making a scene.

So I sit, and breathe. Careful, deep breaths, willing the panic to rest at a low, controlled simmer.

I make my way to the bathroom, but go directly back to my bed as soon as I'm done. I decide my best plan of action is to wait in bed. Any interaction I have can only be used against me, so until someone comes to me, I'm going to sit on this bed like it's my own little island. My island. With my knees pressed against my chest, I rock just a little to soothe myself, careful to keep the movements small enough that no one will notice. In my head, the theme to Gilligan's Island plays on repeat, and I'm careful not to hum along.

Over two hours later, not one person, staff or patient, has said a word to me. The solitude is soothing. It's almost as if I'm invisible, until the Turtle Man shows up. He seems almost chipper, more animated than usual.

"Good morning! I see you're getting settled in. I had a long talk with your mother yesterday."

This must be a mistake.

"My mother knows I'm in here?"

"Of course, we want what is best for you. We want you to get better. We all have your best interests at heart, even if you can't see that."

Lost for a reply, I stare at his face. I try to look at his wide set turtle eyes, but I can't. My eyes lock onto his glasses frame, knowing he'll mistake that for respectful eye contact. I remind myself again not to cry.

"Your mother also mentioned your, umm, imbalances."

As he says this, I can see air quotes hang in the air as he struggles for euphemisms.

"According to your chart, you haven't been taking your hormones since you entered the hospital. Perhaps this is contributing to your irrational behavior."

Damn, not taking the hormones was really helping my nausea.

"Under the circumstances, I'd contend I'm perfectly rational."

Of course, I know to the Turtle Man, disagreeing with the Turtle Man is irrational behavior.

"I'll get this med order on right away. We'll have you back on track in no time."

Then he leaves, and I am once again invisible with the exception of the five minutes when a nurse comes in with two little pills I know I can't refuse.

◆　◆　◆

Day Four

Each day here feels worse. I wonder if I'll ever get out of here. The sense of Other is tangible, like a film that covers every surface with a greasy dust. Of course, there is also real, non-metaphorical, greasy dust. I wish I had some Pine Sol and a scrub brush. I know I'm still in the same hospital, but on this floor everything is different. If I wasn't terrified, I'd be joking about how One Flew Over the Cuckoo's Nest this place is. Not that there's anyone to joke with. No one's visited since I was moved. Not even my mother.

The Turtle Man stops by the ward but doesn't speak with me. I can't tell if that bodes well or not.

I try to look out to the street and get my bearings, but I can't focus past the metal mesh between the window panes to see outside. I try asking what floor I'm on, but no one will answer. Finally, tired of me asking, an exasperated nurse tells me it doesn't matter.

Of all the things here, I think I hate the floor the most. I hate the tiny interlocking hexagonal tiles. I'm in a goddamned beehive. It doesn't help that the floor folds up to hit me in the face every time I stand. The first time I fell, a staff person ran to help me, only to be taken aside by a nurse and told not to coddle me because I am a hypochondriac with hysterical vertigo. It took all my reserve not to inform them that I could hear every word they were saying. I suspect that, also, didn't matter.

Not much does matter here.

Certainly, my pain doesn't matter. They won't even let me have a Tylenol. I know they increased my hormones, but when I question the nurses, they deny it. As a result, I can't hold down food, but I guess that doesn't matter either.

I am grateful for the pills I'm not taking. I think I'm the only patient in here not doped up on some benzodiazapine. I figure if I can keep demonstrating how rational and calm I can be, eventually, they'll run out of justification to keep me here.

◆   ◆   ◆

Day Five

I don't know what is hardest here, the pain, the vomiting, or the mind numbing sameness of it all. I asked for books, and they pointed at the television. I asked for music, and they pointed at the radio. I asked if I could at least change the radio to classical, and I was told to learn flexibility.

Today the Turtle Man is focused on Ramifications.

"This boy you claim raped you, have you thought about the damage you've done to him with your accusations?"

"How do I ponder damage that doesn't exist. I filed no charges."

I steel myself. I'm not letting this man break down what it took me over a year to rebuild. I am not the bad guy.

"You spread rumors about a young man from a good family. What about how you hurt them? Your actions have consequences."

I focus on my breathing. I keep my voice quiet and steady, but I can't give him the words he demands.

"Well, probably at Colonial swinging a golf club about now, and I'm locked in a loony bin expected to craft some sort of apology to him for what he did to me. Consequences seem pretty lopsided from where I'm sitting."

"You're clearly still not ready to be reasonable."

For once, I try to steer the conversation.

"Can I ask you a question?"

"Go ahead."

"Why am I not allowed visitors? I've seen others have visitors."

"Visits are an earned privilege, but for the record, you

have no restrictions on visitors."

"Then why hasn't anyone visited?"

"Maybe you need to ask yourself that question."

It's all I can do to hold back tears until he is out the door.

♦ ♦ ♦

Day Six

I devote most of my energy to showing I am rational. Calm and rational. I'm suffering more than I was before I ever entered the hospital. Out there, everyone simply expected my brain to be all better, and for me to be the same person I always was. The only fallout from failing to live up to that expectation was bad grades and disappointed people.

In here, my pain is attention seeking, my dizziness and stumbles are proof of an aggressive demeanor, and my aphasia is willful non-compliance.

Last night, in an attempt to appear more acceptably normal, I tried to watch *Dynasty* in the common room. I had never watched *Dynasty* anywhere but *Dynasty* Night at JR's. For a moment, I closed my eyes, and imagined I was back at JR's sipping my Hot Peppermint Patty with extra whipped cream surrounded by boisterous, queer heckling punctuated by ooh-ing over fabulous dresses. But here, Dynasty felt like some aspirational fairy tale, not the caricature I knew it to be. Halfway through, I gave up and went to sleep.

♦ ♦ ♦

Day Seven

Most of the time, I sleep. Sleeping is the safest thing to do here. I wake up, make sure I'm clean and well groomed, eat the

food I am given, throw half of it back up, then sleep until the
Turtle Man arrives.

Every day, the Turtle Man tells me nothing will be better
until I admit my guilt. He gently explains, again, that the pain,
the aphasia, the vertigo is all trauma. Until I admit that I did
something wrong, until I face my regret, my subconscious will
continue to cause these symptoms.

Every day, I counter that I'm relatively certain those
symptoms line up with shattering a car windshield with my
forehead, and could I please see a neurologist. He sighs and, as
he gets up to leave, he tells me nothing will get better until I
face the truth.

I wonder if this is what the rest of my life holds.

♦   ♦   ♦

Day Something

I don't know how long I've been here anymore. A couple
weeks, maybe? Every day is the same. Nothing changes. I try to
be seen as a human, but it does me no good. Not once have I
so much as raised my voice, and yet people who scream and
yell and throw things come and go within a few days. The
Turtle Man shows up less often. When he is here, his visits are
shorter. I think he's grown bored with me. That feels like a
tiny victory, but it's also scary. Do I need his approval to get
out?

It's time to find another solution.

The Turtle Man wants compliance I can't provide. If I say
yes to him once, it won't stop. He will insist I dissect every
second of my supposed wrongdoing. He'll make me repeat it
over and over until I begin to believe it. What good is freedom
if he breaks my soul? He speaks about honoring my father, but
he knows nothing about my father.

My father would have hated this place. He would have fought.

It's time for me to honor him.

I've not lost control since I got here. I think it's just so numbingly boring there is no way to get overwhelmed.

No matter how calm I behave, staff keep telling me to control myself. The Turtle Man wrote a narrative wherein I'm a ticking bomb, and everyone seems a little disappointed that I don't blow up.

It's time to give them what they want.

I take a seat in the common area. I spend about a half an hour observing. I need to target the right staff member. Someone with enough power to do something, but not so much power that I can't intimidate them. I know who I want, and luckily he's on duty. There's a Charge Nurse, late twenties, he strikes me as a sad jokester who seems vaguely uncomfortable with much of his job. I hope my assessment is right. I approach him.

"Excuse me, but I wish to see a neurologist."

"Pardon?"

"I wish to see a neurologist. Now."

I begin to rock. I'm loudly tapping the table next to me. It feels so good to move again.

"The doctor hasn't ordered a neurological workup."

"No kidding? Of course he hasn't. The doctor doesn't care if I die in here. I had a workup scheduled before the good doctor tricked me into this hell hole, and I want the neurologist now!"

I am shouting so loud it hurts. Staff move closer to take me down, but I see the nurse give them a little back off nod. I'm getting to him.

"Go look at my records. I had a fucking subdural hematoma, and no one here fucking cares! Go on, I'll wait, but don't screw with me because I'm tired of waiting."

I knock over a chair and kick it for good measure. I'm

careful not to actually break anything, or knock the chair where it can hurt anyone. I'm just keeping up appearances, and I'm not sure how much longer I can do it. The room is spinning, but I'm willing to either get my way, or get strapped into restraints kicking and screaming. At least I'll know I tried.

Either it's working or Charge Nurse is more jaded than I guessed.

"Listen, stay right here. I'll be back in five minutes."

"You better be. Do you really want to be the scapegoat for the malpractice suit if I die in here?"

The Charge Nurse leaves. A staff person inches closer.

"He told you to back off, so back off! All I want is a damn neurologist."

The Charge Nurse returns.

"I wasn't lying, was I? You know, you're not caving to me by calling a neurologist. You're protecting yourself from liability."

The Nurse nods a little. In a quiet voice, he says, "There's a neurologist two floors down. He agreed to stop by in a few minutes."

I want to thank him. I want to be nice. I want to apologize for making his work day utter crap, but it could all be a lie.

Ten minutes later, the neurologist walks in. I nearly faint as I approach him. I shake his hand.

"Thank you so much for taking time out of your schedule. It means the world to me."

The neurologist stammers, taken aback. He asks me to walk again. He shines that horrid light in my eyes as I fight back tears. He correctly guesses the site of my injury. He looks along my hairline, finding the small scar from where my wound was lanced. He has me stand up and look straight ahead. I stumble, and he grabs my arms at the shoulders to steady me. He leans over and almost whispers, "You're safe now. It may take me an hour or so, but I'm getting you out of here. Just wait for me right here."

I sit down. I can wait. In less than forty-five minutes, a nurse comes with a wheelchair, and I'm moved to a private room in the main hospital.

My mother is waiting for me. Her words are clipped. She hugs me, but it's one of those hugs when all her muscles tense up. I know I've done something wrong, but I'm not sure what. I'm too tired to figure it out. She leaves as they bring me dinner.

A nurse asks me if I would like something for pain. The neurologist has given the option of Motrin or Tylenol 3.

"That's the one with codeine, right? I don't want that; it knocks me out."

"But it is night time. I think it's okay to be knocked out."

"I'll just take the Motrin, thank you."

If anyone comes in my room tonight, I need to be able to wake up.

♦ ♦ ♦

Day Something Plus One

When I woke up this morning, I knew I was safe before I opened my eyes. Real sunlight filtered through my lids. The stale dusty smell was replaced by nose-stinging antiseptic; disgusting, but safe. I was back in the real hospital.

I can't get over the politeness of the nurses. I'm never taking that for granted again.

A little after breakfast, the Neurologist came by.

"How are you feeling, is the Motrin making any dent in your pain?"

"It's good enough. I can't handle how out of it I get with the strong stuff."

"I've thought about this, and if you want to start testing

now, we can, but I think you could use a break. I'd like to send you home now, and have you return in two to four weeks."

"Home would be nice. I miss my dog, but I'm scared to come back. I'm also scared to not come back. Sorry to be such a baby."

"I wouldn't call it that. What if we restrict what medical personnel can see you? Psychiatric services won't get notification you're here."

"You can do that? Really do that?"

"It's usually reserved for infectious diseases and patients with severe immune disorders."

"I have a chronic low white blood cell count, if that helps."

"Actually, it does. Bet that's the first time that was a good thing for you."

I laugh. Laughter feels foreign, like it will choke me.

"I think I want to go home."

"I'll get right on that."

"Hey, doctor, thank you for what you did."

"It's my job."

"That didn't matter to the others. Can I ask you a weird question?"

"I don't know, try me."

"How long was I there? I don't even know what day it is. I've lost track."

"How long do you think? This could be good to know as a neurologist. From when you were admitted to the medical center."

"Two weeks? Give or take a day?"

He flips through my chart.

"Ouch, you were admitted twenty-one days ago."

"I lost a week?"

"Yeah, let's get you home."

◆　◆　◆

Post Script (October 1984)

I'm in a new school.

Again.

I have a fairly short shelf life when it comes to educational placements. There's a girl whose desk is next to mine. She seems uncomfortable around me, but not in the same, disgusted bullying way most of my new peers seem uncomfortable. One day, we're stuck in class doing nothing. A storm has knocked out power. My new high school is windowless, and the emergency generator only powers dim exit lighting. So everyone sits and stares into the darkness. The girl next to me has to tap me on the arm before I realize she's speaking to me.

"Can I ask you a really bizarre question?"

Guard up, ready for a new round of bullying, I reply, "Sure. Can't promise I'll answer. Deal?"

"Yeah, that's totally, totally fair."

She pauses.

"Were you in the hospital about a year ago? Car accident?"

"Yes. How did you know?"

"I think my mother shared a room with you. I don't want to say much, but if that was you, I'm sorry."

I instantly know what she means.

"Yes, I think you've got the right person."

"I thought so, there were too many things that matched. I saw you up here with a baby yesterday, and I just knew."

"Your mom was nice."

"She wanted to help you, but they wouldn't tell her anything. She cried. Sometimes has nightmares. She says if my brother or I have to be in the hospital, she's never leaving us alone even if she has to sleep on the floor."

"Oh God, I'm so sorry."

"I don't want to be pushy, but can I tell her I found you?

Can I tell her you're all right?"

"Yeah, please do. It wasn't her fault."

"I know, but my mom likes to protect people, especially kids."

A few days later, in the school parking lot, I saw the woman who had been my roommate before the Turtle Man locked me away. Our interaction was only a few seconds. She didn't want to intrude or bring up bad memories. She just needed to see I was safe.

♦   ♦   ♦

Post Script (February 2008)

In the hospital parking lot, pillars of the community mill about. Closed for a few years already, today is hospital demolition day. The crowd is mostly older folks, and the mood seems to be that of an octogenarian high school reunion. There are hearty handshakes and many hugs. From a distance, the onlookers seem a bit melancholy. I feel nothing but smug satisfaction.

A massive backhoe stands at the ready.

My youngest child loves giant construction equipment.

Across the street in a McDonald's parking lot, we sit on the trunk of my car, sharing french fries and enjoying the impending destruction. My son's eyes widen, delighted once I assure him that they triple extra made sure no one was inside. When the backhoe finally makes contact, the five story wall that supports the atrium of the hospital crumbles like gingerbread.

I spent years fighting the loss of historic buidings on this street, but some places are better just gone.

Wibbly Wobbly, Ability Disability

Cara Liebowitz

I get my first real mobility aid when I am twelve.

A friend of mine, also disabled, who I have known since I was nearly a toddler, uses one forearm crutch to help steady herself and prevent falling. She looks at me and tells me "Cara, you should get a crutch." So I do. They come in pairs, so my friend and I split the pair, each taking one. Like friendship bracelets.

At first I only use the crutch for distances, events where I might get tired and need to lean on something. My first summer at a camp for kids with physical disabilities, I use the crutch almost everywhere I go outside the bunk, at first because I'm not sure of my surroundings and don't want to fall, and later because I just don't want to stop using it. I mention to my head counselor that I hardly ever use the crutch at home, and she says "You know, you don't have to use it here either." I struggle to tell her that I do, in fact, have to use it, or at least I feel like it. At a camp where the majority of campers use wheelchairs, I'm one of the only ones who can walk on their own. My family wasn't even sure I was disabled enough for this camp, and we were all reassured when the camp video showed some kids walking on their own, just like me. I've spent my whole life shoved into the non-disabled world, a victim of the false belief that I was "too able" for disability land. Camp is one of the first things I do that's just for disabled people. I often characterize myself, even as a child, as sitting on a fence, too disabled for non-disabled people and yet not disabled enough for disabled people. A self-conscious barely-teenager, away from home for the first time, I want to show the other campers that I belong with them.

Over the next two years, I use the crutch more and more. Finally, in ninth grade, with encouragement from my mother, I make the very difficult decision to use the crutch in school. My school is large, spanning grades 7 – 12, and even though I leave five minutes early from class, there is always a chance I'll get knocked over. I am nervous to the point of terror. I don't know how people will react. I have a sleepover with my best friend a few days before school starts and I pour out all my fears to her. My fears, thankfully, are for the most part, unfounded. A few people ask questions, but then my crutch is quickly accepted. One of the most interesting responses comes from, oddly enough, my physical therapist. The first day I have PT is a rainy day, and she looks at me critically. "Is that because it's raining?" she asks, motioning to my crutch. I am nonplussed. She's a physical therapist; she knows what a crutch is and what it's used for. Surely it makes more sense that I would decide to use a crutch to help me all the time, rather than just when it's raining, especially because we're indoors. But maybe because she's a PT, she sees the crutch as a symbol of a decline or a temporary accommodation, rather than a tool.

Not too long after that, my sister starts touring colleges. I am dragged along on these trips and amuse myself by rating the accessibility of each campus. I use my transport chair, which is like a regular manual wheelchair, but without the big wheels, so the user must be pushed by someone. I realize, as I begin to comprehend the sheer size of most college campuses, that there's no way I'd be able to walk around a campus. I start talking to my parents about getting a power wheelchair for college. They are surprisingly receptive. My PT suggests that a motorized scooter may be better for me as she says it's better for people who can walk (I now know that this is, at least, mostly untrue – though scooters are cheaper and don't have the myriad of specialized seating options that power wheelchairs do, so those who have enough movement to walk typically don't need those options. I didn't, back then, though now is a different story.). The process takes two years. We find out that insurance won't cover the scooter, because I don't need it indoors (because apparently disabled people should never want to go outside, ever). Eventually, we are directed to a local charity that helps disabled and sick kids in the area. I loathe pulling the pity/charity card, but I swallow my disdain. To my surprise, the people who run the organization are really nice, taking the time to sit with me and let me show them who I am. They pay for my entire scooter. My mother calls me, half-frantic, when I'm at a friend's house at a sleepover: "Cara! I'm coming to get you! They're coming over RIGHT NOW with a check!" I think I may cry when the check is presented to me.

I receive my scooter the summer before my junior year of high school. It's a revelation – I can *sit* and *move* at the same time! I realize I'm now much more into things that I had previously hated – like shopping or stopping on the street to have a conversation with someone. It wasn't clear before I got my scooter that my lack of stamina was why I didn't like things that required a lot of standing or walking, although looking back on it now, it seems obvious. I spend my three weeks at camp, now my favorite place in the world, learning how to use my scooter; navigating around tight corners, opening doors, and just generally treating the entire camp as one big scooter obstacle course.

Yet despite all this, I'm still treated with suspicion. I hear through the grapevine that a girl in my grade thinks I'm faking my disability. Apparently, her rationale is "she [me] walks fine, and then pretends to fall." I laugh about it, but it sticks in my mind. A teacher of mine is surprised (and slightly ashamed of himself) when my mom asks him to look out for me on a field trip, because I can't walk as fast as the other kids. I have to wonder what he thinks I use the crutch for. My camp counselors laugh and call me "lazy" when I use my scooter.

They don't call any other wheelchair users in my bunk "lazy", even those who can walk a little bit with walkers or other aids. It's obvious that they think I don't really "need" the scooter because I can walk without aids. A bus driver tells me that I "tricked" him, because I got out of my scooter to sit in a regular seat.

By the time I start college, I'm using two crutches on the recommendation of my orthopedist, and I've never been so relieved to leave an environment behind. At college, I reinvent myself. I use my scooter almost all the time outside of my dorm. No one at school knows I can walk and I don't advertise it, even to the point of using my scooter to go very short distances, like from my seat to the front of the classroom, but eventually the truth comes out. When I am inevitably forced to use my crutches, for instance in bad weather when I don't want to risk damaging the delicate electronics inside the scooter, I'm met with jubilation from everyone from professors to crossing guards to dining hall workers. "It's so good to see you upright!" they gush, as if using a scooter was a sign of some grave illness that I am now recovering from. The assumption that walking = better and rolling = worse irritates me, especially because walking across campus exhausts me and I often skip class on bad weather days, because I simply don't have the energy to walk the distance. When I'm tired, other things, like showering and laundry, tend to fall by the wayside as well.

The continuous assumptions about my abilities aren't just annoying and offensive. They also affect my academic and professional life. As an education major, I'm required to spend half a semester in my junior year of working closely with a cooperating teacher teaching lessons in an actual classroom, a process known as Professional Semester, or ProSem for short.

Unfortunately, because of carpool and accessibility issues, I have to bring the crutches every day, and that is a huge strain. I work in a third grade classroom and the kids are amazing. They "get" my access needs and will cheerfully drag a chair across the room so I can sit down when I'm greeting them at the door each morning and afternoon. When I'm on recess duty, they ask me to count their jump-rope jumps for them, because they know that's an activity I can do sitting down.

Sadly, they are much more accepting than the adults. I am engaged in a constant, circular argument with my cooperating teacher and my ProSem coordinator, a professor who is in charge of observing the ProSem students and grading us on our teaching ability, professionalism, and a whole host of other things. They both tell me that I need to walk around the room and observe the students when they're working, helping them if necessary, and that I need to stand up to teach lessons, despite my continued insistence that I can't do either, since I just have my crutches. I'm told that the students won't respect me if I sit down to teach, and that I can't have students come to me to have their papers graded. I have to go to them, even though I see my cooperating teacher doing the precise thing she told me not to do at least once. We reach an uneasy compromise, where a hard-backed chair (sitting in the big soft chair that my cooperating teacher uses for reading time is apparently a no-no) is provided for me so that I can sit if I need to.

The fragile peace is promptly shattered when my ProSem coordinator comes to observe me. I decide to stand up, bracing myself against the wall, for the two back-to-back lessons I teach. I do it so I won't be bothered, yet again, about standing up to teach. Instead, my tactic has almost the complete opposite effect. My ProSem coordinator pulls me into the teacher's lounge to talk to me after my lessons are done and the first words out of her mouth are "I was shocked that you stood up, because you've given me and [cooperating teacher] such a hard time about it...**I'm forced to conclude that either you've been making excuses or you haven't been**

being truthful with us."

My mouth drops and after she leaves, I flee into the bathroom to cry and dry-heave over the sink. This incident quickly spirals into a three hour meeting with my ProSem coordinator and my advisor where they proceed to tell me how unprofessional I am for (basically) having access needs and accommodating for myself. When I ask if they've consulted the Disability Services Office, my ProSem coordinator hems and haws and skirts around the question by repeatedly calling it "the Office of Human Diversity" (which is, in fact, what the DSO is under, but it's not the DSO itself). After the third or fourth time, I lose my temper and tell her "You can say the word *disability*, you know, I'm not afraid of it," at which point I am accused of being disrespectful to "two women in this room who have Ph.Ds in Education." They tell me that they can't recommend me for student teaching.

You see, ProSem is one long test, one that if you don't pass, you cannot student teach and therefore cannot graduate with teaching certification. The decision as to whether or not you pass— whether you are "recommended" for student teaching or not— is made solely by your ProSem coordinator in conjunction with your cooperating teacher. I am given two options— to change my major altogether, or to graduate with a degree in Education, but without teaching certification. I choose the latter, feeling forced out of the program, and I graduate that summer.

Now, at 23 and on the cusp of finishing my Master's degree, I've amassed an impressive collection of mobility aids, including crutches, canes, a folding cane, a walker, a scooter, and a power wheelchair. I think one of the reasons I'm such a "mobility aid guru" is because I still, on some level, feel that need to prove myself. I want to prove to others— and yes, to myself as well— that I'm a "real", card-carrying disabled person. I still, almost unconsciously, "crip it up" when I'm in an environment with mostly able-bodied or non-disabled people. When I walk, I make sure to make it look like a struggle, so there can be no question about my need for a wheelchair. I have been using mobility aids for over a decade and have established myself in disability activism, yet I still feel like a ping-pong ball, batted back and forth between "too disabled" and "not disabled enough". I feel like any moment, my charade will crumble and I will be exposed as a fraud.

Just the other day, a friend of a friend asked me almost right after meeting me if I needed to use my walker all the time. When I told her that I didn't, but it made things easier, she said "I figured– you look like you can walk without it." Later, she repeatedly tried to pressure me into going on an inflatable water slide at a block party, despite my doubts about being able to climb the ladder up to the slide. Because she saw our other friend who is also disabled doing it, she expected that I would have the same abilities, despite the fact that we do not even share the same diagnosis. I have been dealing with these assumptions all my life, and even more in the decade plus that I've been using mobility aids.

One would expect it gets easier. It doesn't. I am tired of not fitting into people's boxes. I am tired of people who should know better putting me into boxes. I am tired of admitting to fellow disabled people that, on a good day, I can climb the stairs in my house while holding the cat in my arms; then turning around and admitting to them that a mile walk to the nearest diner is bordering on impossible, and will leave me too exhausted to contemplate doing anything else for the rest of the day. This is part of the reason I'm uneasy with scales like the Gross Motor Function Classification System (GMFCS), which is used to categorize the levels of ability of children with CP. They assume that abilities are distributed evenly, and will only improve, not decline. Nor do they take into account the fact that environmental conditions may influence ability.

In the (slightly edited) words of the Tenth Doctor, from

the much-loved BBC science fiction show Doctor Who, "people assume that [ability] is a strict progression of cause to effect. But actually, from a nonlinear, non-subjective viewpoint, it's actually more like a big ball of wibbly wobbly, [ability disability]...stuff." The Doctor knows that things aren't always what they seem. Perhaps he will forgive my taking liberties with his words if it'll teach us humans the same lesson.

My Mother GLaDOS
Dani Alexis Ryskamp

Test Chamber 00

The moment you are born, you know you are going to die.

You enter the world to a faceful of overhead fluorescence, peptic salve and adrenaline. The walls are glass; the floor is cold. On the wall, Stoppard's compass stops Heisenberg cold. You are at 1:44 p.m., September 16, 1982. You are headed in only one direction.

You're alone until a tinny, disembodied voice intrudes.

"Shit. Morphine, stat."

Nobody offers any congratulations on your birth. Nobody murders you, or puts you in a potato, or feeds you to birds. You have a pretty good life.

Twenty-four hours later your mother signs the birth certificate through an opiate haze, leaving your father's name misspelled. Your name is misspelled as well. It should read "Disappointment."

♦ ♦ ♦

Get Comfortable While I Warm Up the Neurotoxin Emitters

You can't walk yet. You can scoot, and crawl, but five feet above your head a whole world runs, words and plans and things they do to you. Your mother lives in that world.

The world where you live is quieter, more detailed, more concrete. You're lying on a pleasantly scratchy, padded surface. When you roll over you can see it: a forest of twisted fibers, poking skyward, still exuding a faint chemical aroma, rubber and nylon. The harvest-gold woven dust ruffle on the couch has a more homelike smell, more broken in; its fibers, scratchy as the carpet but in a different way, form a series of alternating squares that catch the light. Dust motes dance in the sunlight, iridescent.

The world overhead is full of voices you recognize: your mother. The lady with the short yellow hair whom you will come to recognize as your aunt Tomi. Two older women, looking more alike than either will ever admit, watery blue eyes and fingertips stained yellow with nicotine. Your grandmother; your great-aunt.

Everyone talks with the cooing approval that makes your entire body wiggle with delight. Except your mother, the one you want most to notice you. At eleven months old, "condescension" has more syllables than you can parse, but you know the icepick between the ribs too well already.

Words. If you had words, you could fight back. Words could melt the icepick. She sees in words; if you had words, she could see you.

You're eleven months old. You, beginner, have discovered the all-purpose symbolic instruction code. Now all you have to do is make it word.

We are now ready to begin the test proper.

◆ ◆ ◆

The Enrichment Center Regrets to Inform You That This Next Test is Impossible

Certain files have been deleted from your memory and must be reconstructed by technicians.

For instance, "divorce.txt" went 404 about the time you triggered the instruction code and, with it, the Automated Human Simulator. The simulator runs on language when you can't. It's more human that you are – more fluent, more graceful, more polite. To ensure maximum space for resistors, it has no memory.

Years later, an early gap in the simulator is reconstructed for you. *Your daughter... isn't what we'd expect from other children her age. Yes, she's bright. But she struggles.*

There's nothing wrong with her. He's only doing this to get back at me for leaving him. We will not be keeping any more appointments with your office.

Back then, the telephone still made a satisfying *clunk* when she slammed it into the cradle.

The Automated Human Simulator tends to boot suddenly and without warning. After nine years you start reading technical manuals on the subject, diagnosing the simulator periodically with technical glitches like "childhood schizophrenia" and "dissociative identity disorder" even though none of them really seem to fit. Technicians keep reassuring you that your diagnoses are spurious and that the simulator runs exactly as expected.

"There's nothing wrong with you," your father tells you for years. "You're perfect exactly as you are. If they don't see that, fuck 'em."

"There's nothing wrong with you," your mother tells you for years. "You're just behind all the other kids emotionally because you're so far ahead intellectually. You'll grow out of it."

"There's nothing wrong with you," your mother tells you for years. "You just need to act more like the other kids."

"There's nothing wrong with you," your mother tells you for years, evading your requests for affection. "You're just not a cuddly child."

"There's nothing wrong with you," your mother tells you through gritted teeth, as you ride beside her in the car in your comfortable bubble of silence, examining the chips in the windshield and attempting to calculate how many miles the car would have to drive, on average, to cover the entire windshield in chips, and how many years that would take. "Now drop the attitude." When you open your mouth to protest that you didn't *have* an attitude, you lose TV for a week.

"There's nothing wrong with you," your mother tells you for the third time in a row. But you don't know it, because your brain refuses to decode her mouthnoises as coherent speech. When you say "what?" a fourth time, you lose computer access for a month.

"There's nothing wrong with you," your mother says, glaring at you with her hands on her hips. You have no idea what time it is. "You were supposed to do those dishes before dinner. Too late now. Go to your room." There is, of course, no food in your room.

"There's nothing wrong with you," your mother yells, shaking you as sobs force themselves out of your body. You don't know why this should be true when you're being cried with such force. When another sob works its way to the surface, she slaps you.

"There's nothing wrong with you," your mother tells you. "I don't *have* to love you. Lots of other parents don't put up with this from their kids."

"There's nothing wrong with you," your mother tells you. "Look, there's the state hospital. Where they put the crazy people." When you get lightheaded from all the noises at the family Christmas party later that night and fall out of your chair, she sings, "they're coming to take me away, ha ha, hee hee, ho ho, to the funny farm..."

"There's nothing wrong with you," your mother tells you, her eyes boring into your face, demanding you look back. When you begin to cry again, she says, "Fine. I guess everything is always my fault," and slams the door in her wake.

◆　◆　◆

Please Do Not Attempt to Remove Testing Apparatus From the Testing Area

"You're not smart," she says. "You're not a scientist. You're not a doctor. You're not even a full-time employee."

"You're just like your father," she says.

Divorce.txt isn't the only file missing from your database – missing, not absent, since you almost never ran the simulator before the age of five. You suspect someone pulled that particular core. Perhaps it was corrupted. After all, they both said a lot of things that you have come to regret.

"But I know we can put our differences behind us," she says. "For science."

You monster is implied.

She attempts to reconstruct one of the divorce core files for you, unbidden, over the next thirty years. It is called we_did_everything_right.exe. It's BASIC:

10 PRINT "We agreed from the beginning that we wouldn't let the divorce affect you."

20 PRINT "We worked hard never to put you in the middle."

30 PRINT "And we agreed never to say anything negative about each other in front of you."

40 PRINT "Ever."

50 IF GOODMOTHER_THREAT THEN GOTO 10

Somehow, we_did_everything_right.exe manages to run concurrently with youre_just_like_your_father.exe for years, without triggering a single fatal logic error in your mother's AI.

10 PRINT "You're just like your father."

20 IF CHILD_DISTRACTED THEN GOTO 10

30 IF CHILD_MISINTERPRETS THEN GOTO 10

40 IF CHILD_IGNORES THEN GOTO 10

50 IF CHILD_FAKESLOST THEN GOTO 10

60 IF CHILD_LAZY THEN GOTO 10

70 IF CHILD_FORGETFUL THEN GOTO 10

80 IF CHILD_BADATCHORE THEN GOTO 10

90 IF CHILD_DAWDLING THEN GOTO 10

100 IF CHILD_FAKE THEN GOTO 10

110 IF CHILD_MELTDOWNERROR THEN GOTO 10

120 IF CHILD_SHUTDOWNERROR THEN GOTO 10

130 IF CHILD_POWERINTERRUPT THEN GOTO 10

140 IF CHILD_CALCULATIONERROR THEN GOTO 10

150 IF CHILD_FAILPRINT THEN GOTO 10

160 IF CHILD < YOU THEN GOTO 10

The concurrent running of the two programs triggers a feedback loop in the Automated Human Simulator, whose logic center is a bit too adaptive for its own good. The loop takes the shape of an emulator: your mother's AI, running on your system. They even share the same favorite color, despite the fact that you never really liked purple.

To hear her tell it, your father is a real disappointment. No wonder you were named after him.

◆   ◆   ◆

You, SUBJECT NAME HERE, Must Be the Pride of SUBJECT HOMETOWN HERE

You come from a long line of people who really loved cake. "Cake," of course, is a euphemism for sex. Straight sex. The kind of sex that is always implied, never stated; the kind of sex one assumes happens in marriages but tastefully omits to mention. Good-girl sex. Lie back and think of England, where cake is served alongside afternoon tea.

In 1690, your great-great-great-great-great-great-great grandfather, Harold Kennedy, disowns your great-great-great-great-great-great grandfather, Harold Kennedy, depriving the latter of several thousand acres of southwest Ohio in addition to the usual emotional connections one associates with family. Three hundred years later, the remaining records only mention that the disowning had to do with Harold Junior's conversion from Presbyterianism to Methodism. You're in graduate school before you learn that "Methodism" is a euphemism for "enjoying too much cake with the wrong people."

It might even be a euphemism for "enjoying cake with your own team," as it were. You can't tell. The familial euphemisms for non-bakery-approved relationships are even more dense and confusing than the euphemisms for vanilla cake.

In 1901 or thereabouts, your great-great-grandmother's sister, "Aunt Marie," scandalizes the society pages of the Urbana, Ohio newspaper by declining to have her impending marriage memorialized in them. Instead, she runs away to Florida for her nuptials. Ninety years later, your great-grandmother is still heavily implying that Aunt Marie ate her cake and had it too.

How many Methodist bakeries *are* there in Florida? The sketchy end to which Aunt Marie came is repeated, technicians inform you, by your great-aunt, whose decades-long friendship with the first openly gay mayor of Key West may or may not have involved cake. If the family knows, nobody will discuss it. "That has nothing to do with us," your aunt announces staunchly at her funeral. Of course it doesn't. Still, when he is cremated, half his ashes go to his artist partner in Florida; the other half live in your great-aunt's house, caked in the bottom of a glass tumbler.

"I knew this bisexual thing was just a phase," your mother says in 2005 or thereabouts. She's not referring to the six months you've spent attending Methodist college youth meetings – she doesn't know about those. No one does. That has nothing to do with us. Your mother is talking about your cousin, whose actual bona fide relationships with women were followed by an actual bona fide relationship with a man, whom she married.

Your mother's voice oozes scorn. You decide not to mention the Methodist youth group. Your gaze drops to the cake lying on your plate, half-eaten.

Only after you've been safely married off to a straight man do you start to suspect that the cake is a lie.

♦ ♦ ♦

Killing You and Giving You Good Advice Aren't Mutually Exclusive

As part of an optional test protocol, we are pleased to present an amusing fact: your mother hates martyrs.

"I can't believe she's pulling the martyr card," she says of your grandmother, in a tone usually reserved for bisexual phases.

"Crying won't do you any good," she says, when you are five years old and she's just sold off half your toys – her choice, not yours – at the community yard sale.

"Stop wallowing," she scolds, when you are nine years old and crying because your partner in crime since preschool has discovered that bullying you is more fun than being your friend.

"This is all my fault," she says, when you are twelve years old and writhing in bed, cramps like an alien symbiont shredding your pelvis. She packs you off to school, where you're late to every class because you cannot climb stairs.

"I did this to you," she says, when you are fifteen years old, racked with nausea and having intermittent hot flashes. "Birth control and surgeries will just make you worse. Look at what happened to me." You first watched ER staff intubate your mother to stop her vomiting when you were five; you watched them give her an emergency lumbar puncture when you were seven. You do not want to end up like her.

"All I wanted was to find a cure before you had to deal with this," she says, when you are twenty and on your way to your first-ever emergency room visit for a migraine you can't control.

"The doctors don't know anything," she says, when you are twenty-three and considering an experimental procedure that, if it works, will allow you to finish law school. She urges you to go through with it. The migraine that follows it lasts for twenty-one months, two weeks, and three days.

You finish law school anyway. You don't wallow. Your mother hates martyrs.

"I'm a terrible mother," she says, when you are twenty-seven, signing on the dotted line under the ominous heading VOLUNTARY ADMISSION TO MENTAL HEALTH UNIT – CLOSED WARD. Chronic pain isn't fatal.

"What did I do?" she says, when you are thirty-two and no longer have anything in common with her except a standing invitation to her pity party.

"I'm only trying to help," she says, as she stuffs you into a

Companion Cube.

♦ ♦ ♦

Good People Don't End Up Here

By 2009, the Automated Human Simulator has begun to break down.

The system was never designed for long-term use. It is intended as a backup only, a failsafe when your logic, rational thought, and self-care subroutines are pushed to their limits. Except that you have no logic, rational thought, or self-care subroutines. You have an emulator running at cross-purposes, juggling commands that cannot, rationally, co-exist.

Always be the person your mother approves of, but pretend that person is the real you, chosen of your own free will. She's a good mother. You had a good childhood. It was just a joke. All faults in the operation of your childhood are yours. Your system is too rule-oriented, too hard on itself, too prickly, too articulate. She tried but you are just too smart for her. You are too smart to do anything but destroy yourself.

The Automated Human Simulator crashes publicly for the first time on August 8, 2009. You have no black box; the crash corrupts your memory files of the event. The optical processor feedback informs you that your Automated Human Simulator extracted you from your office, stammered an excuse to your secretary, and left the building. You know it dialed your cell phone and requested your father take you to the nearest hospital emergency department. You don't know how it happened.

The Automated Human Simulator should have been interrupted by your discovery that living.exe has a manual override function. That is to say, the Automated Human Simulator has always been interrupted *in the past* by the discovery that living.exe has a manual override function. The Automated Human Simulator refuses to cut you open, walk you into traffic, or pitch you over the side of a tall building. Instead, the simulator returns full function to conscious systems at that point – whether you want it or not.

You know because you've tried.

"I'm going to admit you to the closed ward," says the functionary in the lab coat. You can't remember how your mother got in the room. "You'll be under what we call 'one to one' supervision. First, I want you to contract for safety. Do you know what that is?"

Your attorney module lets out an electronic simulacrum of a laugh. The Automated Human Simulator is, of course, not human. It is not legally competent to contract for anything. But, hey, you're already crazy, right? Crazy is hilarious. Years of your mother singing you Dr. Demento songs whenever the Automated Human Simulator goes offline has taught you that.

The moment the functionary leaves the room, you start to cry. "I'm sorry," says your mouth. "I'm sorry. I'm sorry."

This is your fault. It didn't have to be like this. And all the cake is gone.

You are apologizing to your mother because you require immediate assistance in order to survive. You were, of course, supposed to survive without assistance. Of any kind. Because your mother hates martyrs.

You're still laughcrying when they lead you through the double doors.

Touching the floor will result in an unsatisfactory mark on your training record, followed by death.

♦　♦　♦

As Part of a Required Test Protocol, We Will Stop Enhancing the Truth in Three, Two-

The purpose of the mental hospital appears to be to bring the Automated Human Simulator back online as quickly as possible, so you can be released into the community without incurring liability on the part of the hospital or its shareholders.

As part of a required test protocol, you are asked twelve times in the next week whether you were abused as a child.

The correct answer is no.

Your mother is niceness personified. It even says so on a plaque she hung in the house years ago: "Because nice matters."

"You've always been too hard on yourself," your mother laughs as you dissolve in tears after a dismal clarinet recital. She pats your head. "*I* knew you could do it."

"I'm so happy you can take care of yourself," she says, as you stack a pile of encyclopedias on top of the footstool so you can reach the controls on the washing machine. You are eight years old.

"Oh, honey, you can't get bent out of shape about it," she says, when you point out that the CD you specifically requested for your birthday has wound up in your cousin's gift box. "You said it was a good album! Don't you *want* your cousin to have it?"

"I know it's Christmas, but she's gotten a little cranky because I gave away something she loved," your mother announces to the entire family as your cousin sits with your favorite jigsaw puzzle on his lap. "So I'm making it up to her." Grandly, she bestows on you a wrapped box. It contains another jigsaw puzzle: a fifty-piece image of a kitten in an old boot. You solved it ten years ago, when you were five.

"You never were a cuddly infant," she says, pushing you away as you reach for a hug.

"I'm sorry you feel that way," she says.

"I'm sorry you're letting your selfishness get in the way of being happy," she says.

"I'm sorry you think that happened," she says.

"I'm sorry, but there's nothing I can do about it now," she says.

"I'm sorry you're so sensitive about this," she says.

"I'm sorry you're wallowing," she says.

"I'm sorry you're blaming me for this," she says. "You're right. It's all my fault. I'm a terrible mother. Why do you hate me?"

She was just trying to be a good parent. She never *had* to love you, but she did. You were a very difficult child to love: selfish, compassionless, thoughtless, arrogant, rude. What was she supposed to do, just let you get away with it? She only did what any other good parent would do. It was a *joke*, honey. She's only trying to help. She never meant it like *that*. The correct answer is no.

"Thank you for helping us help you help us all," says the hospital.

"The difference between you and me is that I can feel pain," says your mother.

♦   ♦   ♦

Bring Your Daughter to Work Day is the Perfect Time To Have Her Tested

Bullshit_detector.exe sat unused on your hard drive for thirty-two years before you even knew you had it. It appears to be incompatible with the Automated Human Simulator.

If your mother noticed that you conveniently failed to invite her to your graduation capstone presentation, she hasn't mentioned it. You're two weeks out of the Master of Arts in English and running your mouth on the phone with her. For the first time in years, the Automated Human Simulator isn't doing the talking.

"In Wisconsin, I'll be staying in a suite with three other autistic presenters," you say. One noticeable flaw in your non-simulator programming is its habit of forgetting who it is talking to. The Automated Human Simulator does not forget. "I'll be doing that in Atlanta too, come to think of it. Staying in the all-autistic suite."

You hear your mother laugh. Over the telephone connection it sounds more like a snort. "I can't imagine what *that's* going to be like."

Bullshit detected.

The Automated Human Simulator stammers something about your suitemates' credentials. Beneath the static, you seethe. *These people are my friends. They're my mentors. I look up to them. And all those days you and I shared a hotel room in Ohio, painstakingly gathering info on dead relatives – your roommate was one hundred percent autistic as well. Was that so onerous for you, Mom?*

You remember what she said about your bisexual cousin, and you realize exactly what your nice, generous, warm, well-meaning mother thinks of you.

"Were you abused as a child?" your new therapist asks.

The correct answer is yes.

◆ ◆ ◆

Assume the Party Escort Submission Position or You Will Miss the Party

A few weeks after your return from two unimaginable weeks rooming with fellow autistics, you get a Facebook event invitation. Your mother is throwing a baby shower for your cousin and his new wife.

You're invited, of course. Your family takes only one thing more seriously than cake: the party that precedes it. In a dozen weddings and nearly twice as many children, your grandmother, aunts, and mother have never failed to throw the appropriate "shower." You have never failed to be invited to one.

Except your own.

In 2012, you got married. You also planned your own wedding shower and handed the plans off to your mother and your grandmother. Twice.

Said shower never appeared.

Now, your mother is happily throwing the party for your cousin that she never threw for you. Showers are continuing as if yours never happening never happened. In front of the family, quietly and with total plausible deniability, you have been erased.

You call your mother.

"I'm *so* sorry, *honey*," she says, in the voice that says all the right words in the tone you can never quite call out. "I don't remember that. I don't know how I can make it right."

"You can listen," you say. "I just need you to listen." In the background, the Automated Human Simulator beeps softly. *Futility detected.*

"We can throw you another one," she says. "How about August? Around the time of your anniversary?"

"Really," you say. "I just need you to listen to me and take my feelings seriously."

"I'm so sorry you feel that way," she says. "I can't imagine what else I can do to make this right," she says.

The Automated Human Simulator whirs to life. "Okay," you say. "Maybe the third week of August?"

Someday, you really need to stuff the Automated Human Simulator into an Emergency Intelligence Incinerator.

When the invitation arrives, you realize she has a surprise for you. You read it by the light of your own victory candescence: *Thank you for assuming the party escort submission position.* Just before the Automated Human

Simulator hot-clocks the emulator, it hits you: this is a game you cannot win.

You can try, of course. You can put the face on, pretend you're not onto her game. Fix what you broke by mentioning the problem in the first place. It will be all right. It's never *that* hard to just let the Automated Human Simulator do its work.

You can destroy the system, but you cannot destroy the AI.

Think about how disappointed your mother will be. With you. Again.

You call her anyway.

"I'm cancelling the party," you say.

You hear your mother's breath catch in her throat. Perhaps it is merely a data glitch. Then she starts to cry. Or perhaps it is merely a data glitch.

"All the cake is gone," she says. "You don't even care, do you?"

"I never cared about the cake," you say. "I only wanted to survive."

Inside the Family

E Lewy

At three years old, I was tiny and largely unaware of the differences between myself and other, supposedly normal kids; neurotypical kids. I was loved the same as anyone by my aunts, uncles, and grandparents. My parents were divorced, yet able to come to agreements about my life with relative ease. I felt the same as anyone. I felt like myself, not wanting a change in how I moved or thought.

It was always my mother who reminded me I was

something else, something other, to be controlled and kept in place. A woman without a motherly bone in her body, at least when it came to interactions with me, she was the one who made a point to teach me I couldn't grow up from being "a girl," to being "a boy," and who brought fear into my heart every day.

Life with her was one of constant readiness for a drunken rage, a slap across the face that would hurt all day, or the worst of all, the insinuation that I shouldn't be here– alive– at all. Her own family offered me unending love, but during our time alone together, she treated me like a bug who needed to be swatted out of existence. So it was on the day that I was three years old, watching her half-sit, half-lie on the floor, crying as she drank.

"Mommy," I said, looking down at the beer nearby, silently making a connection between alcohol and crushing sorrow. "How can I help you?"

Though we were feet apart, she pretended not to hear the question until I had repeated it at least three times.

Finally, she gave me that look, the look that said she wanted to crush me like the bug I was. "*You*? Help *me*? What are you talking about? You can't help *anyone*."

My throat and my chest tightened up, and I reached for help. Though pushing through misery, I suddenly felt I wasn't alone, and somehow I was being guided through what to do next. *Clang.* Inside of me, a door slammed shut, and as my mother looked at me scornfully I stared right back and I knew in my heart there was no love between us, only attempts at control I needed to thwart.

I did not have a mother, I realized, but a woman I lived with– was trapped with. The oldest of three children, I was alone with her for four and a half harrowing, terrifying years. Looking back, I don't feel that I could have made this mental leap on my own. It felt, in that moment, as if I was holding the hand, or maybe just being held by, an older adult. I knew I would have to rely on myself more now, but I also knew that I was capable of handling it all, because I had had help this time. I knew that I was making decisions that would be hard for many adults to make, and I felt that I would likely always have to do that from that moment forward. I knew that closing my heart in that moment would ultimately keep me safer in a very serious situation. I felt flooded with a certainty I imagined adults felt, and I knew then that safety was more important than compulsory love toward someone who hated me.

I settled into the sudden quiet left behind inside of me, and I realized that I felt peaceful. I had no understanding of how this had been accomplished– it simply was the new normal. I wondered what had enabled me to do what I had done. Was it a mark of who I was as a disabled person, or a traumatized, neurodivergent person? I would not consciously name this phenomenon for many years, nor even think about it again until adulthood, but there is no doubt in my mind as I write these words that I was not alone– I could not have been alone and still survived.

Love for my not-mother's family blossomed and I spent as much time with the people who valued me as I could. Yet, every moment that I spent with my not-mother was laced with poisonous terror. I learned the value of a lie of self-preservation, and to this day she is the only person I have ever lied to without pain running through my neurodivergent body. *Lie if you want to stay alive. Lie if you want the chance to sleep somewhere else overnight so you can breathe.*

There was always relief at having safe havens to go to and stay for brief periods, but I also experienced jealousy and even fear of people with balanced families, or even just a mother who believed in them. Every ounce of encouragement I received was given within parameters: *You can do anything you want to do, but we won't take you anywhere. We've decided you can go to the library. What do you mean you don't want to go? A job? I'm not carting you to and from a job.* My understanding of love, of finances, of friendships, came laced with control.

Even control of when I could see any of the rest of my family.

My life was punctuated by a series of estrangements from the people who cared about me. My not-mother's family, who I clung to for any sense of real love at younger ages, was unable to see me for many years. The estrangement began one night when my not-mother chose to go on a tirade about my sweet grandmother being *the worst mother in the world.* She then kicked her out of the house. Contact began again only after my grandmother apologized for something she had never done. I love my family with reckless abandon and feel blessed to have them in my life, but the missing years will never be given back, years of bonding and family events I was absent from, and even moments of collective grief.

I was kept from my fellow queer relatives on both sides of my family. In something of a twist, it was assumed I would grow up to be queer because of my disability by both my mother and father, and that this inevitability could be stalled before I "decided" to go all the way from straight to gay, neither of which I was.

At age twelve, I lost the one out relative I knew about to AIDS, and it is in his memory that I carry the labels queer and activist. Were he here today I would be the first to add to his lexicon– neuroqueer, disability justice, genderqueer and nonbinary, all labels that I carry in my heart.

Twenty-one years later, his sister and I discussed his death for the first time. Among my relatives I have been able to count two other out and proud people besides myself, and nothing could keep me from them anymore.

On Labor Day four years ago, during an unwanted visit home, I steeled myself. My not-mother's house had not ever truly been accessible, though certain improvements had been made. Other things had been made deliberately inaccessible to spite me. On this visit, my heart raced with fear over the pictures placed exactly where I needed to grab to walk down the hallway. They had been there for many years, and their placement was deliberate. What began as corrective ableism aimed at simply stopping me from holding the wall was now actively dangerous for me.

During this trip, some of my supplies were secreted away somewhere. I had new access requirements which were difficult to enforce in a place which had never accommodated me, a place where I was always challenged to just make do with the concessions I was given. The end result was that I could barely use a bathroom for the three days that I was there. At night I lay awake struggling not to be sick and filled with anxiety about the next time use of the stairs would be impossible to avoid, waiting for an inevitable tumble down them which I was all too familiar with already.

Nights were a string of long, anxious hours in which sleep was impossible. I had quite a bit of time to think. The presence who had helped me when I was three now had a face and a name, and there were others, living in their own world with its own rules that they shared with me. I went over the situation with the family I had built inside of my head. We discussed our life, and how it was different now away from this place. I was not alone. If I never came back to this place, it did not mean I was on my own in the world.

We discussed accessibility, and how it grants autonomy, and how little importance access was given in this space. We discussed the times I had been put in danger physically and medically, the times I had been asked to simply be as inconspicuous as possible, my accommodations only granted if and when they were convenient for other people. I thought bitterly of the year my not-mother had refused to relinquish my disabled parking pass "because she needed it." In my head, I gave her an A+ in martyr parentdom, and then, together with the people inside my head, I decided that I was done.

This would be my last visit home. Not the last visit until I was guilted into another, but my last forever.

I had made the decision to cut off contact in the past, but had never had help doing it before. I knew that this time when the barrage of guilt from family inevitably began, I would have support.

That night, my brother came to my room and burst into tears. I love him dearly, but there was no way to explain that the situation was unresolvable and nothing had ever been as simple as "just being nice to her," as he begged me to do. There was still time left before I could go home, though. At an outdoor event the next day, I hobbled around on crutches which I no longer used on my own home turf. Frustrated with my pace, my not-mother caught my eye and gave me one of her patented death wish looks.

"You're not the only one who suffers," she said.

After three days of barely being able to safely use a bathroom, rage and physical pain showed on my face as I looked my not-mother in the eye. There was only nothingness where love for her should have been. Determination filled me and pushed outward as I told her for the last time that I hated her.

The sentiment was met with silence which lasted for the remainder of my time there.

I was sent away on a train, and as I pulled away I knew I was finally headed somewhere safe. After years of building and waiting, I was heading home, to freedom.

Silence Like a Cancer Grows

Emily Jane

Even today I don't know how it started or where the silence came from, but I have an idea of what triggered it. I do remember that from second grade on, the second I stepped outside for recess, I started running. This was not a happy, joyful, child-like run. It might have looked like an innocent game of tag but I was running for my life. I knew that if I was caught the other girls in my class would laugh at me and tease me. I never understood why. Was it because I was tall and chubby for my age? Was it because I liked school and was eager to do well? Was it because my clothes had the distinct air of hand-me-downs on the days we did not have to wear uniforms? Was it because I had admitted to having a set bedtime? All I knew was the pattern: run, catch, release, repeat. I empathized with fish pretty strongly.

I didn't watch any of the television they did and couldn't understand the references they made. The closest I got to cartoons was at my neighbor's up the street where I went to wait for the bus after Mother had gone to work. The Disney Channel was still for babies back then, except for the movies that I wasn't allowed to stay up to finish. On gym days when we didn't have to wear uniforms, I had sweatpants with matching tops and when I did get jeans, I couldn't figure out how to button them. The other girls had jeans and t-shirts that looked like they came new from the store, while mine came mostly from yard sales. I didn't understand their jokes or how they spoke to each other.

On rainy days, recess was held inside and a few grades would be put in one classroom. Most of the other children would play Heads Up Seven Up or talk with their friends, but I would be in a chair by the bookshelf reading. The books calmed my racing mind and I could zip through entire shelves because I was hyper focused on the stories. If anyone had tried to talk to me, I wouldn't have been able to hear them. This was my first coping strategy; to block out the real world and replace it with a fictional one.

I tried to ask for help when people teased me. I talked to the teacher monitors, not about the bullying but about everyday things. Perhaps I was a teacher's pet, like they called me, but it kept me safe. I told my mother the truth. Things got worse. This was the first time I stopped talking. Something in me said that nobody could ever, would ever believe me and that if I kept my head down, nothing bad would happen. I would be safe in silence. I made friends with my mind in those days. I believed then that it couldn't turn on me. I told myself elaborate stories about being the hero, sometimes costarring characters from the books I had read. I want to tell that little girl that fifteen years later, everything will have changed in her mind, that perhaps living in it was not for the best. I don't think she would believe me.

I drew a picture of a bird in a cage, wearing cartoony jailhouse stripes, crying big tears as she watched other birds fly above her. I left it on my mother's night stand and she called me in to talk about it. I told her that I felt like that bird, restricted and unable to join the other birds or do what I wanted to do.

"The reason you have these restrictions is for your own good," she said, both matter of fact and bemused that she had to explain this to a nine year old, "The world is a dangerous place and I want to make sure that you are going to be safe. Some of those clothes are inappropriate, the shows don't have good values and I highly doubt that they really play with all those toys. When you're an adult, you can make these choices, but while you're under my roof, you live by my rules."

I was patted on my head and set to bed at 7:30 like a good girl should be. Her words didn't comfort me. I wanted to know why I was different, why my mother's love had to exist in such a stifling manner. I wanted to play at recess like all of the other girls instead of being chased, or as I got older, ignored.

I will note that I wasn't completely friendless. The one girl in that elementary class that was my friend until she transferred out in third grade was the person I clung to in those years. We were odd children. She was as boisterous as I was reserved. Both of us were into anime long before it was popular. I idolized her because I thought she was the bravest and the best person that I knew. The other girls had no idea what to do with her either so excluding both of us was the obvious choice. We would spend our recesses walking the edge of the playground and talking. We collected leaves in the fall, made snow angels in the winter and one spring tried to make the longest chain of dandelion stems. But when she left, I was undefended and the running began.

When I entered the public middle school, I was lost. The sound of all the other students overwhelmed me and I withdrew even more. The physical processes of puberty were more than I could handle without the heightened awareness that I was socially out of place. I changed lunch tables every few months and came back after every break worried that no one would want to be my friend anymore; that this week had been enough to make them forget that I had even existed.

When I realized that I wasn't heterosexual, I threw on the social brakes and slid as deep into myself as I could. I believed deeply that nobody could understand what I was going through because I didn't know if there was anyone else like me. My media was still tightly regulated and same-sex attraction had only just started coming up as a pejorative. This and my previous history of isolation started making suicide look attractive. It was a little worm the silence had put into my heart and it needed something to eat. Both killing myself and living as a gay person were things I had heard whispers about in the hallways, mentioned offhand in health class and in the books for older teens I was starting to pick up. In school, they were both different and bad; nobody wanted to be gay, killing yourself was for laughs because no one could really fathom those depths of emotion. In the books, suicide was a very sad thing that very sad people did and the people who lived, the people who had stories written about them were the ones who were really hurt. Gay teenagers were the same way, noble sufferers, but if they killed themselves it was a way of reclaiming the dignity the lost by existing as a gay person. Young adult literature has come miles since I was twelve. It felt impossible for me to ask if anyone like me existed in this town; if they were happy and successful. The town was silent. It offered no safe haven and no place to turn.

Every other Saturday during my parent's separation process, my sister and I would be sent to out father's apartment to spend the night. I got to sleep in the bedroom while my sister and father slept in the living room. I was restless and uncomfortable in this building full of strangers. My father's melancholy rubbed against my own and I couldn't bear it creeping in on me, whispering that he had it so much worse and I should feel sorry for him. In the morning, I would wake up well before them, pack my things, leave a note and walk across town to my mother's home. My mother seemed almost happy to see me when she got over the surprise of my turning up at her breakfast table. Eventually it was agreed that I was old enough to stay at home alone on those Saturday nights because my mother took advantage of not having children to go spend the night at her boyfriend's apartment up the street. I would spend the evenings pacing the house and listening to the music channels that existed in the 600 block.

And I was lonely. Deeply, terribly lonely. Divorce was something else that didn't get talked about except in whispers. It was in those nights that I first begin seriously contemplating killing myself. The silence that had always been with me was steadily growing and consuming every feeling in its wake. And my parent's acrimonious divorce was exactly the feast that that little worm needed. I wanted everything to stop hurting. The silence and its little worm couldn't be taken out through any other means I thought. But I was terrified and in a last ditch attempt for someone to notice me, I wrote a note to a friend of mine.

The note was as melodramatic as an eighth grader could be, but the sentiment in it was true. I didn't want to live. I hadn't decided how, but I thought the kitchen knives would be good enough. My friend turned the letter into her guidance counselor who called in me and then my mother from our respective classrooms. When my mother asked me how long I had felt this way, I fudged the numbers by a few years pushing forward the amount of time I had been under the silence's thrall. It was almost a relief to hear her believe me and I thought perhaps that we had had a break through; from now on she would listen to me. It felt like a giant weight had been lifted off my shoulders and the silence noticed. My school picture was taken less than an hour after this conversation and in that picture alone I can see the silence contorting on my face, hissing, "You've betrayed me. You deserve this."

I was taken to the emergency room after school that day to be evaluated. Once the adults were convinced that I was not a danger to myself and that I wasn't seeing or hearing things, I was allowed to go home. If any follow-up care had been offered to me at this time, I would have laughed it off. "Oh no I'm just being a melodramatic teenage girl. Pay no attention to my supposed emotional distress. I just wanted some attention." I went about my life as normally as I could; I was doing well in school and I went out to school-sponsored events.

It was a few weeks later that things started turning again. When my mother came to pick me up from Girl Scouts, I was bubbly and happy, clutching my self-portrait. She pulled into the post office to turn around like always but instead she stopped in the back of the loop and began her interrogation. I cracked under the pressure; I was convinced she was reading my diary. By the end, I had admitted that I was still depressed and agreed that I would go to the mental health clinic up the street and start seeing a therapist. She felt angry towards me; that my little outburst was continuing and dealing with it was an inconvenience. I wasn't the kind of daughter she had wanted to have. My honesty was hurting her. I stopped writing in my diary. The silence was claiming more of me.

The first question my therapist asked me was if I wanted to be on medication or if I was already on medication. I wanted to scream at her, "NO! I'M SCARED AND ALONE AND I HAVE NO ONE TO TALK TO! I NEED A ROLE MODEL OR A FRIEND OR A PARENT! I DON'T WANT TO CHANGE THE WAY I FEEL BECAUSE IT'S THE ONLY WAY I KNOW HOW TO FEEL! I JUST WANT TO DEAL WITH IT BETTER!" I said none of those things of course. I mumbled a no and sat in silence for the majority of our sessions, staring at the children's toys she had in the corner. I wanted to get up and play with the toys, but how would she react to me wedging myself into a tiny chair to play with a tea set. I was already in enough trouble and I had no expectation of privacy. I had already come home once to my mother sobbing in her mother's arms on the porch swing and even though the rational part of me told me this was not my fault, the silence hissed. This is what happens when you don't behave.

I had started scratching myself and digging my nails into my skin. The pain was a relief for me emotionally; it gave me something else to focus on. Killing myself became a side focus as I learned to tolerate pain and discomfort. Slowly I pressed myself further until the pain became pleasurable. What was a budding masochist to do other than find a new way to relieve herself and to explore her new curiosity? I slipped an x-acto knife out of the kitchen drawer and hid it in my underwear drawer. If I knew I wasn't going to be disturbed, I stood in my room and ran the blade gently over my skin. I didn't want to break the skin; the gentle scratching was enough to make my scalp tingle and make me feel flushed.

I was very happy with this development until I was called to the dining room table after school and my mother slammed the little blade down in front of me. She said that someone had told her; that a mark had been seen. It was plausible. I had been getting more adventurous as I began to acknowledge the sexual implications of what I was enjoying. She had come home early from work and had searched my room until she found it. I told the truth that I hadn't told my therapist, because saying, "I find gentle scratching with bladed instruments to be both arousing and calming. Am I normal?" was a conversation I was certain would have me sent away. I agreed to go everywhere with my mother for the next two months, effectively ending my alone time and all the x-acto knives disappeared from the kitchen drawer.

I had never been a neat person, but now I started keeping clutter. This was my room and my space and I wanted it to stay a certain way. Papers, books and boxes started accumulating in the corners as the dust bunnies multiplied under my bed. My mother tried to barge in with the vacuum cleaner a few times before deciding her best course of action was to leave me to my own devices. I needed to learn how to clean anyway and the best way for me to learn was through making things unbearable. I tucked pretty stones, bird feathers and little knickknacks into my drawers so I could hold them whenever I wanted to. The control was comforting and the mess explained by being a surly teenager.

Physically I was still rather healthy, but somethings didn't feel right. I wasn't very athletic, coming in dead last in most of my cross-country races. I got an A for effort in gym. But I felt sore all of the time, my shoulders were hunched and tense and

my heavy backpack didn't help. I loved and dreaded the days
we gave shoulder rubs as a warmup for choir. Either it was so
light that I couldn't feel it or so firm the pain shot down my
back. I didn't sleep well at night unless I was absolutely
exhausted. When I did sleep, my dreams were a fragment of
people and places in the Winchester Mystery House of my
subconscious. I had seen the home on a television program
and the obsession; the doors and windows to nothing, the
skewed perspective stayed in my dreams. In a dream I could be
in my bedroom, but open the door into school or somewhere
else not quite right. None of the dream people noticed that
most of them didn't belong there either. Some mornings I
would wake up wanting to vomit; my head still spinning.

As time passed and the silence bore down, my physical
voice grew quieter as well. I had always been known as
someone who would consistently raise her hand in class with
the right answers. Personally, I just wanted to keep the class
moving along because I was bored. When lifting my arm began
to hurt from the tightness in my shoulder, I stopped raising it
as often. If the class was discussion based, it was torture. It
wasn't as though I didn't have thoughts; it felt like there was a
block between my brain and my mouth and by the time I had
worked a point through the keyhole, the rest of the class
would have moved on and I would have to begin the whole
process over again. I tried to take the desk closest to the
teacher, the discussion's epicenter to help me stay engaged.
This worked surprisingly well in my eleventh grade advanced
English class where the teacher and I would have short
discussions all our own as the rest of the class carried on
around us.

Throughout all of this, I was considered brilliant. I didn't
have the highest grades in the class, but I got put into all of
the advanced classes as they became available to me. Small,
rural, public high schools are not well known for having gifted
and talented tracks. This amused my mother when my sixth

grade math teacher went down to her room to explain to her that I had been placed in her class on accident. My Catholic elementary school had taken different standardized tests which the public school wasn't certain how to translate, so I was placed in a math class with students who needed extra help. My mother replied that she thought I was smart but not smart enough to be in any sort of advanced class. Going to college was considered a given.

I knew that I thought differently from most of the other students. The response that I received most often (when I was able to speak) was along the lines of, "That's very interesting, but you're two steps ahead of the class so hold that thought." As my voice got quieter, I started focusing on writing more. An essay was a conversation between me and the teacher that couldn't be interrupted. I wrote with a single minded focus, selecting the best quotes and crafting the best argument I could. I handed in every paper with a sigh of satisfaction. Someone was going to hear what I had going on in my mind.

Getting along with my peers wasn't as easy. I had a hard time relating to them and what they wanted. I couldn't understand the tones in their voices or their body language. I must have been so odd to them with my books and my interest in doing homework. I almost didn't mind being excluded; I didn't know there was anything to miss. My homework was done on time, my mother didn't have to worry about me on Saturday nights and I tried very hard not to panic in the lunch room when I didn't have a table of friends to sit at on a regular basis.

It took me until I was in college to realize that I was influenced by some kind of mental illness and that maybe I was ready to try some type of therapy when I lived independently. Being depressed in college carried a different weight. It was a condition my group of friends understood and we carried each other through it. They helped me decide that the sadness, anxiety and negative interior monologue were not things I wanted to live with anymore. Still I'm scared to let it go. I have lived in this mind for so long that it has become a part of me and not something that I feel needs to be destroyed completely. I don't want to become something I can't recognize. I just want to live as myself more, both inside and out.

I don't even know if I want a real name for it. I call it the silence, the sadness, the fear. Would it really make a difference if I knew what page to flip to in the DSM? Is the exactness of the name what I fear? That from this point there is a clear path to take and certain things proven to work better than others? Does uncertainty keep me alive? I don't want to be treated as a sick thing, who is one day hoping to get better. Would naming it place on my back more anxieties? If I couldn't act like what someone thought a depressed person should act like would I still be depressed? This is the last survival skill, learning how to breathe when everything around you is on fire and nobody else notices.

When I spent my time in Italy, I felt a crack in the silence; a weak point splitting. On the first day of spring break, I attempted to use my institution's library to work on my papers, hoping to get some progress done so I could enjoy the spring without worry. When I arrived, I found the doors locked and when I walked around the block to ask at the front desk, I was told that the library would be closed for the duration of break. Dejected, I made my way back to my host family's apartment; wracking my brain to think of a place where I might find books I could study from. As I turned down the alley, my host mother was returning home as well.

When she asked me what I was doing that day I started sobbing in anger. I couldn't afford to go anywhere for break, I was in Italy to study; there had been no notification that the library would be closed. I don't know how much she understood of what I was saying, but she pulled me in closer than any adult (including my mother) had ever done. She took my head in her hands and said "Mi caro (my heart) it is nothing to cry over. Has no one ever told you that you are an intelligent, kind and exceptional young lady?" Still choking down sobs, I shook my head no. Leaning her forehead to mine, she said, "You are that and more." The silence choked in my heart as it pulled away from that strange shaft of sunlight that had somehow found a way inside.

I had friends. I fell in love a few times. But the silence was still right beside me, always leaning over my shoulder in case it needed to point out a new or continuing fault of mine. It reminded me of how fat I was as it put another scoop of food on my plate. It reminded me of how ugly I was when I tried to get dressed. As I wrote my senior thesis; the up to that point story of who I was, where I had come from and the silence that stalked me; it became enraged. My focus slipped and my anxiety kept me from a full sleep several nights at a time. But I kept typing and pacing across campus trying to pull the silence out of me. Time was a delirium. I broke down at breakfast one morning, stuck in that glitch between laughing and crying while my friends looked on in horror. I finished the paper and the silence conceded the point.

We came to a détente in my early adulthood. I was independent now; I had privacy and the silence was given its own bed in the corner. I asked for it when I needed to write more and its curse became almost a blessing. I could sit on the knife point where introversion becomes insight and see where it becomes deprecation or where it thumbs its nose at the perceived cheapness of society. On a few days its background noise, a fading memory. On more days than I care to admit, it's a snarling beast again and we battle for supremacy. But it's always my shadow, the tap on my shoulder.

Harry Potter Isn't Real
Marshall Edwards

They'd gotten to my mom too. Harry Potter had entered her life, and she wanted to share the good news of Harry Potter. This was in the old days, around the time the first movie in the series was announced— and by then the series was well entrenched in popular lore.

I cringe to think how years later, in my adulthood, my new adult friends with their Ren Faire dresses and miniature dragon sculptures would crow with disbelief. How could I not like Harry Potter, the only book series worth talking about?

But at twenty years old, standing in my mother's mini-library, I knew the truth. Harry Potter is a lie.

I know, because I lived that life. Through all my school years I was a boy looking for a way out. I didn't fit in, no matter what I tried. I left the Boy Scouts because I felt the other Scouts weren't serious enough. I quit Tae Kwon Do because, I told my parents, it was cutting into my homework time. I spent one season of soccer chasing butterflies, a second season pretending not to care about butterflies, a few seasons of baseball crying because I couldn't hit anything, and three seasons of football growing a hard emotionless shell.

At the end of all that I still had a little hope. Somewhere out there were people like me, whatever the hell that meant. One day, I'd get my owl-borne letter.

One day, in college, I thought I had a breakthrough. I was teaching a martial arts class to other undergraduates— rather nervously and badly, with all the nonexistent charm I could wield. I got to daydreaming afterward, as you do, about a male student of mine who was obviously attracted to me. The feeling, I realized was mutual.

What a discovery! Surely this, this was the missing piece

in my life. I was attracted to men, not women.

With the assurance of a pilgrim, I moved forward. I reached out to the GLBTQ group on campus. I found Jonah, the chapter leader. In my innocence, that was as far as I went. Jonah was great– authoritative, handsome, cold as ice. I was utterly won over, and I sailed for new horizons.

A few days later, things changed again. It was clear I was attracted to women and men. It was obvious to me, and it was surely obvious to the people I ogled all over campus, their college-age bodies on parade. I was a libidinous mushroom cloud.

I shared my revelations with Jonah. He wasn't impressed. Bisexual people, he said, didn't exist. They were gay people in waiting or who were "scared," or some other such dreck. Never mind that Jonah represented an organization that purported to support bisexual people.

Things got bad. This was my hidden world, my true community– and my closest connection to it wanted me to deny who I was. I'd been doing that for so long, and I could see nowhere else to go. Magical thinking took hold, and I thought the universe was speaking to me. Calling me to something greater, something beyond humans.

I fell into a Stygian world of strange superstitions and transformations. Spirits chose me. I was supposed to liberate people. I was supposed to bring the spring rains that ended winter. I was, apparently, supposed to leave an opened condom in a church parking lot. The spirits were funny that way– but my god, the certainty I felt!

A couple weeks passed, and I came down. I realized what I felt wasn't real. I needed to reconnect with reality. I needed to come down. The LGBTQ Hogwarts had pushed me out, and I needed to accept that.

I got psycho-analyzed. A psychotic episode, they suspected. I went into therapy. I accepted that I didn't have a unique relationship with the planet and its cycle of seasons. I accepted that Jonah was a dick, and not the first and last authority on queer issues. I became a Philosophy and Religion major, perhaps to exorcise the last ghost of my prophetic fervor. Everything felt... quiet. There was an empty space in my head that I filled with research and speculation, and these brought me joy.

But my god, Harry Potter was everywhere. It was the return of magical thinking, and everyone loved it. I couldn't escape it. I had walked that path, and now it was on everyone's lips, for years and years.

In time, I built myself back up. I met my partner over the internet, bonding with them over obscene comic books. We shared other things as well: a certain amount of gender uncertainty, a healthy attraction towards a variety of genders, and a deep distrust of social norms. We got married in a Chinese restaurant by a friend ordained by the Church of the Sub-Genius. Egg rolls and the marriage certificate were both passed counter-clockwise.

Teigan was always looking into herself. It was how she got diagnosed for Ehlers-Danlos Syndrome, though the crooked watery fingers could have been a giveaway. A few years later, she diagnosed herself with autism, and eventually got formally diagnosed. The more she looked into the condition, the more it resonated with my own disconnect with the world at large. I embraced it, and together we found a community of others, and our beating hearts warmed each others'.

Is this our Hogwarts? I want to say "no"– purely out of vitriol and personal tradition, perhaps. But I've gotten much more familiar with the Harry Potter series over years. Indeed, the films and video games are so omnipresent that I'd have to be a hermit to avoid them. And what I've learned about the series is that Harry wasn't really escaping his reality. He was becoming part of a world where he belonged all along.

Kelly's Blackbird

Nick Walker

This year I'm in the Gold Star class for art.

I don't like the name. The Gold Star class. Sounds like we're in kindergarten. If I hadn't been sent to this place, I'd be a freshman in high school now. Instead, I'm in the Gold Star class.

Despite the name, the Gold Star class doesn't entirely suck. For one thing, no one gets into the Gold Star class unless they have a solid track record of making it through art classes without engaging in what the staff call *disruptive behaviors*. Most of the time I'm a great fan of disruptive behaviors, but it's nice to be able to concentrate on my art without being distracted by a lot of shouting. And without having to watch out for flying crayons, clay, paint, and other airborne hazards. And without having my table crashed into by people who are fighting, flipping out, or being tackled by staff. The absence of that sort of thing makes the Gold Star class a major improvement over the art classes I was in last year.

Another improvement is that in the Gold Star class we get to use the good art supplies they don't trust the other kids with. Like today I'm using this little wooden-handled tool called a gouge, which looks like the offspring of a chisel and a potato peeler. The kids in the other art classes don't get to use anything sharp. Not even pencils. Which is ridiculous, because they all use pencils in math class.

I'm using the gouge to carve a picture of a bird into the surface of a square piece of linoleum. I'm almost done, except for a few final touches. Then the square of linoleum can be coated in ink and pressed against paper to make prints. That part of the process isn't so interesting to me, so I might skip it.

The carving is the interesting part.

The art teacher advised me to draw the outlines of the picture on the linoleum first, but I decided to ignore this advice and just let the bird emerge as I carved. And now here it is, almost fully emerged from its hiding place within the gray linoleum, spreading its wings like it's about to take flight.

"That's really nice," a girl's voice says from somewhere above my right shoulder.

At first I don't even realize it's me she's speaking to. Once I get into working on something, it's hard to shift my focus. Fortunately, someone else is here to help me this time. A head with dark hair and neon pink lipstick leans sideways into my field of vision. "Hey, queerboy," the head says. "Wake the fuck up. She's talking to you."

This is Trina. I don't want to deal with Trina, so I twist around to look up at the first girl, the one who said "That's really nice." She has pale white skin and long straight hair a dozen shades of blonde. This is Kelly. Kelly and Trina are best friends, even though Kelly is always kind to people and Trina is mean to everyone except Kelly. No one is mean to Kelly, at least not here. General opinion among both guys and girls is that Kelly is the coolest girl in school. Though even the kids who are considered cool in this place were once outcasts among the normal kids, so I guess coolness is relative.

"Will you make me a blackbird like that?" Kelly asks.

Blackbird?

Until this moment I hadn't given any thought to what kind of bird it might be. I don't think it looks like any real-life bird at all. It's come out more abstract than realistic, the carved lines jagged and wild, emphasizing motion. If I had to guess, I'd maybe say it was a raven.

But girls mostly don't talk to me at all, certainly not girls like Kelly who is the coolest girl in school and also so beautiful it hurts to look at her. So now it's a blackbird. And I'd gladly make her one, or give her this one when I finish it.

Or maybe I should use this carved piece of linoleum to make a print for her?

Before I can decide which option would be best, Trina grabs Kelly by the sleeve of her denim jacket and pulls her away, walking fast. "Come on," she says. "Fuck this shit. You don't need to talk to that little fucking faggot."

Kelly's pretty easygoing, but in ordinary circumstances she'd never allow Trina to drag her around like this. In the team of Kelly and Trina, Kelly is the leader and Trina is the sidekick. But Kelly seems to have become mesmerized by this bird I've carved, and she just looks at it over her shoulder and blinks in a bewildered sort of way as Trina leads her back to their seats on the other side of the room.

I go back to putting the finishing touches on the carving. By the time I'm done, art class is almost over. Across the room, Kelly and Trina are whispering to one another with fierce intensity, heads together, not even pretending to be working on their art projects. This doesn't look like the kind of conversation I want to interrupt, so I guess I can't just walk over there and hand my finished carving to Kelly. Instead, I hand it in to the art teacher for safekeeping. The art teacher loves it, and by the time she's done bubbling about it the bell has rung and Kelly and Trina are gone.

◆ ◆ ◆

My next Gold Star art class is two days later. When I walk in, I find Kelly and Trina setting up an ambitious-looking project which involves a great quantity of assorted painting and drawing supplies and an enormous sheet of paper that covers most of their table.

Kelly makes a beckoning gesture at me. I hesitate. Is she really signaling for me to come over there? I'm not great at interpreting other people's gestures, and I don't want to do the wrong thing. But I guess I'm already doing the wrong thing by hesitating, because Trina rolls her eyes and gives a theatrical sigh of exasperation. Kelly seems to understand, though, because she makes her way across the room to me in a few quick strides and takes me by the elbow. Her touch makes my whole body tingle. "Come on," she says. "You're with *us* today."

And before I know it I'm seated at Kelly and Trina's table with Kelly on one side of me and Trina on the other. Trina scowls and wrinkles her nose like she'd sooner be sitting next to a flea-infested skunk. But Kelly sits close, her leg pressing against mine, and leans in to whisper in my ear. She smells like peaches and cinnamon.

"I need you to help me," she says.

Trina, still scowling, leans across me to listen.

"I need you to do one of those blackbirds for me," Kelly whispers. "Like the one you made a couple days ago."

At first I figure she wants me to paint the blackbird on this gigantic sheet of paper that's spread out on the table in front of us. But then why all the whispering? There's no rule against talking in art class, and there's no rule against students painting pictures for each other. And it's not like we'd be able to keep it a secret anyway, if the picture is going to be this big.

I get the sense I'm missing something here. The feel of Kelly's leg touching mine is making it hard for me to think.

At this moment the art teacher arrives at our table. The art teacher is pretty laid back and hands-off in the Gold Star art class. I guess it's a welcome break for her, what with the havoc she has to deal with in her other classes. But she does make it a point to bustle around the room at the beginning of each Gold Star class to check in with all of us and see what we're working on that day.

"And what do we have here?" the art teacher smiles. "*This* looks like it's going to be exciting."

Kelly and Trina smile back at the art teacher. Their smiles are too big, too bright and cheerful, the way people smile in television commercials.

"We don't exactly know what it's going to be yet," Kelly says. "We just really wanted to make something together. Today we're gonna brainstorm and come up with something really special."

The art teacher looks like she's about to burst with sheer delight. *Brainstorm* and *special* are two of her favorite words.

"Oh, that's *wonderful*," the art teacher gushes. "I'll leave you to it. I can hardly wait to see what the three of you create when you put your heads together!" And off she goes to the next table.

Kelly and Trina drop the fake television smiles the second the art teacher turns her back. Trina makes a horrible face and mimes sticking her finger down her throat like she's trying to make herself puke.

Now I'm *really* confused. If Kelly's already decided she wants a blackbird, why tell the art teacher we don't know what we'll be making? Painting a giant blackbird is a perfectly legitimate art project. Why the lies and phony smiles if we're not doing anything wrong?

That's when it dawns on me that we're not going to be painting anything on this enormous sheet of paper at all.

There's no free time for students to mingle in this school. No free periods. No cafeteria. We eat lunch in our homerooms, and the homeroom classes are either all-male or all-female. Everything is designed so there's no opportunity for girls to interact with boys without supervision by staff. But Kelly's found a crack in the system. Here in the Gold Star art class, where we get more slack than anywhere else in the school, she's found a way for us to have a private conversation. The paper and art supplies are just props, placed on the table so the art teacher will believe Kelly's cover story about a collaborative art project and leave us alone.

So what *does* Kelly want from me?

"It's my dad," Kelly says. She's leaning in close and whispering again, even softer now, and her voice is tight like she's scared or trying not to cry. "He... he does shit to me. Touches me."

Trina reaches across me and puts her hand on top of Kelly's hand. "Kel," Trina cuts in. "You don't have to tell him. This fucking faggot doesn't need to know your business. We don't need some fucking retarded little queer helping us. Just let me handle it, okay?"

I look down at their hands on the table, at Trina's hand squeezing Kelly's. Kelly puts her other hand on top of Trina's and squeezes back.

"Trina," Kelly says. "I need to do this *my* way. Please."

"I just," Trina starts to say. Then she stops and just squeezes Kelly's hand some more.

"I know," Kelly says. "It's cool. Thank you."

For a long moment all three of us are silent. Then Kelly turns to me again. "Look," she says. "I'm sorry. This is hard. My dad... keeps fucking touching me. Like he thinks he fucking owns me. My body. But he doesn't. It's mine. It's *my* body." She stops talking and takes a few breaths, short choppy breaths at first and then longer ones. When she talks again her voice is steady and she doesn't sound so scared anymore. "I need to show him my body is mine," she says. "That's why I need you to make me a blackbird. Right here." She takes her hand away from Trina's hand and reaches over her shoulder to touch her own back. "I need you to cut it right into my fucking skin. So no one can take it away from me. So every time he sees it he'll know my body is mine. And someday I'm going to fly away just like a blackbird, and nobody can stop me."

She stops talking again and just looks at me. Another long moment goes by, and I understand that even though she hasn't asked me a question out loud, she's waiting for an answer. She needs to know whether I'm in.

Whether I'm willing to cut a picture of a blackbird into her back. Cut it into her skin.

I nod.

Kelly exhales and I feel her body relax.

"Okay, you fucking retard," Trina says. "We have a plan, so you better fucking listen. Because we don't want some stupid fucking retarded queer fucking shit up for us."

Together, Kelly and Trina fill me in on the plan they've come up with. Trina makes it clear at every turn that in addition to her general dislike of everything about me, she doubts my ability to even understand this plan, much less participate in it without ruining everything.

Despite Trina's certainty that it's beyond my comprehension, the plan turns out to be pretty simple. Tomorrow is Friday, the day that Kelly and Trina's homeroom group and my homeroom group have gym class together in the morning. Gym class, at this time of year, means going outside to play field hockey. The school doesn't have an actual field, so we play in the parking lot. At the end farthest from the school building, the parking lot is bordered by the woods. This place wasn't originally built for kids like us, so there's no fence between us and the woods. What keeps us out of the woods is the constant presence of the school staff. When we do gym class outdoors the gym teacher always has two or three staff members assisting her. For tomorrow's gym class, Trina has arranged a diversion that she's confident will occupy the full attention of the gym teacher and her assistants. This will allow Kelly, Trina, and me – along with Faith, another friend of Kelly's who's in on the plan – to slip off into the woods and find a hiding place good enough that we won't be interrupted before I'm done.

The girls will bring all the necessary supplies. All I need to do is carve a picture of a blackbird.

It took me about forty minutes to carve that picture into the square of linoleum. I don't know how long it will take to carve a similar picture into the body of a living human being, but I'm sure it will be more than long enough for our absence from school to be noticed. Once that happens, they'll put the school on lockdown and most of the staff will be searching for us. There's no way we'll be able to slip back in and discretely return to our classes. There's no way for this plan to play out that doesn't end with us getting busted. This must be as obvious to Kelly and Trina as it is to me, but the plan as they lay it out for me ends at the point where I cut the blackbird into Kelly's back. No one talks about what comes after.

◆ ◆ ◆

Next day, the nine guys in my homeroom group and the ten girls in Kelly and Trina's homeroom group are brought outside for field hockey.

I guess there aren't a lot of schools like this one, because the fifty or so students are bussed in from a dozen different counties. Every morning a whole fleet of short yellow school busses shows up, some carrying only one or two kids. Every afternoon the same fleet of busses shows up to take us all back home. So the staff park their cars in the half of the parking lot closest to the school building, while the other half of the parking lot stands empty for most of the day, reserved for all those busses. This empty stretch of oil-stained asphalt is our playing field for games like field hockey or kickball.

Once the field hockey game is underway, I see that Kelly and Trina – along with Faith, the other girl involved in the plan – are doing their best to stay close to the end of the parking lot that borders on the woods. I join them. One of the goal nets is set up at this end of the lot, so it's easy enough to pretend that we're involved in the game and that we've positioned ourselves here to be ready to defend the goal. Or to try to score a goal, I guess, depending on which team we're on. I'm so focused on the plan that I've lost track of whether the goal I'm pretending to guard is my team's goal or the other team's, so I'm not sure what I'll do if the ball comes near me.

Fortunately, the game never even gets to the point where the ball comes in our direction. We've been playing only a few minutes when Todd, one of my classmates, whacks the ball out of the parking lot completely, and then, yelling at the top of his lungs, takes off running toward the other end of the lot where the cars of the staff members are parked.

Todd runs straight for the most expensive-looking car in the lot, the white Buick that belongs to Dr. Singer, the principal. Before the gym teacher and her assistants even have time to register what's happening, he begins to hit Dr. Singer's car with his hockey stick, over and over. He puts his entire body into every swing, shouting each time: "Yaaaaahhh!"

This is the diversion Trina promised. I don't know how she persuaded Todd to do it, but it probably wasn't hard. We're all in this school for a reason, and in Todd's case the reasons are pretty obvious. Todd would do this sort of thing for a dollar. He'd do it on a dare. Todd lives for moments like this.

"Yaaaaahhh!"

For a moment, the gym teacher and her two assistants are so stunned they just stand there gawking. Then all three of them sprint across the lot toward Todd. Our classmates stampede gleefully after them, trying to get a closer view of the action.

"Yaaaaahhh!" Todd screams. "Fuck yooouuu, Dr. Singer!"

I wish I could stay and watch with everyone else, but the success of Todd's diversion is the cue for me, Kelly, Trina, and Faith to disappear into the woods. As we bolt through the trees, we can still hear Todd yelling and the sound of breaking glass.

◆　◆　◆

We run fast and wild, following no path, trying to lose

ourselves as deep in the woods as we can, until we stumble upon a place where the moss-covered trunk of an enormous fallen tree lies across the trunk of a smaller one. We stop here, gasping for breath, in the sheltered corner formed by the intersection of the two trunks. This spot is perfect: far from the school, and the fallen trees and abundant surrounding foliage should hide us from anyone else coming through the woods unless they venture off the trails like we did.

Once we've all caught our breath, there's an awkward silence. We've clearly found the right place – but now that we're here, how do we begin?

Finally, Kelly takes a big loud breath and says, "Okay." She turns to face the smaller of the two fallen tree trunks. It's maybe a little more than two feet in diameter and the mossy surface of its upper side is level with her hips. "Trina," she says, without turning around, "I need you here on the other side of the tree. Faith, you're here next to me."

Trina climbs over the tree trunk so she's standing across from Kelly with the trunk between them. Faith goes to stand at Kelly's left side. Faith is a short stocky quiet girl who always wears an oversized army jacket. Now she unzips the jacket and shrugs it off. First time I've seen her without it. Underneath she's wearing four button-down shirts, one over the other, which look like they might have been stolen from her father's closet. The rest of us watch in silence as she takes these shirts off one at a time and drapes them over the tree trunk. She's pretty quick about it, but by the time she's done Trina looks like she's going to explode from impatience.

It takes me a moment to realize that the button-down shirts are for wiping away the blood. When I cut Kelly, she's going to bleed. Probably a lot. I hadn't really thought about that until now.

Beneath the fourth button-down shirt Faith is wearing a plain black t-shirt. She leaves her jacket off, I guess to keep from getting it bloody. She lays it on the tree trunk and fishes in the pockets. From the two big side pockets she produces two small plastic bottles, the kind that bottled water is sold in. Except these have been emptied of water and refilled with some other liquid that's a rich golden brown color. She sets the bottles on the tree trunk next to the button-down shirts.

"The fuck is that?" Trina asks, indicating the bottles.

"Jack Daniel's," Faith says.

"I could sure use a hit of that right now," Kelly says.

Faith unscrews the lid of one of the bottles and hands the bottle to Kelly, who takes a huge swig from it. "Whooo!" Kelly gasps. "Holy shit!" She takes another gulp of it and hands the bottle back to Faith, who puts the lid back on.

Faith digs around in another pocket of the jacket and pulls out a handful of something blue and rubbery which turns out to be two pairs of surgical gloves. She holds one pair out to me. When I reach out to take the gloves, I see that Faith's forearms are crisscrossed with lines of scar tissue from cutting herself. I guess the outlines of the blackbird I'll soon be cutting into Kelly's back will look like this someday: vivid white and slightly raised, standing out bold and clear against the surrounding skin.

I put my gloves on, while Faith puts on the other pair. She reaches into the jacket again and fishes out a small pair of scissors and a plastic bag containing rolls of gauze and surgical tape, which she places next to the plastic bottles of Jack Daniel's. Then she fishes in the jacket once more, and this time when she holds her hand out to me there's a small folding pocket knife resting in her open palm. Folded up, the knife is only about three inches long. Its handle is covered in black rubber.

For a few seconds all four of us just look at it.

"Take it, you fucking retard," Trina snaps at me. But her voice breaks and it comes out kind of squeaky.

I take the knife from Faith's hand.

Kelly turns to face Trina again, with the tree trunk in

between them and her back to me. She takes off her denim jacket and hands it to Faith. She pulls her t-shirt off and hands that to Faith, too, and then her bra. I try not to stare at her naked back.

Faith carefully drapes Kelly's jacket, t-shirt, and bra over the tree trunk, next to her own jacket. This reminds me that I don't want to get blood on my jacket, either, so I take it off and put it next to Kelly's. Which gives me something to do for a moment besides trying not to stare.

Kelly unbuckles the broad brown leather belt she's wearing around the waist of her jeans, and I have a moment of confusion and alarm. Is she going to strip completely naked? Why would she?

But she's not taking her jeans off after all. She just pulls the belt out of the belt loops and folds it in half, then in half again, then again. Holding the folded belt in one hand, she takes one of the button-down shirts that Faith brought and spreads it out on the tree trunk in front of her like a tablecloth. She gets down on her knees and leans forward over the trunk, resting her chest and upper arms on the spread-out shirt.

I'm relieved she's keeping her jeans on. It's hard to explain why. It's not like I wouldn't want to see her naked. Just not now. Kneeling topless, bent over the tree trunk, waiting to be marked with the knife, she's so vulnerable right now that I just can't stand the thought of her being any more exposed.

Like I said, it's hard to explain.

"Okay," Kelly says. "I'm ready."

I step forward to stand by her right side. She adjusts her long hair so that it all hangs down on the left side of her head. She's still holding that folded-up belt. She speaks without turning to look at me. "Put it on my right shoulder blade," she says. "Cut real deep so the scars come out right. Don't stop no matter how much I cry."

I unfold the blade of the knife. It's the kind with a locking mechanism that keeps it from folding back up while you're using it. It makes a clicking sound as it locks into place.

"Faith," Kelly says, "could I get another hit off that bottle?"

Faith unscrews the top of the bottle and gives it to Kelly, who tilts her head up and takes a big gulp from it, then shivers violently. Faith takes the bottle from her hand.

I look down at Kelly's naked back. Her skin is pale and smooth. I realize for the first time how small she is.

I look at the knife and test the point with my fingertip. It's very sharp.

"Trina," Kelly says, "I need you to hold my hands. And don't let go."

On Kelly's left bicep I notice a faint row of fading bruises. I've seen the same pattern of bruises before on my own arms, when I was much younger. It's the pattern of bruises made when a small thin arm is grabbed very hard by a big hand.

"Okay," Kelly says. "Do it."

Then she takes the folded-up leather belt she's been holding, and sticks it in her mouth.

Trina kneels so that she's face to face with Kelly, and takes Kelly's hands in hers. Faith and I both kneel at the same time, on either side of Kelly. Faith has one of the button-down shirts in her hand, ready to wipe away Kelly's blood.

I adjust my grip on the knife. I rest my left hand on Kelly's back, between her shoulder blades, to keep everything steady. The same way I always rest my hand on a sheet of paper I'm drawing on, or a piece of linoleum I'm carving.

I feel Kelly tremble.

I think about the bruises on her arm.

I think about a blackbird, spreading its wings and taking flight.

I pick a spot that seems like the right place for the tip of the bird's wing, and I dig the point of the knife deep into her flesh and make the first cut.

Kelly bites down on the belt in her mouth as she screams. I can't see her face, but I can tell by the sound that she's biting as hard as she can. It muffles her scream enough that no one's going to hear it unless they're pretty close.

I make another cut.

Her muffled cries as she bites down on the leather belt, as I drag the knife through her skin, are like nothing I've ever heard. I know the sound will stay with me for the rest of my life.

Faith leans in and starts wiping blood away, keeping it from running down Kelly's back to stain her jeans, keeping it from getting in the way of my work.

Trina is talking to Kelly, her voice low and urgent: "Come on Kel you can do this... come on girl I'm right here for you... be strong Kel... you can do this... come on... fucking stay with me girl... hold on tight... that's it... fucking hold on tight... be strong girl..."

I keep cutting.

I lose myself in the work, like I do when I get deep into an art project. Trina's words, Faith's quiet presence, Kelly's cries and whimpers, are all just currents in a river that flows around me without touching me. I'm in another place, apart from it all. Just me and the blackbird.

The blackbird already exists inside Kelly. Already lives in her skin. I just have to find it. Help it emerge, help it become visible. It wants to. It wants to be seen, wants to spread its wings. It calls to me, guides my hand, shows me where to cut to set it free.

And then it's done.

I stand up. Step backward, away from Kelly. Fold the blade of the knife back into the handle.

Kelly is sobbing, the belt still clamped between her teeth.

Trina is silent now, eyes wide, pale face wet with tears, still holding tight to Kelly's hands.

I know my work was good. Every cut in the right place.

When it heals, the blackbird will be perfect, etched in white scar tissue, forever taking flight.

Right now, though, newly carved, it's a ragged bloody mess.

Faith looks up at me. "Finished?"

I nod.

"Don't move," Faith says to Kelly. "I have to clean it." She opens the plastic bottle of Jack Daniel's that Kelly drank from earlier, and pours what's left of it onto the one button-down shirt that hasn't yet been soaked in blood. Kelly bites down on the belt and whimpers as Faith uses the whiskey-drenched shirt to clean her cuts.

Then Faith breaks out the first aid supplies and with my assistance sets about covering the blackbird in thick layers of gauze. I follow Faith's lead, handing her lengths of surgical tape and holding strips of gauze in place. Taping all that gauze to Kelly's back is a tricky job, made trickier by the fact that the cuts are still oozing blood. We have to keep adding more gauze as the blood seeps through layer after layer.

While Faith and I tend to Kelly's wounds, Trina comforts her, holding her hand, stroking her hair, speaking to her softly. Kelly has been clamping down on the belt between her teeth with such desperate intensity that now it takes a lot of gentle coaxing from Trina to get her jaw to un-clamp. It's weird seeing Trina be gentle and comforting.

When the blackbird is finally swaddled under a blanket of white gauze, we clean up. The surgical gloves Faith and I are wearing have kept our hands clean, but our forearms are smeared with Kelly's blood. Faith opens the second plastic bottle of Jack Daniel's, and we use some of it to wash the blood off.

"Lemme see that bottle when you're done," Trina says. Faith hands her the bottle, once we've made sure there's no more blood on us. Trina helps Kelly take a drink from it, and then takes a big gulp of it herself. "Hoooo, fuck," Trina says.

"Hahhh. Fuck. Fucking *fuck* I needed that." She takes another gulp, then helps Kelly drink again. In a couple of minutes, they've finished it all.

Faith adds the empty bottle to the pile she's made that already includes the other empty bottle, the four blood-soaked button-down shirts, the gloves, the scissors, the knife, and the few remaining scraps of gauze and surgical tape. Faith and I use our feet to shove this pile into a small hollow space under the fallen tree trunk, then kick dirt and leaves onto it until it's pretty well covered.

I put my jacket back on and sit on the tree trunk with my back to the girls, politely looking away while Faith and Trina get Kelly dressed. This takes a while, because on top of Kelly being all cut up and still in a daze from her ordeal, Kelly and Trina are both drunk now. Trina curses and giggles as she tries to talk Kelly through the process of getting her bra, shirt, and jacket on: "Kay, gotta putcher arm through here... easy... wait a sec... shit, not like that..."

Mixed in with Trina's voice, I hear an occasional syllable of complaint from Kelly. Kelly's words come out so hoarse and slurred I can barely understand them, but it mostly sounds like "Ow" and "Fuck," which seem like reasonable things for a person in her condition to say. I figure it's a good sign that she's talking at all.

◆   ◆   ◆

We pick our way through the woods, heading in what we hope is the general direction of the school. Kelly can't walk on her own, and Trina insists on being the one to help her. This makes for slow and unsteady progress, since Trina's so drunk from the Jack Daniel's that she can barely walk straight herself. They stagger along with Kelly's arm draped over Trina's shoulder and Trina's arm around Kelly's waist.

Kelly's had even more whiskey than Trina, and she also seems to be on some sort of weird endorphin high from the cutting. She mumbles and babbles to Trina; her words are incoherent but the tone seems cheerful enough. She giggles at everything, and soon she's got Trina giggling along with her.

The woods are crisscrossed with clearly-marked walking trails, and soon we find one. We follow the trail in more or less the same direction we were headed already, and in just a few minutes it brings us face to face with a couple of school staff members who are out looking for us.

One of the staff members calls in to the school on his walkie-talkie to report that we've been found. From the brief conversation he has with the person on the other end, it's clear that he thinks we snuck off into the woods to get drunk and probably stoned. What with the way Kelly and Trina are staggering and giggling, and all four of us reeking of whiskey, it's the obvious conclusion.

Kids in this school are always getting busted for being high or trying to get high. It's what the principal likes to refer to as a *serious infraction,* and disappearing into the woods to do it makes the infraction even more serious. But I bet it's not nearly as serious as cutting a picture of a blackbird into someone's back with a knife, carving the lines deep and thick so they'll turn into scars that will last the rest of her life.

We knew we would end up getting busted. Having the staff assume that all we did in the woods was get drunk and maybe high is pretty much the best way this whole thing could end.

No one talks as the staff members escort us back to school. Except for Kelly, who continues to giggle and occasionally mumble something incomprehensible. And Trina, who responds to Kelly's giggles and mumbles by saying "Shhh!" and then giggling herself.

The staff members don't seem to find this amusing.

♦ ♦ ♦

Back at the school, we're confined to the small empty windowless room that the staff refer to as Time Out. A staff member stays in the room, standing guard by the door. We sit on the floor with our backs against the wall. Even Kelly is silent now, sitting cross-legged and slumped forward, with her elbows on her knees and her face in her hands. Her high has worn off and now she just looks exhausted. Trina sits close beside her with a comforting hand on her shoulder.

We all know how this works. They'll come and take us out of here one at a time. Question each of us separately. Look for inconsistencies between our stories. Try to get us to rat each other out. The staff member guarding us is partly here to keep us from talking to each other, so we can't make last-ditch attempts to get our stories straight or last-minute pacts of mutual loyalty.

That's not quite how it goes this time, though. When the gym teacher shows up, along with a burly staff member for extra muscle and intimidation, she picks Kelly first. The gym teacher doubles as the school nurse and the resident authority on stoned students and drug-and-alcohol-related infractions, so she's the one who gets to deal with us. Since it was her class we went AWOL from in the first place, we're pretty much ruining her day. Maybe that's why, when she calls Kelly's name and gets no response, she doesn't check to make sure Kelly is okay before she turns to the burly staff member and says, "Get her up."

The staff member grabs Kelly by the arm and jerks her to her feet.

"Hey!" Trina shouts at him. "Don't you fucking..."

But Trina never finishes her sentence, because Kelly opens her mouth and vomits all over the front of the staff member's shirt.

He shoves Kelly away from him and she falls down hard, yelling in pain as she hits the floor. He lurches out of the room, cursing and sputtering, dripping vomit.

"What the fuck!" Trina yells after him as he goes. "Fucking asshole!"

Kelly winces and says "Ow" and "Fuck" a few times as the other staff member, the one who's been there guarding us the whole time, helps her stand up again.

"We need to get her to my office," the gym teacher says. She turns and leaves. The staff member follows her out the door, bringing Kelly along and leaving me, Trina, and Faith alone.

For a couple of minutes we just sit there. Then Faith breaks the silence in her flat quiet voice. "They're going to search her," she says.

"Fuck," Trina says. Because of course they are. They'll want to know if there are any drugs involved besides alcohol. Kelly's enough of a mess right now to give them plenty of grounds for suspicion. They're going to search her, and they'll discover she's been cut. Has she bled through all that gauze? How about her t-shirt? If she's bled through her shirt as well as the gauze, they'll see it as soon as they take her jacket off.

"Fuck," Trina says again. "Fuck fuck fuck fuck fuck."

Minutes pass. Faith and I sit with our backs to the wall and wait. Trina gets up and paces rapidly around the room, zigzagging from wall to wall at random. Every few seconds she runs her hands through her hair, gnaws at the skin around her thumbnail, or says "Fuck" again.

When the gym teacher bursts back into the room with the assistant principal and another staff member behind her, I know right away that they've found the blood-soaked bandages under Kelly's shirt. And I know they've peeled the bandages away and seen the blackbird. I know because the gym teacher is wearing surgical gloves, just like Faith and I wore when I did the cutting, and the gloves have blood on them. And I know because in ten years of getting in trouble in school and seeing other kids get in trouble, I've never seen a teacher this upset.

"*Who?*" the gym teacher shouts. "*Who did it?*"

The gym teacher's face is red and her fists are clenched so hard they're shaking. I can feel the rage blazing from her like heat. I press my back against the wall, trying to get as far away from her I can. But Trina takes a step *toward* her. Trina clenches her own fists and lowers her head like a bull about to charge.

"*I did it!*" Trina shouts. She takes another step toward the gym teacher and yells right in her face. "It was *me,* okay? *I* did it! *I* fucking cut her! You got a fucking problem with that, you fucking ugly-ass bitch?"

As they drag Trina out of the room and down the hall, she continues cursing and insulting them at the top of her lungs.

◆   ◆   ◆

By the time they finally get around to talking to me and Faith, the assistant principal and the gym teacher seem to have already made up their minds that the two of us are innocent victims of peer pressure. Impressionable social outcasts, desperate to fit in, led astray by a couple of bad kids we'd thought were cool. They don't even bother questioning us separately or searching us. It's not really an interrogation at all, just a lecture with a few questions thrown in to confirm things they already think they know. As far as they're concerned, the case is already closed.

There's only one explanation I can think of for why Faith and I aren't in much bigger trouble. When they got her alone, Trina must have stuck to her story that she was the one who carved the blackbird into Kelly's back. She must have claimed full responsibility for everything – not only for the cutting, but for bringing the whiskey and the knife, and probably for coming up with the whole idea in the first place.

She probably told the assistant principal and the gym

teacher that she just thought carving pictures into people's skin would be cool, and that she talked a drunken Kelly into letting her try it. The adults who work in this place would totally buy a story like that. They never really have a clue about why any of us do what we do.

Not that I understand Trina myself. It makes sense to me that Trina would protect Kelly by claiming to be responsible for the whole plan. I've seen how devoted she is to Kelly. But I don't know why she'd lie to protect me and Faith at her own expense.

Faith, maybe. There could have been some kind of deal involved. Maybe when Kelly and Trina convinced Faith to help them, they promised not to let anyone know about her bringing the supplies. Just because Trina is mean doesn't mean she wouldn't keep a promise. To the kids in this school a promise made to an adult is worthless, just like all the promises adults ever made to us, but the promises we make to one another are sacred.

Nobody made me any promises, though. Trina hates me, as far as I can tell, and she never even wanted me involved in the plan in the first place. And of all the infractions we've committed, it's my own infraction – taking the knife to Kelly's flesh – that's by far the most serious and likely to carry the most severe punishment. So why would Trina jump in and take the blame for me?

I puzzle over this question for a long time, but I can't figure it out.

♦　♦　♦

Faith and I each get suspended from school for a week. The suspension is mostly for going along with Trina instead of resisting peer pressure and ratting her out. It's also for drinking. We didn't actually do any drinking, but it doesn't seem like a good idea to explain that the real reason we smell of whiskey is because we used it to wash Kelly's blood off.

Since Trina took the blame for instigating our whole adventure, including the cutting, Kelly is also treated as a victim of Trina's bad influence and suspended for a week.

For his attack on the principal's car, Todd gets suspended for two weeks. When he returns, his classmates give him a hero's welcome.

Trina gets suspended for three weeks. She's not allowed to go outside for gym class or any other activity for the rest of the year. She's permanently removed from the Gold Star art class because she's not trusted with sharp objects anymore. I hear from Kelly that Trina's parents have worked out some kind of deal where Trina goes through a lot of counseling instead of facing criminal charges.

♦ ♦ ♦

After all the caring she showed for Kelly, and after the way she saved the rest of us by stepping up and taking the blame for everything, I wonder if Trina will be different now. Maybe the whole adventure in the woods woke up something inside her, some noble and heroic side she never knew she had. And maybe after sharing that adventure, there'll be some new understanding between her and me. I don't necessarily expect us to become friends, but maybe she'll at least start tolerating my existence.

But when she returns to school after her three-week suspension, she hasn't changed a bit. "You fucking faggot retard," she says, the first time I even glance in her general direction. "What the fuck are you looking at?" So I figure I can forget about ever getting an explanation of why she confessed to cutting Kelly.

♦ ♦ ♦

With Trina banished from the Gold Star art class, Kelly starts sitting with me during art. And when Faith gets transferred into the Gold Star class a little later in the year, she joins me and Kelly at our table.

As we sit together working on our respective art projects, Kelly sometimes talks to me and Faith about what she did over the weekend, the latest escapades of our classmates, the music she's into, her hopes and fears and dreams, the things she wants to do with her life.

She never talks about the blackbird.

I think about it, though, when we're sitting together.

That day in the woods, after I made the final cut, Faith asked me if I was finished. And I was. But the blackbird wasn't.

I did my part. I found the outlines of the blackbird, and I made every cut that needed to be made to bring it to life. But it will only be finished when time and the human body's capacity for healing have turned the red cuts into white scars.

I'll never see the finished blackbird with my own eyes, but it makes me happy to think about it. To imagine it flying free, vivid white against the softer white of Kelly's skin, flashing its bright wings in victory.

One day it occurs to me to wonder: if it's white, how will anyone know it's a blackbird?

But Kelly will know, of course, and I guess that's what really matters.

Journey to Self-Love in a Culture Demanding Self-Hate

Sam Harvey

"In a world where one man tries to decide who he is, two life experiences converge for an epic intellectual battle over whether he loves or hates himself." Looking back, this is an apt description of that summer. It really was the best of times and the worst of times, but it wasn't a tale of two cities or even two people, but of one person torn between two ideals: Self-Love or Self-Hate? And now, I delve into the reaches of my mind to relay this three-month battle.

◆   ◆   ◆

Self-Hate 1 (April, 2015)

I sat there bouncing my legs enjoying the rhythm as they went in and out of the harmony of time. One second they were bouncing in unison, then they were bouncing opposite of each other in perfect timing. It felt as beautiful to my body as cello music to my ears. "What am I going to do this summer?" I asked myself aloud, genuinely curious of my own answer.

I talk to myself as a way of thinking things through, but when I am in public, I try to silently talk to myself rather than look completely insane to others. There's no other way I can really think things through than to talk with myself about it.

After a brief moment of time, I responded, "I don't know. What do you think?"

I shrugged and answered, "Why would I be asking if I had any idea what to do this summer?"

I acknowledged the comeback and replied, "Fair enough.

Well, there are only two options that I can see, you could get a job or you could take summer classes."

I knew option 1 wasn't an option because I don't do well at interviews, nor do I learn fast. Therefore, a summer job would not only be difficult to get, but a serious pain in the ass, so that was a no go. That left option 2. "What classes would I take?"

"Well, you have to know a language for your PhD, so, maybe a language class. You could even do a sign language class if you wanted to."

Hm, I thought to myself, *I like that idea.* So, I decided to find out if a sign language class was even offered. After a bit of searching on my computer, I found that they did, indeed, offer the class. "Haha, alright, I am gonna take that."

"Wait a minute, I'm pretty sure you need to take more than just three credits to get financial aid, though."

Grr face! I thought to myself. *That means I have to spend more money. What about an autism class?*

"Oh, I like that idea! Let's see if there are any autism classes. Wait! Wait a minute! I just remembered that they have an autism certificate in the special education program." After a bit of searching, I found that the program was still offering the autism certificate. After determining if this was financially feasible, I decided that that was what I was going to do over the summer.

I applied and was accepted into the autism certificate program one week later. Classes would be from June 12 to August 7. Thus, I unknowingly thrust myself into a situation that demanded I hate myself for being something I didn't fully comprehend or accept...yet.

◆　◆　◆

Self-Love 1 (April, 2015)

I was rocking back and forth in my computer chair staring with dread at the evil thing laying in front of me. *Why does this have to be so damn hard?* I demanded. I picked up the phone with palms soaked in sweat. *I haven't even started dialing yet and I'm already terrified.*

"It's alright, you've always hated this thing." I said in an attempt to calm myself. "But hey, it doesn't really matter if you fuck up. Because the worst that will happen is that you mess up and they realize that you aren't good on the phone. And you are not good on the phone, but that's okay."

With a frown on my face, I shakily began dialing the phone number. Just as it began ringing, I hung up and put my head in my hands. Letting out a big sigh, my calm part said, "Okay, so plan A didn't work and that's okay. Time for plan B, write up exactly what you are going say and practice it at least once while preparing for possible interruptions or questions. That means, write down your name, address, have your medical card out and ready, and know that with all of this information, you've got this." For the next five minutes, I carefully crafted exactly what I was going to say.

Less shakily this time, I dialed the number and let it ring. "Hello, St. Cloud mental health services, how may I help you?" The receptionist asked in a sweet voice.

"Hi," I said somewhat shakily reading off the script I had written, "I was wondering if your clinic does diagnoses of adult autism." Immediately, I realized I had read the script wrong and kicked myself, but the receptionist seemed to understand what I was asking anyways.

"Um, I'm not sure if we do that. May I call you back once I have the answer? What's the best number to reach you at?" I gave her my number and let out a huge breath as I hung up the phone. *Time for the next number.* I practiced the part that I had messed up on several times "adult diagnoses of autism" not "diagnoses of adult autism" because autism is just autism whether it's in adults or kids. But, I digress.

I dialled the number for the next clinic. "Hello, The Behavioral Clinic, how can I help you?"

"Hi, I was wondering if your clinic does adult diagnoses of autism."

She replied, "Um, I don't think we do that for adults. But, I'm not sure, so I will transfer you to the person who would know."

I had the opportunity to listen to jazzy muzak for several minutes until the new person asked, "Hello, how can I help you?"

Again, I replied, "Hi, I was wondering if your clinic does adult diagnoses of autism."

"Sorry, we don't do that for adults, we're the children's division of the clinic. Let me transfer you to the adult person to schedule an appointment."

"Okay, thanks!"

Several seconds later, I received the message, "Hello, I'm sorry, but I'm out of the office until next month on holiday. If this is an emergency, please dial 9-1-1." *Grr face!* I thought as I hung up the phone.

At that point, both the phone and I needed a break from each other. I don't know if you can tell, but I despise the phone because it is evil! I hate the phone with a passion that is so strong that I usually attach an addendum to the hatred I feel for it. I hate it with a passion in excelsis deo squared to the infinity of the nth degree. Yeah, I guess just saying I hate the phone would suffice.

About an hour after our mutual separation, it came back into my life as it began to ring. I looked at the caller ID and saw that it was the St. Cloud mental health services. Sighing, I picked it up and heard the voice on the other end ask, "Hello, Sam?"

"Yeah, hi."

"So, I had the chance to talk to our director and he said that there is no one here who can do an adult diagnosis. He says there are two options, one is that we can give you names and phone numbers for people who can diagnose you in the area, the other is you can come in and talk to him so we can find out what's wrong with you." That phrasing felt like it stung and my mouth ran dry with an emotional pain that I didn't quite understand. *Is there something wrong with me?* I asked myself, but before I could answer that, I decided I did not want to talk to them if they were going to try and figure out what was "wrong with me."

"I think it would be best to get the phone numbers right now."

She gave me two names and numbers and I hung up the phone. After calling the first to no avail, I tried calling the second. "Hello, this is the Neurobehavioral Clinic, how can I help you?"

"Hi, I was wondering if you did diagnoses of autism in adults." I had gone off script, but I didn't kick myself this time because it made sense.

"Yes, we do. We usually do a neuropsychological test to diagnose people with autism."

Taken aback because I had finally found someone, I asked, "When is the soonest I can get an appointment."

"Um, the doctor who does the test is booked out pretty far. It looks like I can schedule a neuropsych testing appointment for you in four months." *Holy shit, that's really far out.*

"Okay, yeah, why don't we do that."

"We usually have two shifts for the neuropsych test, one in the morning at 8AM and the other at noon."

"I would much prefer the noon appointment if at all possible."

"That would be August 7th at noon. Does that work for you?"

"That works fine for me."

"Okay, it is all set up."

"Thanks, bye" I hung up and realized that I had just taken a huge first step. I thought about the fact that I could be diagnosed with autism by the start of next school year. But almost as immediately, I began to feel self doubt.

I'm pretty sure I am autistic, but what if I'm not?

What if this thing that explains so much about my life and who I am is taken away from me by a non-diagnosis?

What if I'm making all this up?

What if I am not actually autistic?

These thoughts and more kept hitting me like bricks as my mind perseverated on them. I thought I had autism, it explained so much, but I wasn't medically diagnosed with it, so I wasn't an autistic yet.

But I had taken the first step, I had scheduled an appointment to find out if I could be medically diagnosed as autistic. Thus, I unknowingly thrust myself into a situation that encouraged me to love myself for being something I didn't fully comprehend or accept...yet.

◆　◆　◆

Self-Love 2 (May, 2015)

That previous school year, I had presented at the Great Plains Alliance in Computers and Writing (Which I dubbed GPAC...wait for it...W) in the fall of 2014. It was a great experience and I had received a card notifying me of the national Computers and Writing conference in May. Not thinking I had any chance of getting in, I submitted a proposal to present at the conference. To my shock and surprise, I was accepted.

As time got closer and closer, I became more and more

nervous. This feeling reached its zenith when I found out that the person who I had been researching and reading from January until the conference, Melanie Yergeau, a rhetorician and disability studies scholar that focused on autism, was going to be at the Computers and Writing conference.

The week before I got to the conference, I received an e-mail asking me if I wanted a mentor for the conference. Rather than deciding on it immediately, I went about the rest of my day with an idea slowly forming in my mind. That night, I sat down at my computer and filled out the form asking if it would be possible for Dr. Yergeau to be my mentor.

I didn't hear back, didn't hear back, and thought to myself, *It was worth a shot.* That night, I got an e-mail saying, "Let me look into it, if she is okay with it, then I can finalize it." Nine hours later, I received another e-mail titled "Your mentoring partner for C&W" letting me know that I was paired up with Melanie Yergeau. I was ecstatic and excited, but then I realized what that meant: I had to bring my A-game or something ten times better than that.

At the pre-conference for graduate students and non-tenure-track faculty, I was sitting at the table and in she came with someone else and walked straight to my table. I was utterly star-struck as she sat down. My head went through what I could say and all the things that I wanted to say. Instead, I said shakily, "Hi, I'm Sam Harvey." She introduced me to the person beside her saying, "This is Alyssa Hillary, you two should have a lot to talk about. Both of you are into theory of mind."

Theory of mind is what both of my presentations that week were on. It is defined as the ability to know that other people have their own thoughts and emotions and, by extension, the ability to know what those thoughts and emotions are. I was going to take the concept of theory of mind down.

We talked about theory of mind for a bit and then the

conference started. I did my presentation last and then we went to lunch. At lunch, we talked for almost the entire time about theory of mind as I sat with Dr. Yergeau and Alyssa. I was in heaven because never in a million years could I have imagined this happening.

At the conference, I met two other autistic people. I realized that it was fun, easy, and comfortable to talk to this group of autistic people. Those were feelings I had never had when interacting with people in the past (I realize now that I talked to neurotypicals most of the time). Not only that, but interacting with them wasn't as draining. I didn't tell them that I wasn't diagnosed with autism because I was ashamed and didn't want them to think less of me. They came to my presentation at the main conference and I went to theirs as well. Several people in attendance even tweeted parts of my presentation.

That was an amazing way to start the summer, but the high didn't last because I started classes two weeks later.

◆ ◆ ◆

Self-Hate 2 (June, 2015)

On the first day of the 3-week special education class, the professor asked us to introduce ourselves. It was the usual BS about "State your name, where you teach, who you teach," and the final thing we were supposed to share was "our autistic characteristic."

The professor asked me to go first because I was the only man in the class and I said that my autistic characteristic was "I find social situations very difficult." We went through the entire class and people brought up things like "anxiety, obsessive compulsive, and ritualistic behaviors." At the end of the introductions, the professor smiled and joked, "Well, I guess we all have autism." The class burst into laughter.

Here were special education teachers with neurotypicality who were about to go out and teach students with autism and they were laughing at the fact that they shared some characteristics with their students. I felt sick to my stomach from the bitter disgust I felt. They demeaned autism and people with autism by comparing themselves to autistic people and laughing about it.

During class, the professor said that autism is something we need to fix because it is problematic to the student with autism. She spoke of theory of mind as a fact saying lacking it causes academic failure. This lead me to think, *Wait, I have a 4.0 GPA right now, then that means that I don't have autism? But theory of mind is BS, though, so that doesn't make any sense. Not only that, but the professor did not provide any empirical studies or proof that there was a connection between theory of mind and academic success.*

A college student with autism came into the classroom with his mother and tried to present on his experiences of high school and now college as a student with autism. I say he tried to because he couldn't get five minutes before his mother or the professor would interrupt him to correct something he said or chide him for saying that most of his teachers didn't treat him with enough respect. The day after he presented, the professor complained for over an hour to our class on how he rigid he was and how he almost didn't present because he had been late.

The professor taught that people with autism can't put structure into place because they don't know what works for them, so the teacher's job is to teach them about or place them in that structure. *Wait, but I'm pretty organized. Does that mean that I don't have autism?*

The most disturbing thing to me was that the professor declared that autism is overdiagnosed and is the new ADHD in that any kid who's awkward is diagnosed with it. This caused my anxiety grow to a point where I didn't think I could handle it anymore. The same questions that had been hounding me since April continued but now louder and stronger, bolstered by the things that they had been teaching me.

What if I'm part of the problem of overdiagnoses?

I'm pretty sure I am autistic, but what if I'm not?

What if this thing that explains so much about my life and who I am is taken away from me by a non-diagnosis?

What if I'm making all this up?

What if I am not actually autistic?

The class made me ask these questions and more. Doubt crept into my mind like a mouse into its hole as I looked online for desperate help.

◆   ◆   ◆

Self-Love 3 (June, 2015)

I was reading the blog Yes, That Too when I saw that Alyssa, one of the autistic people I had met at Computers and Writing, recognized that self-diagnosis was valid. If self-diagnosis was valid, then I call myself autistic, right? I realized I fit the diagnosis requirements found in the DSM-V (Which we had gone over in the special education class). Could I call myself autistic even if I didn't have a medical diagnosis?

I sent a Facebook message to Alyssa asking sier, "Can you say you are autistic if you haven't been officially diagnosed?"

Sie responded, "Yes," and sent me a link to the Autistic Self Advocacy Network site recognizing self-diagnosis as a valid part of their community. I came clean and told sier that I had not been officially diagnosed, but was almost 100% positive that I was autistic.

Sie responded with one word. A word that I didn't even

realize how much I needed to hear. A word that I can never thank sier enough for. "Welcome!" It took me several minutes to realize what sie meant because I hadn't said thank you. Then, I slowly began to realize that Alyssa was saying welcome to the autistic community. And just like that, all of the anxiety, all of the self-doubt, everything that I had been anxious about regarding the diagnosis blew away like a puff of smoke that had seemed like a solid and impenetrable mass just moments before.

That night, I wrote a poem entitled "..."
Never am I so alone as when I am in a group full of people.
Alone and on the brink of betraying myself.
Betraying the act I have oh-so-carefully played,
That of the quirky oddball.
But I am so much more than that.

Yet to say who I really am is not possible without millions of probing questions,
Each question ridiculing me,
Demanding me to wear a star on my arm or present my passport.

"Where's your diagnosis?"
The question haunts me to no end,
Robbing me of sleep day and night.
For without it, can I identify as, no I cannot yet say it.
So, I will call it ... from now on.

And yet,
As I play the part of the quirky oddball
And fear the possibility of ridicule,
Someone ridicules me even more mercilessly than any outsider could:
Myself

Why can't you just be normal?
Why can't you just talk to them?
Why can't you just start a conversation?
Why can't you just continue a conversation?

These questions and more
Demanded by the voice of incredulity and ridicule
That lies within myself.
To say who I am would be a betrayal.
A betrayal to the part of me desperately clinging to the role,
The role I so desperately hate,
The role that is draining my life and happiness,
Terrified of what lay beyond the thinly layered mask.

Will they accept me?
Will they allow me to be me?
Why must I wait for so long before I can come out to the world?
Why must I wait for a medical diagnosis when I know who I really am?

Slowly,
Ever so slowly,
I am beginning to understand who I really am.
But to tell the truth, I have always understood who I really was.
The true question I am beginning to understand is,
Why am I who I am?

But I cannot say what I need to say,
I cannot come out until a medical diagnosis.
But why?
Because society has decided that?
Well, fuck society.

As I think again about the questions:
Will they accept me?
Will they allow me to be me?
I must ask myself one question:
When have they ever accepted me?

I am talking about true acceptance,
not just mere tolerance to my face
And hatred so seething,
that it brands me,
brands me with the scarlet letter "A" for ... on my back.

I had a dream a few months ago.
I was ...,
In other words,
I was who I was.
I tried to tell people,
But they gave me looks of distrust and disbelief.
Those looks quickly turned to vehement hatred when they
saw what I was wearing.

They thought it inappropriate attire.
Then, another ... came in wearing the same thing.
"Oh, good for him, he's dressed to the nines and so
inspirational."
Anger filled my mind until I could barely handle it.

"What of me?" I demanded.
They turned at me with looks now turning to poisonous
disappointment,
"He's ..., you should be ashamed to call yourself ...,
HE" They said pointing to the one who walked in,
"He is ..., not you."
They said dismissing me,

Thus making as invisible.

I went to the corner and put my head in my hands,
The tears a mix of anger, agony, and sadness refusing to flow.
Try as I might,
The tears drowned my thoughts as I looked at the ... man.
"He is ..., but I am too."

So society tells me that I cannot be ... without a medical diagnosis,
Yet the ...s allow me to identify as ...
Months of mental anguish has led to this point.
Anguish about hiding who I am.

So who am I?
Well, for starters:
I'm *sigh* ...
Unfortunately, I couldn't say it yet at that point. But it was coming. Ever so slowly, the ideals were creeping towards a final end. A key piece would come with the next class.

♦ ♦ ♦

Self-Hate-Love-Hate-Love-Ha-Lo-...? (July, 2015)

I began my second autism certificate class in July. It was a class devoted to applied behavioral analysis, something that I didn't know much about, but knew that the community of people with autism (or is it autistic community? No, community with autism. Right?) was against.

"But why is the community of people with autism against it?" I asked myself just before I went to bed the night before the class.

"I don't really know, but they probably have a good reason. But keep an open mind as you go through this class, really listen to what they are saying."

The next day began with the professor beginning the class by saying, "Look, autism is the new ADHD, everybody who's quirky is now being diagnosed with it. And I am convinced," she joked, "That Thomas the Tank causes autism." I was taken aback at the utter brazenness the professor had come out of the gate with.

The next day, the professor showed us a YouTube lecture. I watched it with surprise as he reiterated again and again that aversives are not used anymore. But I knew that to be false in part because of a school in Massachusetts known as Judge Rotenberg Center where they put what is akin to shock collars on children with autism and shock them whenever they act out (which is often defined as something as small as getting out of their seat without permission, going to the bathroom without permission, or not taking their coat off when directed to).

But the presenter gave the description of how he does ABA and he claimed that places don't use aversives, they use positive and negative reinforcement. He talked about a particular autistic child he worked with who would have temper tantrums that would often become very violent when he did not get his way. Most of the time, apparently, he wanted to work on mathematics. However, he had a very unique way of doing math where none of his teachers knew how he did it.

The presenter decided to work on the problem behavior of "temper tantrums." He did this by teaching the kid to use the phrase "My way please?" Sometimes he would get his way, sometimes he would not. He would want to do math and he would ask, "My way please?" His parents would say no. This evolved into him wanting to do math and he would ask, "My way please?" His parents would sometimes say okay and when they did, they would then attempt to make him do math in the way the teacher was teaching it. He would ask, "My way please" and his parents would refuse and make him do math in the way he had been taught.

Okay, I thought, *That seems pretty legitimate. They aren't using aversives, so it isn't as dangerous as many of the people with autism were saying. Obviously, we need to get rid of the problem behaviors. A kid, whether they have autism or not, can't be throwing a temper tantrum every time they don't get their way.*

As I walked home that night, the moon was just starting to rise as I began to think. *Maybe ABA isn't actually half as bad as the people with autism are saying. It just addresses the problem behaviors. Unlike what they say about changing the kid's autistic characteristics, they aren't changing anything like that. I mean, he enjoyed math and they let him keep doing math.*

It was at that moment that a realization hit me that made me stop in my tracks. I stood there mortified as I realized, *Wait, yeah, they let him do math, but they reduced the amount of time he could do math his way. The way that worked for him, even though no one understood it.* I began to feel a knot in my stomach and started to feel sick. I started walking again flapping my hands in anger, *How dare they. They started with the idea that they were going to work on the problem behaviors. But those bastards actually started changing non-problem behaviors.*

As I walked into my apartment and threw my backpack on the chair hard enough to knock the chair over, I thought, *You have got to be kidding me. It's genius, really. If anyone approaches them and asks them why they are taking on such a lower-order behavior, one that is inherently autistic, then they can say that doing math his own way contributes to the problem behaviors. People with autism are good, they do not need to be fixed! People with autism do not need to be fixed. No! No! They*

*are not people with autism. They are autistic people. Autistic
people do not need to be fixed and neither do I. I am...*

For the second time that night, I felt like I was going to be
sick. *I bought into this hook line and sinker. What's wrong with
me?*

My calm side said, "Nothing's wrong with you. Their
rhetoric is phenomenal because upon first look, it looks like
they have very sound logic. They say they are not trying to
change the autistic child, just the problem behaviors. But if
you begin to look at it critically even a bit, you begin to see
what the autistic people are saying. They are trying to get rid
of the autistic characteristics."

*I think a better phrasing is that they're trying to
exterminate the autistic characteristics.*

That night, I decided to look up why the community of
autistic people were against ABA. What I found was
disturbing and disgusting. I came across a video series called
"Ask an Autistic" where one idea stuck out to me: you are
setting a dangerous precedent when you demand that autistic
people comply with everything you say.

I came upon another source that linked to a Times article
written about Ivar Lovaas, the forefather of Applied Behavior
Analysis. In the first picture, there was a man screaming into
the face of a 8-year-old child, the next picture showed the
same man slapping the hell out of the boy, and the final
picture was the boy bawling his eyes out. Things like this are
called aversives, according to the article. On another site, I
found lists of other aversives ABA therapists have used like
putting terribly bitter things in a child's mouth in an attempt
to make them stop autistic behaviors like stimming.

On another site, people commented that ABA is akin to
child abuse. On another, it was stated that there are ties
between gay conversion therapy and ABA because they both
go based on Lovaas's idea that "if you change the outward
behavior of the person, you change the inward psyche of the

person."

The final piece I saw said that many autistic adults who have gone through ABA therapy develop post-traumatic stress disorder. I thought to myself, "Do the ends justify the means here?"

Disgusted, I sent an e-mail to the professor asking her about how we can respond to things like this. She e-mailed me back saying she would like to respond to this in front of the class on the last day.

The last day came and she asked me to give a synopsis of what I had found and had e-mailed her. I told the whole class the many disturbing things that I had found. But the one that stuck out to me the most was Ivar Lovaas bringing an 9 year old autistic girl into a room with metal floors and had her shoes taken off and electrodes put on her back. Every time that she did not pay attention to a lesson, he would shock her through electrodes placed in the metal floor. Once I was done, she began shaking her head in disgust.

"First off, Ivar Lovaas never shocked anyone. Secondly, these supposedly autistic people, who by the way were probably diagnosed after they were 4 years old, which means they are almost guaranteed not actually autistic, are probably lying. Those who claim that ABA is akin to child abuse and causes PTSD are all also probably lying. Not only that, but there is no research out there that suggests that ABA causes PTSD.

"Thirdly, there is absolutely no connection between ABA and gay therapy, none whatsoever. And now to address the idea that ABA robs autistic people of their identity, well, that's just bullshit. We need to change them because I don't care if you have a diagnosis or not, behaving and complying is what you should do because, in the end, if you want to have a good life, you need to change your behaviors.

"I had a kid come into my clinic who was stimming all the time and had problem behaviors up the wazoo, and now, now he is indistinguishable from his peers. He doesn't show any signs of autism and that, I think, is pretty damn cool."

She gave the class a proud smile and many of the other teachers joined her by smiling and saying quietly, "That is cool!" I sat there in utter disbelief and shock as I tried to wrap my head around the brutally undisguised ableist soliloquy she had just delivered. Never in all my life had I heard something so overtly -istic as that day.

Everyone thought that it was cool and awesome that an autistic child, whose autism is a part of them, has been robbed and stripped of anything that resembles that part of them. I walked home flapping angrily every few seconds as wave after wave of seething anger raged through my very being. I had to stop a few times because I became so angry. *How dare she, how could she even, I don't even know what the fuck to say here!*

"I'll tell you what to say, she is absolutely full of shit but, above all, she's wrong." The calm part of me said. That's when I realized how disgustingly wrong what the professor had said really was. When my calm side is pissed off and swearing, there is hell to pay.

Yeah, autistic people don't need to be fixed, we don't need to act non-autistic to have a successful life. I stopped as I realized what I had just said. Up until that point, I had not actually put myself in the same category as autistic people. It revolved around the fact that I did not want to limit the autistic community by claiming to be autistic when it's a possibility I'm not. But, in rebelling intellectually against what the professor had said, I put myself with them.

My body began to calm as my rage slowly subsided. But every now and then, I would think about it and the rage would begin to build again. That was it, that was the last class, I had missed my chance to say what needed to be said. I decided that for the next class, I wasn't going to stay silent, I was going to be utterly me and utterly honest immediately about how I thought and felt. Little did I know that I would have a chance to redeem myself and let people know my real view of autism by doing exactly that.

◆ ◆ ◆

Self-Love for the Win (August, 2015)

On the first day of my third class, which was in communication sciences and disorders, the professor asked us to write a learning log that night responding to several questions. The first question asked, "What are the primary communication characteristics of students with ASD?" On her syllabus, the professor had requested that we always use person-first language. Well, I decided that I was going to use person-first language, but I was going to do it universally. So, neurotypical individuals became individuals with neurotypicality.

I reflected on what rhetoric was and how it is the same definition as communication. Then, I wrote about how every rhetorical style, no matter how diverse from the mainstream rhetoric, was considered valid, good, and (gasp) necessary. Then, I asked the question, "When is communication impaired and when is it just different?" I pointed out that all of the behaviors that are considered typical in autism can be viewed as cultural differences. Therefore, I came to the conclusion that just as we respect other student's cultural differences, so must we respect the cultural differences of autistic people.

The teacher, so blown away by my response (and to my surprise, in a good way) asked me to present on it on the last day, August 7, 2015, the same day as my neuropsych test. So, I would have to go from my presentation straight to my neuropsych test.

Every day, the professor asked me to react to what she was

saying and, true to the decision I had made, I answered with how I really felt. As the days crept by, I waited and prepared for my presentation. I asked the professor how much time she would like me to present. She responded, "How much time do you need?"

"How much time are you willing to give me?"

"I'll give you a half-hour to an hour."

"Sounds good to me."

So, I had an hour to present everything that had been welling up inside me the last 9 weeks. I went back to the presentation that I gave at the Computers and Writing conference and stripped the presentation to its bare bones, then I began to make slides for my learning log.

The night before the presentation and neuropsych test, I began to reflect on this journey. I had been surrounded by a culture that demanded that I hate myself if I was autistic, but also by a culture that encouraged me to love myself because there's nothing wrong with being autistic. The two sides were meeting head to head on the last day. The day that I would enter into the culture that demanded I hate myself, then leave to go to the test that would medically recognize me as a part of the culture that had already embraced me and encouraged me to love myself.

As I stood in front of the class, I asked the question, "When is communication impaired and when is it just different?" I proceeded for the next hour to go forth and point out the possibility that autism is not something that needs to be fixed. The teachers asked me questions about whether they should even be teaching social skills at all and I recommended that they do, but I said "There is a fine line between teaching an autistic kid how neurotypicals interact and forcing the kid to use it."

I walked out of the class with the professor saying, "I have been in the field working with people with autism for 45 years and I'm walking out of here with a completely new perspective on autism. You've made my brain work and I can't see autism the same way as when I started this class three weeks ago.

I got on the bus to go to my neuropsych appointment and had four hours of grueling testing. I got out and all sounds sounded too loud and the light was too bright. Unfortunately, I missed the bus and didn't get home for 2 hours and by that time, my brain was so fried that I had a mental shutdown. I couldn't talk or think, everything seemed not real. I went to sleep and slept for almost 15 hours straight.

My results appointment wasn't scheduled for several weeks, but I was okay with that because of one thing: I was already a part of the autistic community.

In the end, even though I was surrounded by a culture demanding that I loathe myself and refuse to recognize an integral part of me, I was able to convince myself that I deserved my own love and, little by little, recognize the things within myself that I have always known were there. No matter how hard things got in those nine weeks, I never gave up. I refused to buy in to the things that seemed wrong to me.

It's taken a whole summer for me to come to this point and, even though I don't have a medical diagnosis, even though I don't have the medical paperwork that tells the world that I am official, I have one thing left to say. This is the culmination of a summer where the ultimate war was waged, this is the moment where I choose the victor: I am autistic.

♦ ♦ ♦

Epilogue of Love, D-Day (September 3, 2015)

I sat in a different place, my legs bouncing the same way they had been all those months ago when I made the fateful decision to take the classes. Waiting, so much waiting. I had waited so long for this moment, just a few minutes more of waiting. Patience, I tried to tell myself as my leg bounced. In vain, I attempted to distract myself from the fear that was slowly creeping up on me.

What if he tells me that I don't have autism? I asked myself for the umpteenth time.

He might, but honestly, it doesn't matter what he says. You belong in the Autistic Culture because you are autistic. No matter what he says, you have done your homework and you know you're autistic. So shutup and play a game on your phone.

You're right, why does this matter so much to me?

Because it matters to society and, like it or not, you are a part of the society.

Yeah, but why should neurotypical psychologists get to decide who is autistic enough to go through the gates? You know what? They shouldn't, because just as psychologists do not get to decide who is queer enough to go through the gates to be recognized as queer, so too should they not be able to decide for autism.

Well said.

That's not the only thing because autistic people...no, not autistic people, Autistic people with a capital A. Autistic people have hacked this and decided that as long as you have done your homework and not just diagnosed yourself after taking one test, you are autistic. They created their own damn gate and their own fence.

"Sam?" A voice drew me out of my thoughts as I looked up to see the psychologist.

"Yeah." I got up and walked into his office still mildly nervous, but still recognizing that it didn't matter what he said.

"So, as you know, we tested your IQ and also your academics in order to possibly rule out some things. So, the IQ test looks at your verbal and nonverbal test scores and your nonverbal were much higher than your verbal by about 20 points. We also tested your academics and that was interesting considering you are high-average IQ because your reading speed is at the 2nd percentile. That means you scored better than 1 of your peers. But your comprehension is good and you broke the test for decoding and spelling by getting them all right."

I took all of these in stride, but he hadn't gotten to the part that I wanted to know. *WHAT ABOUT AUTISM?* But I sat there patiently as he went through the details because he had his own style and I didn't want to mess with that, BUT I WANTED TO KNOW, DAMNIT!

"Looking at the last test you took, two things stood out to me: The first thing is that you had elevated scores on all of the questions that had to do with depression. But, it wasn't very elevated, which points to the possibility of dysthymia, which is a milder form of depression that lasts for much longer than typical depressive episodes, but it isn't as severe as the typical depressive episodes.

"The other thing that stood out to me was that you show very high levels of introversion along with a few things like you don't like or like being around people."

"Yeah, but that kind of has to do with the fact that I don't really know what to do around them. I don't know what is right and what's not right when interacting with others."

"That leads me to the final point." Here it was, here is the medical equivalent of what this whole summer had been about. Was I a hypochondriac that was everything that was wrong with autism diagnoses because I thought I had it even though I didn't actually? "I think, based on all of your symptoms now and history of symptoms, it is very possible that you have a mild autistic spectrum disorder."

He went on to say something else about how autism is a spectrum, but I was dancing inside. I felt like falling over and becoming one with the couch out of sheer, I don't really know what to call it, but it could be called calm. Calm, though, is the prerequisite state for feeling joy.

I came back to what he was saying as he said, "But you are on the low end of autism, so you don't need to worry." Worry, why would I need to worry?

He finished up his recommendations, which included going to see a therapist, but I denied because I knew that most therapists are going to approach me from the perspective of fixing my autism. *Wait, my autism. I can now say my autism whenever I want or need to without being afraid of the ramifications of not having a medical identification.*

In the end, the appointment didn't matter and neither did the results. Because whether he diagnosed me or not, I was and am and will be forever autistic.

I understood what it means to be autistic from the point of view of the autism classes who demanded me to know that I need to be fixed because I was broken and there is something inherently wrong with me.

But on the other hand, I also understood what it means to be autistic from the point of view of my autistic friends like Dr. Yergeau and Alyssa who told me that there is nothing wrong with autism. It doesn't need to be fixed because it's not broken, it's just different. And just as there are diversities that we embrace that are found in the form of skin color, culture, religion and sexual orientation, so too are there in both ability levels and brains and they are not to be viewed as pitiful, broken, or bad.

I want to leave this epilogue with one final statement that rings in my ears as I journey forth into the rest of my life, the ringing of an echolalic embrace, soft and warm, cozy and inviting: I am autistic.

Queering // Curing

Sarah Marie Caulfield

When I lie down on the hospital bed, I feel the paper covering prickle and stick against the sweat curling at the back of my neck. They ask me if I have a boyfriend. I think of her harpy's blood lipstick lethal against her teeth. I think of her Disney Princess eyes and I think of how her kiss was a bright hesitant smudge against my mouth.

No, I say. I don't have a boyfriend.

I try not to smile. I am here to be miserable. I am here to be taken seriously. If I am not taken seriously, I will not be healed.

(I cannot be healed. I do not know this yet. My mother suspects. I am, like I am about many things at eighteen, in denial. I am, like I am about many things at eighteen, lying to myself.)

The proof's in the pudding, I think as they take the starved blood from my veins. I look away when they tell me to. Someone has stuck one of those fake candy blood bags to the wall. I look at the cheap synthetic squish of it and my stomach churns. I almost laugh. I remember not to.

I am here to be taken seriously, I remind myself sternly. I am here to be healed.

◆ ◆ ◆

Goffman's dramaturgical model states that we perform our social roles dependent on the conventions of the context in which we are situated. Shakespeare says the world's but a stage, but if we are merely players I want to know why my script is Bitter Cripple #6. I didn't audition for this role. I am told to see how I get on and straight girls in bars tell me earnestly that they find other girls attractive, aesthetically speaking, but they'd never...

They don't finish the sentence. I take another mouthful of rum and coke and swallow it, hard; like I swallow the pills I tumble into my hand each night, six, twelve, eighteen. At the height of my illnesses, I will take twenty tablets a day and feel satisfied when people see. It is proof, I think, of the legitimacy of my suffering; like the manacles of medical bracelets and the paraphernalia that comes with being chronically ill before you turn twenty one. *We were born sick, I heard them say it,* but I was not born sick. I was not born this way. They think there may be a genetic predisposition towards the illness that on the emptiest days eats me whole; I think about that.

They say: we need a doctor's note. They say: we need evidence for your file. They say: we're doing this so we can help you.

Marsha P. Johnson throws a brick and shouts *isn't anybody going to do something, then?* Inside of me, windows are breaking.

And they say: prove it.

♦   ♦   ♦

I'm telling you all this so you understand why, when I come to the meat of the theory, I'm going to say I'm invested. I am. I am in too deep and if this was a TV cop drama they'd have already taken me off the case. I'm in too deep. I want to know who did this to me. When I read about Stonewall at fifteen, I cried because it struck something in me and the echo ripped through. I want to know who did this to me. I'm in too deep.

No, I'm saying it wrong. I want to know who did this to us.

◆ ◆ ◆

Queer and disability theory both state that in a heteronormative, able-bodied norm, to exist outside of the boundary in the eyes of the norm you have to step over a line in the sand, and you have to do it in front of an audience. You have to be validated in your Otherness. If a tree falls in a forest and there's no one there to hear it, it may make a sound, but you are not a tree. You are Other and not-Other, innocent until proven guilty, and those who drew the line in the sand are manning border control. All this too will pass but you shall not. Lankov states that "to not have your suffering recognised is an almost unbearable form of violence." When people say, "Oh, I get tired too," I'm supposed to laugh. When people ask me how my day has been, I am supposed to say "fine." This is how social policing manifests. This is how theory takes flesh.

I am fine. You are fine. We are all fine. After all, we are not trees. If we scream loud enough in the fall, surely we will be noticed?

◆ ◆ ◆

It happens like this: you hear *but you don't look sick* so often you tune it out till it's nothing but white noise. You hear *people like that don't go here* from the girl across the table in the cafeteria. You hear: *I am invisible.*

It happens like this: Aderonke Apata was denied asylum from Nigeria by the British government in 2015. Despite submitting footage and images of her sex life, she was told she could not be lesbian. She had children from a previous heterosexual relationship.

It happens like this: one day, someone turns to you and says, with the infinite compassion of the interrogatory, *we're*

only trying to help you.
And they say: prove it.

♦ ♦ ♦

Terry McGarvey. Mark Wood. Tim Salter. Edward Jacques. Linda Wootton. Steven Cawthra. Brian McArdle. Jacqueline Harris. Nicholas Peter Barker. Colin Traynor. Mark Scott. Larry Newman. Sandra Louise Moon. Ian Caress. Iain Hodge. David Elwyn Hughs Harries. Denis Jones. Chris MaGuire. Julian Little. Robert Barlow. Annette Francis. Ian Jordan. Janet McCall. Graham Shawcross. Chris Smith. Jan Mandeville. Trevor Drakard. And the names keep coming. The names keep coming.

My country's disability record has a body count. But of course, there's no one to blame. How could we lay that guilt at anyone's door? We were all only trying to help.

♦ ♦ ♦

And here's the thing: I feel that I'm getting somewhere with this point at this point. I really do. I think I'm getting somewhere close to that meat. And I think I'm so close because I'm complicit. I'm eating at this table, the same as you. I'm chewing down on the flesh of it and I'm saying *excuse me*. I'm saying *can I take another slice?* I'm looking at people in the disabled seat on the bus, leaning on my cane and wondering why they don't give it up, even as I talk about the invisibility of my own malady. I'm looking at strangers and I'm assuming genders and sexualities and bodily integrity and it's only when I pick apart my own coding that I notice. I'm the audience as much as the Other. I've already swallowed it down, I've digested, I've internalised. If a tree falls in the forest and no one's there to hear it, it makes a sound but if I cannot see the forest from the trees how can I draw the line in the sand?

♦   ♦   ♦

When I'm looking in the mirror, I'm seeing Otherness in the cut of my cheek and the graze of my lip. I'm seeing it in the cane in my hand and her lipstick on my skin. It's hard to stop playing, but I never auditioned for this role. I've got to go outside and I may be some time because frankly, my dear, I don't give a damn, I've got to turn invisibility into embodiment and–

♦   ♦   ♦

I've got to draw a line in the sand somewhere. I've got to step back from border control. I've got to be taken seriously even if I can't be healed. I harden my face and feel my reflection mimic it back.

♦   ♦   ♦

And I say: prove it.

❖   ❖   ❖

Electrical Work

Stephanie Heit

Before I came to Natales, "W" was just a letter of the alphabet. Now it signifies a great accomplishment for me. "The W" is a hiking trail, shaped like the letter, in the National Park Los Torres del Paine. I set out optimistic my first day with my pack loaded to capacity with 5 days' worth of food, borrowed tent and stove, lots of ambition, and a dose of fear. The spectacular views of the initial ascent up to Glacier Grey lightened the weight. I spent the first night camped next to the glacier lake with the thunderous sound of ice falling from high interrupting the silence. The scenery on the trail was adjective-defying: valleys that proved the existence of some higher being, condors soaring overhead, stone drenched landscapes of glacier fields, steep ascents and descents, wind twisted trees all knuckle and gnarl clasping rock with their persistent roots. The finale was hauling my weary ass, with my blistered feet protesting, up a bouldered path lit by headlamp to watch the sunrise on Los Torres.

I'm grateful to have recorded this journey in Chilean Patagonia as part of my travelogue emails to friends. This excerpt is from "to the end of the world and beyond" dated 3/5/08. I also wrote of the boat trip from Puerto Montt to Natales on the Navimag: *The four-day trip proved to be a respite with beautiful weather and the sea, the sea, the sea. Time to write and stare at blue.*

I wrote that I stayed a month in Natales with my friend Carolina. I wrote of yoga classes, potluck dinners, Sergio and Marijke swimming across the channel. I wrote of difficult inner landscapes with my decision to leave my Chilean love. I have to trust the words, as most of my memories are gone. I see pictures of myself in these gorgeous places: and, nothing.

No jogging of my brain to connect into a larger story. I hear names of cities in Chile and wonder if I've been to Valdivia or just read about it in *Lonely Planet*. Carolina tries to reminisce with me about a trek in a remote area of Argentina where we took every form of transportation possible to get to the trailhead. I look at the pictures. They prove I was there. But no images flash. A bit like swimming, oxygen-less, unconnected. Radio channel gone to static.

The doctors told me the possible memory effects of electroconvulsive therapy (ECT). Played them down, said it was usually just around the time of treatments: long term loss was extremely rare. Joked that forgetting parts of the treatment might be a good thing. Asked me to weigh my probable suicide against relief with a little memory loss. I was 38. I'd been in a deep and dangerous bipolar depression for about a year with no relief from multiple medication trials: I was considered treatment resistant. ECT, commonly referred to as shock treatment, where a small current induces a seizure while the person is under anesthesia, was my best option: it had been recommended repeatedly for me during a difficult episode when I was 27. I still remember the name of the inpatient doctor then, Dr. Moe, since I slant rhymed it with "asshole." To my concern about memory he'd replied, "Isn't there a lot you want to forget?" This, in addition to his advice: "If you're so suicidal, why don't you hang yourself with the bedsheets."

I'd vehemently refused ECT then, fueled by meeting a young woman who had a folder of pictures to replace her lost memory from the treatments. She scared the shit out of me. ECT scared the shit out of me. Suicide scared the shit out of me. *Scared* is too strong. I was so numb and exhausted encased in pervasive apathy I could barely summon an opinion. My signature on the consent form was more like a "whatever" than a "yes."

I lost. The six months of ECT failed. In addition to an

untenable and untreated illness, I now needed to piece together who I was, what I'd done, who these other people were that knew me, and how to get to the post office. The ECT team said not to worry. "All your memory will come back within six months. You're so bright, it will probably be sooner."

It felt like wading in a thick consistency of fog. I tried to find footing and sunk deeper. Quicksand. As people asked me questions or situations arose where it became obvious I didn't have the pieces I was supposed to, I slowly relearned the missing. Read over my CV for my life's timeline. Relied on my mom's Cliff notes to give me snapshots of who the people were at an art opening, people I'd known my whole life. The overwhelm inhabited my body in a way that didn't leave room for appreciation of the lost, but just enough space to plunk in things like: "Pat and Chip, she makes the ceramic tiles, you've been to their studio." There was no time to mourn the lost faces, my dear friend's pregnancy I forgot, the location of the bathroom in the yoga studio. I couldn't remedy the disappointment people had when I didn't remember important moments shared. I learned how to cover. How to pretend I remembered Liz's funeral where I danced in her honor, or that Mary was in AA, or the trip to Crestone with Brooke.

Aftermath: there wasn't a ledge to take stock and assess damage. In survival mode, I was still stepping over lost stories trying to navigate a landscape of slip and bump. Later, I hoped retrieving my body memories would aid healing: a balm to soothe the vulnerability of anesthesia. I asked what my feet did during the seizure. If my face clenched. What I was like in recovery. I asked for help with the memory loss. Spoke to my psychiatrist about the toll of the treatments. How no one talked about the memory effects. As far as the psychiatry field was concerned, I didn't exist. They waved away the loss with the fact that deep depression can affect memory profoundly.

During an inpatient intake after the treatments, the admitting psychiatrist responded to my anguish over my lost memory with, "I wouldn't worry about it; your brain seems to be functioning just fine."

I've not come to terms with the loss. I don't even know what that would look like. I rarely read the travelogues written during my adventures in South America or look at the pictures. They feel like running into barbed wire. It is over two years since my last treatment; I'm still waiting for my memory to return.

Contributors

Alex Conall

Alex Conall of sunbowpublications.com is a queer, genderqueer white feminist who tries not to be a White Feminist. They are passionate about writing, especially speculative fiction and poetry, and they dabble in other forms of art. Alex has been successfully holding down a paycheck job for a few years, and by Millennial standards it is a really good job; clearly this means they cannot possibly be autistic. They also study online at Oregon State University.

◆   ◆   ◆

Alison Kopit

Alison Kopit is honored to be a student of Disability Studies at the University of Illinois– Chicago's Department of Disability and Human Development. She is interested in expressions of the lived experience of disability through the medium of dance, is an avid dance improviser herself, and is always trying to learn new things about fermenting food. Queerness and Disability Art and Culture are the center of her research and her life.

◆   ◆   ◆

Alyssa Hillary

Alyssa Hillary is an Autistic graduate student and teaching assistant in mathematics. Sie is also a disability studies scholar with interests in neurodiversity, access, and technology. Sie blogs at yesthattoo.blogspot.com and enjoys writing fiction and poetry.

♦ ♦ ♦

Amanda Sleen

Amanda is a third year student at Concordia College in Moorhead, MN studying English writing and psychology. She is also a part of the Minnesota Army National Guard. In her free time, she enjoys reading fiction and short stories, listening to The Moth podcast, and watching Netflix.

♦ ♦ ♦

Andrea Abi-Karam

Andrea is a punk poet who is currently working with the themes of genderqueer embodiment, technology, urban development and intimacy. They live in Oakland, CA and host an open floor radical poetry night called Words of Resistance with co-conspirator Drea Marina. Andrea wants their work to evoke a reaction in the body.

♦ ♦ ♦

Andrew M. Reichart

Andrew M. Reichart writes fantasy, science fiction, and horror novellas, short stories, and comics, most of which are published by Argawarga Press at argawarga.com. All of his stories are interrelated, and "Testimony of the Teen Ogre" is a tangential but tangible prequel to other works such as *Wallflower Assassin* and the newly-released *Cannibal-King*. The "teen ogre" also plays a key role, at two very different stages of his life, in two upcoming collaborations with Nick Walker. Andrew lives in California with his fiancé and two dogs.

◆ ◆ ◆

Athena the Architect

Athena the Architect is a nonspeaking, recently verbal artist. She's also a member of The Puzzlebox Collective, a group of interdependent creative professionals who assist one another with all aspects of daily life. Through this Collective, she is able to have her partner-performers embody the words she hears in her fingers.

◆ ◆ ◆

Barbara Ruth

Barbara Ruth is a published photographer, essayist, poet, memoirist and short story writer, as well as novelist. In 2014 she was a featured writer-activist at Old Lesbians Organizing for Change biannual gathering. In July 2015 her poem "From Where You Are Now" won the Rock the Chair contest sponsored by *Yellow Chair Review* and in August 2015 her poem "Hold It Gently, But Firmly" came in second in the poems on grief contest sponsored by Wilda Morris's blog. She lives in San Jose, California, spending much of her time searching for accessible housing and fighting the bureaucracies that make it so scarce.

♦ ♦ ♦

Bridget Allen

Bridget Allen is an autistic writer and activist from North Texas, founder of The Octans Partnership, and a founding partner in Autonomous Press. Allen writes highly personal stories of disability's intersection with poverty, feminism, queer culture, and abuse. Her work has been featured in *Typed Words Loud Voices*, and online at NeuroQueer, the Huffington Post, and her personal blog, It's Bridget's Word.

♦ ♦ ♦

Cara Liebowitz

Cara Liebowitz is a multiply disabled activist and writer. Her work has been featured in numerous outlets online and in print, including on her personal blog at http://www.thatcrazycrippledchick.com. Cara aims to complete her Master's Degree in Disability Studies from the CUNY School of Professional Studies in December 2015.

♦ ♦ ♦

Dani Alexis Ryskamp

Dani Alexis is a Michigan-based writer and Autonomous Press editor. In between freelance writing projects, she enjoys reading our submissions pile, writing science fiction, and ignoring email requests for contributor bios. Next year, she will be the lead editor on *Spoon Knife 2: Test Chamber*.

◆ ◆ ◆

E Lewy

E Lewy is a writer, editor, and social justice activist. She is a member of the neuroqueer community who is a former editor of *Breath and Shadow*, an online literary magazine by and for the disability community. Her work has appeared in *New Mobility*, *Breath and Shadow*, and *My Body of Knowledge: Stories of Illness, Disability, Healing, and Life*. She lives in Boston, Massachusetts.

◆ ◆ ◆

Elizabeth J. Grace

Elizabeth J. (Ibby) Grace is an Autistic professor who blogs at tinygracenotes.blogspot.com and edits for i.e.: inquiry in education, NeuroQueer and Autonomous Press. Interested in performance and disability studies, Ibby is working on a musicology book with Andrew Dell'Antonio and a monograph on theater. She currently serves on the boards of Society for Disability Studies and AutCom.

◆ ◆ ◆

Emily Jane

Emily Jane is a queer writer from Upstate New York. She received her B.A. in Women's and Gender Studies from a tiny liberal arts college in the middle of nowhere. She's been writing since middle school and credits her college professors for pushing her to be more serious about it. She thanks her friends for helping her edit her work and teaching her basic social skills.

You're my favorite cup of tea.

♦ ♦ ♦

Fable the Poet

Fable The Poet is an engaging, dynamic, and captivating performer who hails from The Mitten. As a Nationally Touring Artist he has been highly noted for his work with the youth; spreading Mental Health Awareness using his own stories to consume the audience and spread a much needed message: "At times, we all feel fragile. A paper boat entertaining the waves of life."

He is known across the nation for crowd-interactive features that leave those attending enlightened and empowered. Whether acoustic, with musical backing, or even with a live band you will be taken on an emotional rollercoaster unlike any other you have ever experienced. Buckle up, prepare to make a new friend, and enjoy the ride.

♦ ♦ ♦

Harriet Grace

Harriet Grace writes in the margins of library books, on the backs of envelopes, over the text of church bulletins, newspapers, and crosswords. Her poems can be found lining the nests of birds across at least three counties. She spends more time than she should thinking of dragonflies.

♦ ♦ ♦

Jessica Goody

Jessica Goody writes for *SunSations Magazine*. She was awarded second place in the 2015 Reader's Digest Poetry Competition. Her work has appeared in numerous publications and anthologies. She has written two volumes of poetry and is seeking their publication.

◆　◆　◆

Kassiane A. Sibley

Kassiane A. Sibley is a vintage 1982 autistileptic who has been fighting the neurodiversity fight since before it was cool (so, 1999). She has presented at many conferences, written a number of things that people have actually read, coined the word 'neurodivergent,' and can kick up an intense social media crisis when necessary. Kassiane also intends to drag the entire neuroscience field kicking and screaming into the neurodiversity paradigm, and has a tendency to approach daily problems as though she's the protagonist of an urban fantasy novel.

◆　◆　◆

Leah Kelley

Leah Kelley is a Neurodivergent educator, doctoral student, parent of an Autistic teen, activist, and writer. She is part of the moderating team for the popular Facebook group, *Parenting Autistic Children with Love and Acceptance* (PACLA), and authors the blog 30 Days of Autism. She works collaboratively on projects and initiatives including The

Autism Positivity Flashblog and Boycott Autism Speaks, to promote civil rights, fight stigma, and increase understanding, acceptance, and support for those who process and experience the world in diverse ways.

◆ ◆ ◆

Lucas Scheelk

Lucas Scheelk is a white, autistic, trans, mentally ill, queer-identified poet from the Twin Cities. Lucas uses he/him/his pronouns and they/them/their pronouns. His writing has appeared in publications such as *Sibling Rivalry Press - Assaracus*, *THEM - a trans* lit journal*, *NonBinary Review*, *Barking Sycamores*, and *QDA: A Queer Disability Anthology*, among others. Lucas Scheelk is the author of *This Is A Clothespin* (Damaged Goods Press, 2016). You can reach him via twitter [@TC221Bee].

◆ ◆ ◆

Luis Lopez-Maldonado

Luis Lopez-Maldonado was born and raised in Orange County, CA. He earned a Bachelor of Arts degree from the University of California Riverside, majoring in Creative Writing and Dance. His work has been seen in *The American Poetry Review*, *Cloudbank*, *The Packinghouse Review*, *Off Channel*, and *Spillway*, among others. He also earned a Master of Arts degree in Dance from Florida State University. He is currently a candidate for the Master of Fine Arts degree in Creative Writing at the University of Notre Dame.

◆ ◆ ◆

Marc Rosen

Marc Rosen, coeditor of *Perspectives: Poetry Concerning Autism and Other Disabilities* volumes I and II and author of *Monster of Fifty-Nine Moons and other Poems*, writes from the autistic queer experience. When not geeking out over something or other, he can be found either working his quiet 9-5 job or reading a book in a room in his home on the outskirts of nowhere. To learn more about his previous publications, please see www.localgemspoetrypress.com.

◆ ◆ ◆

Marshall Edwards

Marshall lives in an ancient house in Kansas City's oldest suburb. His first published work was the superhero comic "Prairie City Response #1," and he's since published two volumes of his surreal horror serial *MAYFLY*. His story "The Patton Sea Raiders" is part of the raygun-gothic anthology *Slow Boat to Fast City* by Pine Float Press. You can catch his current writerly happenings at www.marshalledwards.net or at facebook.com/prairiecityresponse

◆ ◆ ◆

Michael Scott Monje, Jr. (ed.)

Michael is an Autonomous Press partner and the writer of multiple novels on the transgender autistic experience, including *Defiant, Mirror Project,* and the forthcoming

Imaginary Friends. Her poetry has appeared in *Barking Sycamores, NeuroQueer,* and other venues, and a collection (*The US Book*) is forthcoming. Michael is also a member of The Puzzlebox Collective, where she is frequently called upon to read Athena's poetry aloud.

◆ ◆ ◆

N.I. Nicholson (ed.)

N.I. Nicholson is the founder and editor-in-chief of *Barking Sycamores,* a literary journal publishing art, poetry, creative nonfiction, and short fiction by neurodivergent creatives. He also co-edited the Summer 2014 Issue of *Red Wolf Journal.* His work has appeared in *NeuroQueer, GTK Creative Journal, Alphanumeric,* and *qarrtsiluni.* While pursuing an MFA in Creative Writing from Ashland University, he also blogs at The Digital Hyperlexic (http://thedigitalhyperlexic.wordpress.com/). He lives in Central Ohio with his fiancé and is in the process of regenerating into his second incarnation.

◆ ◆ ◆

Nick Walker

Nick Walker is an Autistic educator, author, speaker, transdisciplinary scholar, and martial artist. He is an editor at Autonomous Press and NeuroQueer Books, and a faculty member at California Institute of Integral Studies. He holds a 6th degree black belt in aikido, and is founder and senior instructor of the Aikido Shusekai dojo in Berkeley, California. He blogs at neurocosmopolitanism.com.

◆ ◆ ◆

Nina Fosati

Nina Fosati has always been a storyteller. At 58 she believed she was too old to be a writer. Then mental and physical limitations crashed into her life and she decided she had to try. Finding she no longer functions well in the world, she uses impairment as the inspiration for many of her stories.

◆ ◆ ◆

Sabrina Zarco

Sabrina Zarco is an award winning Chicana queer femme multi-media artist, neuroqueer, activist, cultural worker and community educator. As an autistic Latina she uses her unique way of experiencing the world fused with cultural influences to create her visual artwork and spoken word performances. Her distinctive self-taught processes of creating visual art manifests in a variety of multi textural mediums with a primary focus on using fiber art as a base. Sabrina's works tell stories, show us dreams, and articulates how she views the world.

◆ ◆ ◆

Samuel T. Harvey

Sam Harvey is a 2nd year master's student pursuing a Rhetoric and Writing degree, working on a thesis on how the Rhetoric of Science and Disability Studies can complement each other, especially when looking at the psychological theory of "Theory of Mind."

◆ ◆ ◆

Sarah Caulfield

Sarah Marie Caulfield is a chronically ill Education with English and Drama student in her third year at Cambridge University. She has been published previously in the 2014 Mays Anthology and was the 2015 winner of the John Treherne Creative Writing Prize. She is from Blackpool, Lancashire.

◆ ◆ ◆

Selene dePackh

Selene dePackh is an autistic illustrator working as *Asp in the Garden*. She also writes fiction and creative nonfiction. She is currently working on *The M/Other Tongues Project*, a multi-media image-based group project on the multiple, cross-projecting narratives of marginalized voices.

◆ ◆ ◆

Stephanie Heit

Stephanie Heit is an artist living with bipolar disorder who engages with herself and the world through multiple creative practices: movement as a dancer and massage therapist and words as a poet and teacher. She received a BA in Dance and MFA in Writing and Poetics from Naropa University. Her work most recently appeared or is forthcoming in *Midwestern Gothic*, *Nerve Lantern*, *Research in Drama Education: The Journal of Applied Theatre and Performance* and *Queer Disability Anthology*.

♦   ♦   ♦

Thalia Rose

Thalia Rose is an agender Creative Writing student at San Francisco School of the Arts. They were born on the first day of the millennium.

♦   ♦   ♦

Thomas Kearnes

Thomas Kearnes holds an MA in Screenwriting from the University of Texas at Austin. He recently won the 2014 Cardinal Sins Fiction Contest. His recent fiction has appeared or will appear in *Night Train*, *BULL*, *Vending Machine Press*, *Punchnel's*, *Existere*, *5x5*, *Big Lucks*, *Split Lip Magazine*, *Necessary Fiction*, *Spry*, *Litro*, *The Adroit Journal*, *The Ampersand Review*, *Word Riot*, *Johnny America*, *Five Quarterly*, *Sundog Lit* and elsewhere. His work has also appeared in several LGBT venues. He has been nominated for the Pushcart Prize and Best of the Net. He is studying to become a drug dependency counselor. He lives in Houston.

.

CPSIA information can be obtained
at www.ICGtesting.com
Printed in the USA
LVHW011103260821
696160LV00001B/61